Diamond Rings Are Deadly Things, Book #1

"Mystery, suspense, murder and romance all intriguingly tied together in one very fun walk-down-the-aisle cozy mystery!"—Shauna Wheelwright, reviewer

"As a longtime fan of Rachelle Christensen, I always love her stories and characters, and this novel is another thrilling mystery to add to my collection. Adri faces bridezillas, wedding dress disasters, and murder. Find out what mashed potatoes and crafts have to do with suspense in *Diamond Rings are Deadly Things*—and don't be surprised if you have to stay up all night to finish the book!"—Rachel Ann Nunes, author of *Before I Say Goodbye*

"This is a terrific story with quirky characters, fun crafty ideas, and a mystery that will keep you wondering through all the twists and turns."—Heather Justesen, author of *Brownies and Betrayal*

"*Diamond Rings are Deadly Things* pulled me right in from the first page and held me captive until the very end. Great characters, a compelling plot, a surprising twist at the end ... Rachelle Christensen knows how to craft a great mystery."—Tristi Pinkston, author of the *Secret Sisters Mysteries*

"A cunningly crafty mystery with just the right mix of romance and do-it-yourself inspiration. Readers won't be able to get enough of Adrielle Pyper, stunning party-planner turned heroine who could lose all her expensive supplies one day, and still pull off the perfect wedding the next."

—Nichole Giles, author of *Descendant*

"Author Rachelle J. Christensen has created likable and realistic characters. She blends the drama of a mystery with the allure of weddings mixing in a good dose of humor, suspense, and of course, a touch of romance."—Mason Canyon, reviewer

Praise for

Veils and Vengeance, Book #2

"I love a great mystery that keeps my interest and keeps the pages turning. I loved the Hawaiian setting, that was a character on its own. As the story progressed, I enjoyed where the author went with the mystery, doing a perfect job of planting the right amount of seeds to try to throw me off the trail of who the killer was."—Mindy Holt, reviewer

"Packed with danger and romance, enchantment and entertainment, Rachelle Christensen's Veils and Vengeance takes you on a suspenseful Hawaiian vacation without ever leaving your chair!"

~Maria Hoagland, Author of The ReModel Marriage (Romance Renovations series)

". . . the perfect blend of romance and mystery so that you were kept interested through the whole book. . . I also loved that everything involving the murder and the romance was kept real and believable. Rachelle Christensen does an excellent job of pulling you into her story and making you want to keep reading to find out what happens next! I can't wait to read the next one . . ."—Melissa, reviewer

"Do you crave a good, clean romantic read full of mystery and intrigue that's smart and fun to read? Then grab Rachelle's books! I thoroughly enjoyed this book and couldn't put it down. She mixes a murder mystery with romance in the beautiful setting of Hawaii very well and enjoyably."—Stephanie, reviewer

Proposals and Poison

Other Works by Rachelle

The Soldier's Bride

Diamond Rings Are Deadly Things (Wedding Planner Mysteries #1)
Veils and Vengeance (#2)

Wrong Number
Caller ID

Novellas:
Silver Cascade Secrets
Hope for Christmas: An Echo Ridge Romance
Double Take

Nonfiction:

What Every 6th Grader Needs to Know: 10 Secrets to Connect Moms & Daughters

Lost Children: Coping with Miscarriage

Proposals and Poison

A Wedding Planner Mystery #3

RACHELLE J. CHRISTENSEN

Proposals and Poison

Original Cover Design: Kelli Ann Morgan
Cover Art Illustration: Kimberly Anderson

Interior book design: Heather Justesen
Editing: Jenna Roundy
Publisher's Note
This is a work of fiction. Names, characters, places, and incidents either are the product of the author's imagination or are used fictitiously, and any resemblance to actual persons, living or dead, business establishments, events, or locales is entirely coincidental.

ISBN-13:
978-0692639702

ISBN-10:
0692639705

Published by Peachwood Press, April 2016

Dedication

To
My writing family at LDStorymakers and Indie Author Hub.
My writing career exists because of these fabulous
organizations. I'm so grateful to have such wonderful friends!

And to Idaho, my home state once again. I'm singing of you,
ah, proudly too. Singing of Idaho.

Chapter 1

DATE IDEA JAR

Set a jar with popsicle sticks next to a sign that says:

DATE JAR

Share your BEST date idea for the new Mr. & Mrs.

Instruct guests to share their ideas and put each popsicle stick in a decorative jar to give to the bride and groom.

Courtesy of www.mashedpotatoesandcrafts.com

The afternoon sun had the asphalt steaming when I closed the door of my wedding shop on my way to run errands. Summer was notoriously busy for weddings, and July promised no respite from the work ahead. I couldn't complain about my workload, though, because it made me happy to finally be in a place where my life was falling into a somewhat predictable routine. It also kept me from obsessing over my relationship status with Luke Stetson.

At the moment, Luke was in court, working a messy divorce case that was ballooning into so much drama he'd had to cancel on me three times in the past two weeks. The case involved the sister of Lily Rowan, one of my new clients. Lily was the happy part of the story, because she just got engaged to Tim Esplin—the vet I would take my cat to this afternoon. Lily wanted a November wedding, and since it was already July ninth, I was pushing to get the most important decisions made so we could progress with the rest of her plans.

My phone beeped, and I looked at the reminder on my calendar. In one hour I would be meeting with Lily to talk about the theme she and Tim wanted for their celebrations.

Sliding my finger across the screen, I dismissed the reminder, only to once again see the text from Luke. He'd canceled our lunch date by text this morning and still hadn't called. I wondered when the case would be over, and if he'd have more free time or get bogged down in another case.

Well, my work almost kept me from obsessing about Luke for, like, two minutes, I thought, frowning. As I slid into my car, I considered the question that had entered my mind right after Luke canceled our lunch date. Would Luke Stetson, divorce attorney, ever be able to love again? And should I, Adri Pyper, wedding planner, be spending time (a.k.a. pursuing a relationship) with him?

The elusive answer shimmered like the heat from the pavement, just out of reach. I shook off thoughts of Luke and cranked the air conditioner up on my way to the consignment store located just a mile from my shop. Everybody's Closet had a summer fling sale going on with new merchandise, and Necia kept me in the loop since I was always on the lookout for vintage and unique decor to use in my weddings and parties. It was the height of yard-sale season, and Necia usually got in all the leftovers from people's garage sales. I loved going to yard sales and finding great bargains, but too many weekend weddings had me missing the early morning sales. Everybody's Closet was the next best thing.

The parking lot only had one other vehicle, a single-cab white pickup that didn't belong to Necia. She usually walked to work in the summer months. I pulled in next to the pickup, right in front of the store, and put my car in park. When I looked up, my eyes locked with those of a man standing in front of the doors, holding a rifle.

The silver metal of the stock gleamed in the hot afternoon sun, and I blinked, waiting for my brain to catch up to the strange sight before me. The man was short and stocky with dark brown hair, and as I studied him, he smiled and moved his rifle, pointing it toward the sky. I sucked in a breath when the man stepped forward. My windows were down, and the sound of robins trilling cheerfully carried across the parking lot. He said something in a different language. It wasn't Spanish—I spoke a little, and his words had a Slavic sound to them. Regardless of the language, I was pretty sure he was swearing.

I fumbled for the window and door lock controls. My throat went dry as the man looked at me again and fired a shot into the air. I covered my ears and screamed, reaching for the gearshift to back out of the parking lot. My hand slipped and my car went into neutral. When I moved to put it in gear, the car died.

By then I was in a full-on panic. I turned the key, and thankfully my car started back up. I pumped the gas and put the car in reverse, but the gunman was faster than my frightened wits: by the time I backed out of my parking space, he was already peeling out of the parking lot, heading for the main road.

What had just happened? I wasn't sure whether I should call the police department or dial my friend Tony Ford, the local detective. Then, with a start, I thought of Necia. What if something had happened to her? I jumped out of my car and ran through the front doors of Everybody's Closet, the bronze bell clanking as I charged in. "Necia!" I called out.

"I'm right here, and I'm okay." She came around the corner, wearing a red-white-and-blue-striped apron. "Did you see that man with the gun?"

"Yes, and my brain froze. I didn't know what to do. It all happened so fast. Was he in here?" I pummeled her with questions, breathing hard.

"No, I just came from the back and saw him standing there holding a gun," she said, her breaths coming in short gasps. "Then he walked off and I heard a gunshot. I already called the police and they're sending someone over." Her light-brown hair was pulled back into a messy bun, and a few strands framed her heart-shaped face. She was in her late thirties and practically lived at her store.

"That was so weird. What do you think he was shooting at?" I turned to look at the parking lot. My hands shook, and my heart thumped hard in my chest. I took a deep breath, proud of myself for not freaking out after witnessing the man discharge his gun.

Necia raised her eyebrows. "I have no idea, but I don't suppose it would hurt to go outside and look around."

We stepped outside and I shielded my eyes against the sun, tucking one of my blonde curls behind my ear. The parking lot was empty, and a few trees lined the edge of the property. The birds were quiet, and besides the occasional passing car, there was hardly any noise. Necia and I looked at each other, and my fear was mirrored in her eyes.

"I can't imagine what he was doing with a rifle in town like this," I said. The Sawtooth Mountain Range that loomed around Sun Valley attracted its fair share of hunters, but that guy was completely out of season. I didn't know of many hunts held in the sweltering heat of July.

"Let's go back inside while we wait for the police." Necia held the door open for me and followed me inside.

"I came here to look at your new items, but now I don't feel like I can concentrate." I glanced at my watch—already past two—and grumbled. "I'm going to have to reschedule an appointment, because I'm sure Tony or whoever comes from the police will make us fill out a statement."

"That's true." Necia took out a ballpoint pen and clicked it a few times. "Wasn't it last year around this time that a policeman came to my store to see you?"

"Uh, yeah, and now Tony is dating Lorea, so I've been seeing even more of him lately."

Necia chuckled. "That's good to hear. She's a great match for him."

"I think so too." Lorea Zubiondo was my assistant and partner in crime when it came to planning weddings and creating stunning wedding gowns. Over the past year and a half, we'd helped plan over twenty weddings, solved a few mysteries, and created fantastic crafts and recipes for my website, Mashed Potatoes and Crafts. Her first date with Detective Tony Ford had been sort of a pity date to her sister's wedding, but they'd hit it off, and I'd never seen Lorea quite so twitterpated before.

The clanging of the bell interrupted my thoughts, and I looked up to see Tony standing in the doorway. He was well over six feet tall, with a full head of light-brown hair. In his dark suit and tie, he was an imposing figure, but his boyish smile was what made Detective Ford so good at what he did. He disarmed people with that smile and the smattering of freckles across his nose, but I knew better than to underestimate him. Tony was smart, and an excellent detective. "Good afternoon," he said. "I'd say it's a pleasant surprise to see you here, Adri, but it's not a surprise at all. You are always in some kind of trouble."

"I am not." I held up my hands. "I didn't do anything. Didn't even get out of my car and some crazy guy started shooting."

"Hmm. Why don't we start with a few questions?" Tony gave us his signature smile. "Necia, were you inside the store when the incident occurred?"

"Yes." Necia told him what she had seen.

"What about a description?" He looked at both of us. "The most important detail I need right now is his vehicle. Did either of you see what he was driving?"

"Yes, I pulled right up next to his pickup." I pointed out to the parking lot. "It was white."

"I thought it was gray," Necia said.

"No, I'm sure it was white." I looked at Tony and then at Necia. She furrowed her brow and looked at the ground, as if trying to conjure up an image of the vehicle.

"Extended cab?" Tony asked.

"No," both of us answered in unison. I smiled at Necia as I added, "I'm pretty sure it was just a two-door, regular bed." I paused, trying to recall any other detail about the pickup. By that time, my blood pressure had skyrocketed and my memory was saturated with fear, not leaving much room for other details.

"Ford, Chevy?" Tony prompted.

I shook my head. "I don't know. Maybe a Ford?"

Necia rubbed her forehead. "I didn't get that good of a look, and I'm not really great with truck models, anyway."

"Anything else in particular you remember about the vehicle?" Tony pushed the button on the radio attached to his shoulder and gave a quick description of the pickup, citing that it was possibly white or gray. That sort of bugged me since I knew it was white, but maybe he had to report what both witnesses thought they had seen.

Thinking about the pickup cleared away some of the fuzziness in my head. I willed the memory to come into sharper focus. "I think there was something in the back of his pickup. Maybe something red?"

"Something?" Tony repeated, and he gave me a half smile.

I resisted the urge to smack him in the arm like I did so often to my older brother Wesley, who happened to be Tony's best friend. "I know it's odd, but I don't know what it was. Just that something was in the back of his pickup, hanging over the edge."

Tony nodded. "That could actually be an easy thing to spot if it was there. Necia, did you notice anything?"

"I can't be sure." She clasped her hands together and rocked back on her heels. "My view from inside the store was limited."

"Hang on." Tony spoke into his radio again, reporting the possibility that I'd just brought up. How many policemen were roaming the semi-quiet streets of Hailey right now, looking for this mystery vehicle?

"Now, how about a description of this guy?" Tony asked.

I closed my eyes and focused on the memory of the man standing in front of the store. "He was short. I think shorter than me." I held out my hand to indicate about how tall I thought the man was.

"So probably about five-six or five-seven?" Tony looked at Necia, and she nodded.

"And he had bushy, dark brown hair," Necia said.

"Receding hairline?" Tony asked.

"No, a full head of hair, but no facial hair," I answered. "And he had on a white T-shirt with some kind of green picture or logo on the front. I didn't recognize it. Oh, and he spoke a foreign language. Not Spanish. Maybe German?"

"Do you speak German?"

"No, but I've heard it plenty of times and it reminded me of those sounds."

He was about to ask another question, but stopped when a second police car pulled into the parking lot. "That'll be Hamilton. He'll have you fill out a statement."

I held in my groan when I saw the police officer get out of his cruiser with a clipboard. I'd gone my whole life without so much as a speeding ticket, but in the last few years I'd had so many dealings with law enforcement, I knew just what to expect. Officer Hamilton would repeat most of the same questions and get us talking in the hopes that we'd remember something significant, some clue that maybe we didn't already mention. And then we'd have to fill out the witness statement and possibly answer a few more questions.

"Let me make a phone call and reschedule an appointment," I said. "Then I'll get that filled out."

I dialed Lily's number and rescheduled our meeting for Thursday—another two days to wait. "I'm really sorry about this, Lily, but I have an appointment for my cat next. I've already had to reschedule the appointment twice. Do you mind?" I would be taking my cat, Tux, to the vet, who happened to be Lily's fiancé. I'd probably be fifteen minutes late after running home to get Tux, but I was banking on typical waiting room delays to make up for the detour in my plans.

"No problem. I understand," she replied. "It'll give me some time to talk to my stepdad about our plans."

"Thank you," I said. "Maybe I can ask Tim what he thinks about the wedding colors." I laughed at my own little joke.

"Tim is actually pretty good with details," Lily replied. Her voice wasn't as chipper as usual, and she didn't even chuckle when I mentioned Tim and the wedding colors.

"I could possibly go over some things with you in the morning before work since you're right next door," I offered. Lily Rowan had been my neighbor since I'd moved back to Idaho from San Francisco, and we often chatted in between our comings and goings from work and life.

"Okay. That might work," Lily said.

"I'm looking forward to showing you some of the designs we have in this season. And Lorea has three new gowns that just came in." I infused extra brightness into my voice, hoping it would lift her spirits and have her more eager to meet with me.

"Thanks, Adri. That'll be fun. I'll talk to you later." She still didn't sound super excited, but at least we had an appointment.

With a frown, I ended the call and submitted myself to another round of questions. While Necia and I related most of the same information, the Blaine County sheriff pulled up in a black Ford pickup. He talked to Tony and then headed our way. He asked us a few questions about the description of the rifle, and we did our best to answer.

I took the clipboard from Officer Hamilton and hurriedly wrote down every detail that I could remember. I included all of my contact information, even though I wanted to write *You know where to find me!* on the dotted line.

I filled up the page and handed it back to Hamilton before Necia finished writing details in her neat and tiny script. Hamilton took the form over to the sheriff and Tony walked back toward us.

Hopefully I could leave now. I glanced at my watch. It was nearly three thirty; if I didn't hurry, I'd be late to the vet. I was disappointed that Lily hadn't been able to reschedule for later today, because she hadn't seemed herself over the phone. I wanted to talk to her to see if I could reassure her about planning her upcoming wedding. Maybe Lorea could help me think of a way to cheer Lily up.

"Is that frown work-related?" Tony asked.

I rubbed my hand over my frown. "Yes, your paperwork made me miss an appointment and I had to reschedule."

"Sorry about that. I know summer is a busy time for you wedding gals."

I laughed. "Yes, and you seem to be taking up quite a bit of time lately for one talented seamstress I know."

Tony grinned, and it was the kind that had the edges of my mouth pulling up in a smile to join the happiness in his face. Man, he had it bad for Lorea, and that was a good thing. "We've been dating for five months now. I surprised Lorea when I remembered that."

"She told me. I can't believe how fast the time has gone. It doesn't seem that long ago that I was in Kauai." Beautiful beaches graced by rugged mountains and the smell of plumeria had my toes itching for the Hawaiian sand, where I had planned a destination wedding earlier in the year. Those thoughts led to Luke, and my heart did that silly little stutter again.

"Hello?" Tony waved his hand in front of my face, jolting me back to the present. "I can see those wheels turning in your mind. Don't be planning my wedding already."

This time I did smack him. "Not thinking about you."

"Oh? Who's on your mind?"

"Never mind. Are we done here?" I interrupted him before he could follow that line of questioning.

"We're taking this seriously." Tony took the clipboard that Necia handed him. "I don't know what that guy thought he was doing, but discharging a gun within city limits is a misdemeanor at best. Since he fled the scene, he's looking at a few more charges. We'll be in touch, but let us know if you think of anything else." He handed Necia his card. "There'll be some officers coming and going today, keeping an eye on your store."

"I appreciate that," Necia said. "Maybe you can come by tomorrow, Adri?"

"I'd like to. I'll have to see what my schedule looks like. See you two later."

I gripped my keys and waved with two fingers. My car had been baking in the sun for over an hour, and heat emanated from the interior when I opened the door. I started it and cranked the air conditioner to full blast. My phone chimed with an incoming text just before I put the car in drive, so I slid my finger across the screen and saw Luke Stetson's smiling face.

Luke: ***Want to meet me for dinner?***

Me: ***What? The mighty attorney has time for dinner?***

Luke: ***:) Yes, and I want to see you.***

Me: ***Would love to.***

Luke: ***Rocky Mountain Pizza?***

Me: ***Sounds delicious!***

Luke: ***Pick you up at 6:30?***

Me: ***I'll be hungry.***

Luke: ***:)***

I suppressed the girlish squeal I wanted to let out. Okay, maybe I did squeal a little and immediately forgave Luke for being so busy the past few weeks. When he'd canceled our lunch date earlier, I'd been annoyed and sort of depressed, but now even the sun seemed to shine brighter. I reminded myself not to get my hopes up—after all, it was still a date with a divorce attorney. Hunger and a rapidly increasing pulse did funny things to my brain.

With the upcoming date on my mind, I forgot all about the gunman in front of Everybody's Closet and drove to my house to pick up Tux.

Chapter 2

PAPER & LACE HEART BUNTING FOR GUEST BOOK TABLE

Cut out 15-20 hearts in varying sizes from papers matching your wedding décor. Glue or mod podge lace on every other heart. Hang the hearts from twine, ribbon, or cording. Attach to the guest book table. You could easily create the bunting with other shapes to highlight your wedding colors.

Courtesy of www.mashedpotatoesandcrafts.com

The veterinary clinic in Hailey smelled like dog food and antiseptic spray, but it couldn't overpower the smile that kept coming back whenever I thought of a date with Luke. A rumbling purr and a nudge from Tux brought me back to the present. I was sitting in the vet office, holding my cat and dreaming about Luke, instead of working on the new weddings I had booked for the fall. Maybe I shouldn't let myself get too excited. Luke's capacity for a relationship was still questionable.

Tux meowed and stretched his little white paws forward, a contrast to the sleek black fur covering his entire body, except for the V-shaped patch of white on his chest that looked like a tuxedo cravat. He pushed his black head against my hand. Cats were simple and so easy to love. Maybe I should get Luke a cat—it'd be a good place to start for someone who made a living helping people tear apart their love stories.

The bell above the door jangled, and Tux hissed at the chocolate Labrador that had just entered. The dog's tongue lolled to the side in the summer heat. He looked like he hadn't even noticed my cat.

"Hush, Tux, or I'll have to put you back in the carrier." I held firmly to the scruff of Tux's neck until he settled back onto my lap. The dog snuffled at the floor, straining against his leash.

The vet assistant swung a door open and checked her clipboard. "Tux?" she asked, looking toward me.

"That's us." I stood carefully, cradling Tux and keeping his face away from the dog.

"You're late. Follow me," she said in a curt tone.

I hurried after the short-haired blond assistant—her name tag said "Vickie"—into a small room scrubbed clean, with lingering scents of the various animals who filed through every day. "I'd recommend putting your cat in the carrier on your way out," she said. "You were lucky he didn't get mauled by that dog."

"I'll do that," I responded. "I'm very sorry about being late." I'd waited for about ten minutes despite being twenty minutes late, so I wasn't sure why it bothered her.

Vickie seemed especially grumpy, so I pasted on a smile to combat her negative wavelengths. She didn't smile as she entered in the information I'd given her on Tux. Looking her over, I noticed that her nails were neatly trimmed and painted bright purple.

"I like your nails." Maybe a compliment would soften her. I really did like her nails, because purple was one of my favorite colors.

"Thanks." She looked up and glanced at me, and then at my cat. "It makes me smile on those days when I don't want to." She finally smiled, but it looked kind of grim. I wondered how many animals she'd worked with today, and what she seemed to have against me or my cat.

I held Tux and spoke to him in soft tones while Vickie took his vitals. I think we both took a deep breath when she left the room.

"I wonder what was eating her," I whispered to Tux. He didn't have a chance to answer with his usual plaintive meow before the vet, Dr. Tim Esplin, entered the room. He was just barely taller than my own five feet ten inches, and he had a full head of wavy brown hair with neatly trimmed sideburns. Tim didn't wear scrubs; instead, he wore a classic snap-closure cowboy shirt, Wranglers, and boots. He fit the part of a down-home country vet, and his upper-class fiancée, Lily, didn't want him to change one bit.

"Good afternoon, Tux," Tim said as he approached my cat. "Adri, it's nice to see you. I wasn't sure how much you got away from all those gowns and doilies."

I laughed. “I manage to sneak away once in a while. Just running errands today.” I placed Tux on the table. “He sure has grown since I found him last year.”

Tim nodded. “You’ve done well with him. Most strays aren’t this lucky. I just had to put one down yesterday that someone brought in.”

I grimaced. “That’s true. I’m lucky to have Tux too,” I said. “We watch out for each other.”

“Pets are the best for that.” Tim examined Tux carefully, and my cat purred.

I thought of how he’d mentioned putting down a stray, and frowned. “Do you have to do many euthanizations?”

“Usually only a couple per month,” Tim replied. “It never gets easier.”

“Does it hurt the animal?”

“No. It’s just like a shot, and they go to sleep. We make them as comfortable as possible.” Tim carefully administered a shot to Tux, who mewed in protest but then quieted.

“That’s a hard decision to make.” I rubbed under Tux’s chin as he purred.

“We do all we can before we go to that point, but if we can’t find a home for them, we’re required to euthanize. In the case of a sick animal that’s suffering, it’s what we do to provide peace.”

“My uncle used to say that’d be the way to go,” I said.

Tim arched an eyebrow. “Unfortunately, some people agree with him, and it’s become a problem in recent years.”

He refocused on Tux, but I felt like I’d put my foot in my mouth somehow. So I decided to change the subject to something less grim. “I’m meeting with your sweetheart to talk shop and get some things on the calendar this week.”

Tim smiled, but something around his eyes hinted at an underlying concern.

"Is something wrong?" I asked.

Tim shook his head. "Not with us, but ... well, sort of. Lily is so upset about this whole divorce mess with Rose. Has she said anything to you?"

"No."

"I don't know what to do. She's talking about postponing the wedding because she doesn't want to get married on the heels of Rose's divorce. I don't want her to feel pressured, but I do love her." Tim hesitated, and then let out a breath. "I want Lily to be my wife. I can't lose her." He handed Tux to me, and I moved my cat into his carrier and shut the door. "I'm heading out early today to spend some time with Lily to get her mind off Rose."

"I didn't realize she was that close to her sister."

"Actually, she's not." He threw away some paper towels from the exam table and washed his hands. "Lily is the one who told me Rose was an unfit parent for Jasmine."

"Oh?" I wasn't sure how much I should pry, but since they were my clients I decided to venture. "How old is Jasmine?"

"She's six, and Rose *is* a terrible mother. She has never put her daughter first in anything. That poor little girl has had to ride the parade of Rose's boyfriends while she and Javier have been separated, and then Rose is busy slinging mud at him and turning Jasmine against her father."

"Oh dear. I'm sorry. I can see why Lily is concerned. Divorces are always difficult."

Tim put a hand on the back of his neck. "That Luke Stetson is a cutthroat attorney. Javier definitely picked a good one. He's fighting for full custody of Jasmine, and he just might get it."

I cringed, and then coughed to hide my surprise at hearing Luke's name with the term *cutthroat*. He was good at his job, but I hadn't heard him described that way before. "What makes you say that about Luke?"

"He works overtime to find the nitty-gritty details. Just yesterday, I heard—"

Vickie knocked on the door and opened it. "We have a dog that just came in—needs stitches, heavy bleeding."

Tim straightened and headed after Vickie. "Sorry to run, Adri."

"No problem. We're done here anyway. Good luck." But I wished we hadn't been interrupted. I would have liked to know what he was about to say concerning Luke.

Chapter 3

CORNHOLE GAMEBOARD

Find two boards 48" x 24" made from plastic corrugated cardboard, foam core, plywood, or OSB depending on what kind of durability you'd like. Have it screen printed with wedding images like bells, a cake, gifts, etc. or use stencils to paint the design desired. Cut one hole 6 inches in diameter with the center of the hole 9 inches from the top of the board and 12 inches from either side of the board. Make your own toss bags filled with corn to be authentic or you can fill with beans or rice. Create a stand for the boards or prop up with another board. Set up two boards side-by-side for the game and start playing.

Courtesy of www.mashedpotatoesandcrafts.com

I kept running through my conversation with Tim. In a small town like Hailey and the surrounding Sun Valley

Resort, most people knew each other, and consequently, events like Rose's court battle for her daughter were whispered about. Luke didn't like working a case with two local residents—that put him on the wrong side of people's Christmas card lists—but it was a hazard of his business. He couldn't talk about the case to me, but Tim's comments had my curiosity burning, and my fingers were twitching with the desire to text Luke and ask him what he thought of Rose Benavidez.

I drove to my condo and returned Tux to the comfort of his quilted cat bed. He perked up when I set some special cat treats in his dish. "That's for behaving so well at the vet. You're a good boy." I rubbed behind his ears and down his silky back; his purr rumbled under my hand. "See you later."

My wedding shop was a cute fifties-style bungalow that had been remodeled into an office space years ago. Almost two years ago, I'd carefully applied the vinyl sign in my window that read *Adrielle Pyper's Dream Weddings: Where Happily Ever After is Your Destination.* I drove around back and entered Lorea's workroom, piled high with boxes and bags of gowns and fabrics. Last year, we'd ventured into the dress business together, and although we hit a few snags, Lorea was in her element, designing and remodeling several gowns each month. Andean pipe music played in the back room and filtered out to the front of my shop, but I didn't see Lorea anywhere in the piles of satin, tulle, lace, and beadwork draped from every table and surface.

I heard giggling and walked through the sewing room to the front of the shop. Lorea was just coming in the front door with another of our clients, Jessie Wilder. Lorea held the door for her and her son. Jessie's long, straight blonde hair fell to the middle of her back and always looked sleek and stylish even as she wrangled with her young son. She clutched Gavin's hand as he dragged his feet across the threshold of my shop.

Lorea and I had been working with Jessie to plan a September wedding that was out of the norm. Jessie was engaged to a Croatian man named Drago Kovacevic, but that wasn't really what made this wedding different; rather, Jessie was a traditional young woman and she wanted a traditional wedding, but she had a four-year-old son and she'd never been married.

Gavin was born when she was only seventeen years old, and though some thought it was unconventional, she wanted to wear a wedding gown and have a beautiful marriage ceremony and celebration. I didn't think there were any problems with her plans, and I had told her so at our first meeting. Marriage at any stage was a beautiful choice, and I was happy that she saw the significance of a ceremony. But Drago's family was concerned about this American girl and her son. Apparently, they'd always hoped he would return to Croatia.

"Good afternoon Jessie, Gavin, and Lorea." I greeted them all with a smile that belied the bit of adrenaline still burning off from my earlier episode with the crazy gunman and Luke asking me out on a date. Weird how I could group those two incidents in the same thought.

"Did you get all your errands done?" Lorea asked. Her black hair was styled in a short cut that left her neck bare, and around this time every summer I thought about cutting my own shoulder-length hair. Jessie was just taller than Lorea's five-foot-two frame, but that was only because Lorea had on four-inch wedge sandals.

"Almost." I thought of the couple things on my list that would have to wait until after work.

"Gavin is so excited to hear about his new daddy's special game he has planned for the wedding." Lorea winked in my direction, and I gave her a subtle nod. The planning stage had been full of fun games and treats, because we were planning a kid-themed wedding with all sorts of delightful activities for Gavin and his buddies to enjoy as well as the adults in attendance.

Gavin stood on his tiptoes, a miniature version of his mother with light blond hair and blue eyes. "What is it? What game? Is there a prize?"

"Well, it's a surprise, and I can only give you a clue," I said.

He furrowed his brow. "What clue?"

"If you know how to throw a ball, then you might be able to play this game."

His eyes lit up as he glanced at Jessie, Lorea, and me. "I can throw a ball so far!"

I smiled. "You'll love all the games we have planned."

"There's more games?" He grinned and bounced on his toes.

The cornhole game had been showing up all over Pinterest lately, and Lorea and I were designing a board that would be screen printed with wedding bells and gifts, with a large hole cut out in the middle. Kids would throw toss bags filled with corn through the holes. We'd discussed whether we should do bean bags or corn-filled bags, but Lorea was a traditionalist when it came to old-fashioned games, so she'd won that argument. She had already talked to her sister and asked her to help make the toss bags for the late-September wedding.

"I'm going to work with Jessie on getting the pattern right for her maid of honor," Lorea said. She walked toward the back, where all of her sewing and design supplies were stored.

"Work your magic," I said.

Lorea wiggled her fingers toward Gavin. "Did you hear that? We have lots of magic in this shop."

Gavin stopped walking. "You do? Where is it?"

Jessie ruffled his hair. "It's the kind of magic that lives in your heart. The kind Mommy feels for Drago."

Gavin put his hand on his stomach. "My heart feels it too." He grinned.

"Ah, he's such a cutie," Lorea said. Usually she poked fun of sentimental statements like the one Jessie had just made, but with Gavin in the room she looked like she was about to melt. Maybe my friend was starting to come around to the idea that true love really did exist. And maybe she and Tony were getting more serious than I thought.

I filed away some receipts and checked the mail before venturing toward the back to see how things were going. Gavin stood on top of a box and stacked spools of thread in a tower on Lorea's worktable. When he'd stacked about six, they all toppled over. He squealed and clapped his hands.

Jessie rolled her eyes. "You know what they say: why waste money on toys, right?"

I nodded. "My niece and nephew would play in the garbage all day if their parents would let them."

Gavin threw an empty spool into the garbage and jumped up and down.

"Speaking of," Jessie said with a laugh.

"The activities we've come up with will definitely help with his high energy," I said.

Jessie smiled. "It's going to be such a neat experience for him and his cousins. I just wish that Drago's family could be there."

"That's hard. Isn't there any way that his parents at least could make it over?"

Jessie looked down at the carpet and nudged a spool of thread with her sandal. "There might be, but they don't want to come. They think Drago is making a mistake marrying me."

Lorea made a growling noise. "Those *txori burus*. Why can't they see what a gift you are to him?"

Jessie laughed at Lorea referring to her future in-laws as birdbrains. Whenever Lorea got upset or excited, she would slip in a few words from the Basque language, Euskara, to emphasize her point. Lorea probably understood the dynamics of Drago and Jessie's relationship because of her own Basque heritage. Her mother had been trying to set her up with other Basque men for years, and although Lorea was proud of her ancestry, she was a holdout for love, no matter how many times she scoffed at the notion that marriage was in her future.

"Lorea's right, of course." I looked over at Gavin to make sure he wasn't listening; he was across the room under a pile of scrap material. "I'm sorry they feel that way. The only advice I have comes from what I've seen: Love them as hard as you can and they'll come around eventually."

Jessie threaded her fingers through a section of her hair. "That's what Drago says, too. Well, that and when we have another baby. The first Kovacevic grandbaby will not be ignored." Jessie studied Gavin, and it was obvious what she was thinking.

"They'll love Gavin," I said. "It might be hard at first, but how could they resist him?"

Jessie smiled. "Thanks. You and Lorea have been great. I know Drago loves me and Gavin, and whatever happens in the future, he won't love Gavin any less. I just need to keep my fears under control."

"Yes, enjoy this time. You deserve this beautiful wedding. I think you and Drago and Gavin will be very happy," I said.

I thought about our conversation after Jessie and Gavin left the shop. Lorea and I would have to come up with an idea that would help the new family see just how special their life together would be.

At five thirty, I left the shop to get ready for my date. Lorea closed up the shop for me a few nights a week, and at other various times as well because she often stayed late to get a few more stitches in her latest gown. It was only on my drive home that I realized I hadn't told Lorea about the incident with the crazy-looking man holding a rifle this morning. It had been such a busy day that Lorea and I weren't able to chat much. The story would have to wait until tomorrow.

"Hey, Tux." I patted my cat. "I'm going on a date with Luke tonight."

Tux didn't care if I spoke in a sing-song voice; he just mewed and followed me in from the garage.

I hurried to change out of my clothes and into a

mint-green tank top with a sheer white blouse and denim capris. The ninety-five- degree desert heat didn't let up until after sundown, and by then I was ready to relax and enjoy Luke's company.

A knock sounded on my door just as I was slipping my feet into a pair of white sandals. Luke was early. I ran my fingers through my hair as I headed for the front door and swung it open. "You're early—" I stopped when I saw Tony standing on my doorstep. "Lorea's working late at the shop."

Tony bit the inside of his cheek and shook his head. "I came by to see you. Do you mind if I come in a minute?"

There wasn't any laughter in his eyes. Something was wrong. My first thought was of Lorea—but no, she probably hadn't even left the shop yet. I stepped aside and motioned for Tony to come in. "Is something wrong? My family's okay, right?"

Tony nodded. "Yes, your family's great as far as I know. Could we sit down?"

"Oh dear." I clasped my hands together and followed him into the little sitting room off my front door. The wedding ring quilt my aunt Dana made me hung over a stand in the corner, and I focused on the different shades of green blending together. I didn't want to look at Tony's face.

"I'm sorry to barge in on you. It sounded like you were expecting someone?"

"Yes, Luke Stetson is on his way over to take me to dinner."

Tony lifted one corner of his mouth in an attempt at a smile. "That's good. He's a great guy." He looked down at the carpet and then back at me.

"It's okay, just tell me. I know it's bad." My insides tightened. I leaned back against the love seat and reminded myself to breathe.

"You're right, it is bad. I'm really sorry." Tony swallowed. "I hate this part of my job." He blew out a breath. "Lily Rowan died a couple hours ago."

Chapter 4

CHILLED QUINOA SALAD WITH LIME VINAIGRETTE

2 cups cooked quinoa, cooled

1 chopped red bell pepper, 1 cucumber chopped, 1 tomato chopped. Toss together for salad.

Lime Vinaigrette:

Juice of 1 lime, juice of 1 lemon, zest of orange, 2 minced garlic cloves, ¼ cup chopped onion, 4 fresh basil leaves, 2 Tbsp chopped fresh parsley, ¼ cup olive oil, ¼ tsp sea salt.

Combine the citrus juices and zest, garlic, onion, basil, parsley, and oil in a food processor. Mix into the quinoa salad. Chill and serve garnished with avocadoes and lime.

Courtesy of www.mashedpotatoesandcrafts.com

I covered my mouth, sucking in a breath as my vision blurred. The tears rolled down my cheeks as Tony's words echoed in my mind. Lily was a sweet person, a good friend, and I had been thrilled when she became my newest client. Lily had caught the bouquet at Natalie and Brock's gorgeous wedding last year. I still remembered the surprised look on her face, which changed to a demure smile as she'd turned to her date, Tim Esplin.

"I'm sorry, Adri," Tony said. "I wanted to tell you before you heard it somewhere else, because I know she was your neighbor."

"What happened?" I asked.

"She was out in the stables at her stepdad's place. It looks like a heart attack." As Tony spoke, each word grew quieter.

My throat felt like it was bound with cords and my voice box was a steel drum. Too many possibilities collided with each other and my brain felt like a scattered jigsaw puzzle, struggling to fit the pieces together.

I shook my head. "She was too young for a heart attack."

Tony pursed his lips, took in a breath, and said, "I know. We're investigating. I remembered you saying you had an appointment with her earlier today that was canceled. Did you talk to her?"

"Just briefly to reschedule the appointment for Thursday." I shook my head.

"Did she say anything that seemed out of the ordinary?" Tony asked.

"No, we probably talked for less than a minute," I said. "Although she did seem kind of down about something."

Tony flipped his notebook open and wrote something down. "Hmm. Any idea what that would be?"

"Well, Tim mentioned she was really worried about getting married because of Rose's divorce. She hadn't said anything to me about it, though."

Tony nodded and wrote something else in his notebook.

"Poor Lily," I said. "And Tim ... he's going to be crushed."

Tony blew out a breath. "He is out of his mind with grief right now."

"You were the one to tell him?"

Tony nodded. "Yes, Detective Hamilton and I went out to his house and then we split up to notify the rest of the family. We haven't been able to reach her stepdad yet, but someone thought he'd gone up to the mountains and would be back down about now. I was headed up that way and decided to stop by here first. As soon as Phil is notified, it'll be in the news. Probably tonight."

I clasped my hands together and looked at Tony. "Thank you for telling me." My chin wobbled, and I felt my eyes well up with tears again. "I'm so sorry for her family."

Tony nodded. "Well, I'd better go. Are you going to be okay?"

"Yes, Luke should be here any minute." Just saying those words gave me a measure of comfort; I wouldn't have to be alone to think about Lily's death. I swallowed my tears and stood. "Are you going to tell Lorea?"

"Yes, as soon as I can."

"Thanks, Tony. It means a lot that you came to tell me." I put my hand on his arm. He was probably about six foot three, which meant that he was nearly a foot taller than tiny Lorea, but they looked so cute together. "I'm glad you'll be there for Lorea. She really liked Lily."

"Take care," Tony said.

I stood in the doorway watching his police cruiser drive down the street. Life didn't make sense. How could beautiful, young, vibrant Lily be gone?

After Tony left, I realized that he had another reason for stopping by. He'd asked me about my conversation with Lily and taken out his notebook to write notes. The only reason he would do that was if something wasn't sitting right with him. Something about Lily's death must have looked suspicious to Tony.

Before I could step back into my house, Luke pulled his Harley Davidson Road Glide in front of my condo and swung his leg over the motorcycle. He wore stonewashed denim jeans and a gray V-neck short-sleeved shirt. He hurried up the front walkway and grasped my hands.

"Are you sick? You look like you're going to pass out." He wrapped his arm around me and led me back inside the house. His gentle actions undid me, and I began sobbing again. Luke held me, leading me toward the love seat. "What happened?"

I wiped my eyes and struggled to speak. "Lily died today. Tony just came and told me that she had a heart attack."

"A heart attack? Lily?" Luke held my hand and squeezed gently. "I've seen her. Isn't she about your age?"

"Yes, and she's healthy too." Lily rode horses, biked, and seemed to always be on the go. Her cheerful demeanor had made it easy to get to know her, and I had been looking forward to planning her and Tim's wedding. Every time I thought of Tim, it was like a knife twisting in my gut. His words from earlier echoed in my mind: *I want her to be my wife.*

I turned and cried on Luke's shoulder, and he held me, rubbing my back in slow circles.

"I'm so sorry," he murmured. "What can I do?"

I heaved in a breath that caught between the edges of my sobs. "Just hold me."

"I can do that." He pulled me closer to him and rested his head against mine.

We sat that way for a few minutes until my tears subsided and I could breathe normally. When I looked at Luke, I noticed moisture around his eyes, and it almost undid me again. That was something about him that I would never take for granted—he understood loss.

When his wife died of Hodgkin's disease a little over four years ago, it had turned his world upside down. He'd moved from North Carolina to Idaho and started a practice in marriage and family law, far away from the memories of what once was. He kept his past private; most people still didn't know that he was a widower. But he'd confided in me, and I'd kept his confidence. I saw him differently than others did. His prickly exterior had been hard to get past at first, but we'd been through enough that Luke trusted me, and crazy as it sounded, I trusted and really liked the local divorce attorney.

"Are you hungry?" I asked.

"Not as much now."

"Me neither."

We sat there for probably twenty more minutes, talking about Lily and the strange incident of her heart attack. Luke's stomach grumbled, and he shifted to the edge of the couch, probably trying to hide his hunger.

"How about some quinoa salad?" I said. "I made a batch yesterday with orange bell peppers from my mom's garden."

"That sounds great."

We didn't say much about Lily for the next half hour while we ate the chilled quinoa salad with lime vinaigrette and chatted about work. Instead, Luke settled on a different topic. "Tell me about your summer schedule. How's it looking?"

I appreciated that Luke knew instinctively what would help me feel better. Even though he teased me often about my profession as a wedding planner, he knew how excited I got about my work. "I have three more weddings coming up between now and September."

Luke nodded. "And I have three new potential divorce cases."

"You're terrible. You know that, right?"

Luke held up his hands in mock innocence. "Just doing my job."

"Anyway, I'm excited about this girl named Jessie. Her wedding is going to be so much fun." I scooted up to the table and leaned my elbows on the surface. "She has a four-year-old boy, and we're planning sort of a kid-themed wedding with stuff that kids *and* adults will love."

"Like what?" Luke leaned forward and mimicked my pose.

I smiled, noticing what he was doing. "Well, there will be a table full of bowls of treats and scoops. Each guest gets a bag and goes along and fills their bag full of candies."

"Kind of like the candy bins at the grocery store, but the kids can have at them?" Luke straightened. "I want to come to this wedding."

"You should. It's going to be in September, while the autumn nights are still so nice."

"Will there be games too?"

"We're thinking about cornhole. It's kind of like a bean-bag toss."

"This Southern boy knows what cornhole is." Luke infused a drawl into his voice that made me want to kiss the five o'clock shadow on his jawline.

"Well, Southern boy. Maybe you can give me a few more ideas." I added my own twang to my voice. We both laughed, because neither of us were Southern. Luke had moved to North Carolina when he was a kid, so he had a little bit of an accent, but it only crept in when he was tired or said certain words like *y'all.*

Luke pushed his chair back. "I need to get a move on; there's plenty of work left for me to do tonight."

"I was afraid of that." I stood next to him. "When is this case going to be over?"

He sighed. "I was hoping for this week, but I'm sure the judge will grant an extension because Lily is Rose's sister." The skin tightened around his eyes, and I winced. Lily's death had far-reaching effects for the entire Sun Valley community.

"Does it usually take this long for a divorce?" I asked.

Luke cleared his throat. "We should have been done already, but then Rose and Javier decided to fight for custody. Because of all the garbage that's going along with it, it doubles the time in court and triples it in my office."

"Do you think Rose should have custody of her daughter? It seems pretty harsh to try to take her away completely."

"Well, Javier was willing to work with Rose, but then it's like she switched gears completely and went nuts. She didn't want him to see Jasmine at all, so he decided to fight her. I can't say much, but some things have come out that I think has the judge considering Javier's request."

"That poor little girl." I didn't know Rose's daughter, but I felt bad that she was trapped in the mess of her parents' divorce. "And now to have Lily gone. I know she was close to her niece."

Luke adjusted his glasses. "I just have to hope that whatever is best will work out for kids in these situations. It's tough, because sometimes I think I can see so clearly what should happen, and it doesn't."

"That's why you're a good lawyer." I stepped closer to him and put my hand over his heart. "You really are good deep inside."

Luke covered my hand with his and smiled. "I feel the same way about you."

We were teasing each other again, but it felt like more. Something was happening to the air inside my kitchen. Something like sparklers on the fourth of July. Something like heat rising up from the asphalt in summer. Luke's eyes looked like the sky before a thunderstorm and I wanted to reach out and grab onto the emotions he was sharing before he bottled them up again. I wanted to kiss him, and maybe he was thinking about it too. All I had to do was lift my face to his ... but I chickened out and settled for circling my arms around his waist. "Thanks for being here. I really needed you tonight."

Luke hugged me for a moment. Then he released his hold on me and stepped back as if shaking himself from a trance, probably realizing just how close the air felt around us.

"Let's try this again in a few days, okay?" He brushed a strand of hair back from my face. "Call me if you need anything."

"I will."

After the sound of Luke's Harley faded in the distance, I had to admit that there was something happening to my heart. I couldn't stop thinking about him, and I already wished that he was back, or that I was riding behind him on his decked-out motorcycle with the extra purple glitter helmet he'd ordered just for me.

Chapter 5

WEDDING SNACK BAR FOR KIDS

Purchase decorative cellophane bags or paper bags for each guest, twist ties or ribbon, and at least 10 different kinds of candies or snacks. Fill glass jars with various candies and sweets like chocolate-covered cinnamon bears, yogurt-covered raisins, dried fruit, M&M's, Trix cereal, etc. Put a scoop or spoon in each jar. The guests start with a bag and go along the snack bar to fill their bags. Use a twist-tie with a thank-you from the bride and groom for an extra-personal touch.

Courtesy of www.mashedpotatoesandcrafts.com

Lorea greeted me with a hug and misty eyes when I went into work the next morning. "I still can't believe that Lily is gone," she said. "I keep hoping Tony will call me and say it was all a mistake."

"I know. It hurts right here–" I placed a hand over my heart. "–every time I think about her and Tim." I shook my head to ward off the tears. I didn't want to cry anymore.

"The funeral is Saturday morning," Lorea said.

"What can we do to help?" I straightened the table near the front window of my shop, fixing the brochures I'd had printed up about my wedding planning services.

"I'm not sure ... Well, I did have one idea." Lorea hesitated.

"What? You can tell me."

"I didn't know if it would be too painful, but maybe you could put together a little booklet with some of the information you'd gathered already about Lily and Tim." Lorea followed my lead and moved toward the table where clients helped me see the vision of what they wanted their wedding to be. She busied herself with fixing some of my fabric swatch binders and paint chip cards.

"That's a great idea." I walked back to the cash register and pulled out a cream binder with teal and purple accent colors. Each one of my clients filled out several pages of information in their own event binder, and I used it to keep track of all of their ideas, color schemes, dress details, bridal shower favors, addresses, wish lists, and more. "I hadn't started a binder for Lily and Tim yet–they were hoping to get married in November–but I'll print out all the emails she sent me with her wish lists and see what I can come up with."

"I think Tim would like that," Lorea said. She grabbed a catalog of wedding gowns that had several sticky notes protruding from the edges. "On a different topic, tell me what you think of this dress for Jessie." She pointed to a wedding gown in a creamy organza that hung straight down and flared at the bottom.

"Wow, that's gorgeous. I don't know what Jessie's looking for, but from what she's shared, I bet she'll like it." I tapped the page and looked at Lorea. "How do you do that?"

"Do what?"

"Meet someone and know the kind of dress they'll like? You're like a wedding gown genie."

Lorea laughed. "Thanks. I don't know. I just see people and think of different styles that would suit them. With Jessie, I know she always wanted a traditional wedding, but she feels self-conscious because she already has a kid. I haven't looked at any of the frilly, poofy gowns—my eye keeps being drawn toward these sleek lines with a flowing train."

"It'll be interesting to see what Jessie thinks."

"I already ordered it because I know someone will want it. I may make a few alterations," Lorea said.

I could tell she was visualizing the dress. Remembering something, I snapped my fingers. "That reminds me. Trixie called wondering if you were ready for the next fitting on her gown."

Lorea rolled her eyes. "I know. She called again and is bringing Mike over for his fitting, too."

I bit my lip. "This is a first for my business."

Lorea smiled and we both busied ourselves with the work at hand. We were purposely concentrating on our work and not on Lily's death, but it was the only way I knew to cope with the situation. The work still had to be done, but maybe later I could help the family by sifting through the information I had from Lily. I made myself focus on the next appointment I had and the deadlines with my upcoming weddings.

A few minutes later, the chime on the front door signaled that someone had arrived. We both turned to greet Trixie Kincaid, the very person we'd been discussing.

"Trixie! Perfect timing. We were just talking about Mike's tux." Lorea glanced at me, and I had to bite the inside of my cheek to keep from laughing.

"I'm so excited!" Trixie bounced with enthusiasm as she walked toward us. Her dyed-red hair contrasted with the bottom layer, which was highlighted in a deep purple shade. She wore a wide black headband and dangly earrings with multicolored beads that jangled as she walked. In her thirties, Trixie was about five foot six—taller than Lorea, shorter than me—a little on the plump side, and easy to work with.

"Come back here. I know you're dying to see it," Lorea said to Trixie. She motioned for me to follow her to the sewing room in the back of the shop.

Trixie grinned, and I smiled too. It was fun to satisfy my clients. Trixie and her fiancé met at a dog obedience course where they had enrolled their boxers, so this wedding had an interesting flair to it.

"What do you think?" Lorea held up a tuxedo in two parts. The back had a long tail coat, and the front had a zebra-striped satin bow tie.

"He's going to look so dashing," Trixie said. "Everyone will love this." She clapped her hands together and then gave Lorea a side hug. "You're a marvel. Thank you for doing this for me. Shall I bring Mike around back to try it on?"

"Yes, I have a space ready for his fitting," Lorea replied. When Trixie turned to go out the door, Lorea raised one eyebrow in my direction. "This is a first for me too, you know," she whispered.

"I'll help you get things ready. I wouldn't miss this for the world," I said.

A few moments later Trixie knocked on the back door, and I held it open while she brought Mike in. "What do you think, Mike?" Trixie asked as she held up the front part of the tux with the bow tie.

Mike actually looked excited, and he made a little yipping sound.

"Well, Mike," Lorea said. "Let's get started on our fitting for my first canine client." She patted Mike on the head, and his tongue lolled to the side. Mike was a brindled boxer, his coat covered with interesting brown and black stripes that reminded me of a zebra; the pattern worked perfectly with the zebra-striped bow tie.

The dogs were part of the love story in this wedding. Trixie's dog fell in love at first sight with Derek's dog, Mike. After the dogs hit it off, Trixie and Derek scheduled a play date and found that they were meant to be.

Trixie was estranged from her father, so Mike the dog was going to walk her down the aisle—in a tux. If my dad could see this, I'd never hear the end of it. Our dog Samson was a farm dog that chased rabbits, dug for gophers, and barked at the wind. He was a good dog, but there was no way he'd ever wear a tux, or attend a wedding for that matter. But Trixie and Derek's wedding planning had been a lot of fun. They had ordered special chocolate-dipped dog treats—the chocolate was made especially for dogs so it wouldn't damage their kidneys, as Trixie had explained to me. The invitations had been sent with pictures of Sadie and Mike on one side and Trixie and Derek on the other. All dogs were invited to the bash this Saturday night.

Mike's fitting went well. He was surprisingly calm for a boxer, or maybe Trixie's enthusiasm overshadowed his. Lorea had to do a few alterations, and I worked with Trixie on ideas to keep the variety of dogs attending the wedding in a pleasant mood.

"The dog treats will help," Trixie said. "And since we're adjacent to the dog park, people will be able to walk their dogs right after."

"We'll keep things short," I said. "You've talked to Pastor Rogers, and I'm bringing in extra help to rearrange seating for the reception. I think it'll work." I didn't tell Trixie that I was a little more than worried about dogs doing their business on the wedding decor.

But she had anticipated my worries. "I'm glad we decided to purchase everything instead of rent and risk losing our deposit. We'll clean everything up and sell what we don't need," Trixie explained.

"Yes, that was great thinking." I made a note in Trixie's binder. "I think that's all we needed to cover for today. I guess I'll see you at Mike's final fitting on Friday."

After Trixie left, Lorea finished up Mike the dog's tuxedo, and we both laughed when she hung it up in the closet labeled "Trixie/Derek." I went back to work on the project for Lily. It took about an hour to cut and paste all the email conversations and attachments Lily had sent me into one file. She and Tim had been dating for over a year, and for the past month she'd been in contact with me about potential wedding venues and dates.

When she and Tim had started talking marriage, she didn't wait until the ring was on her finger to start planning. She had wanted to be married in the Sun Valley Pavilion, and had even put a deposit down to hold a date in November. Working with people like Lily was what made my job rewarding. She was so happy and excited about the next step in her life and wanted everything to be perfect like she'd dreamed of since she was a little girl. Fresh pain seared my heart as I thought about her life, all of the plans I held in my hands, gone.

I worked on Lily's information until my next appointment and then stayed busy the rest of the day on the events I had coming up in the next few weeks. First there was Trixie's wedding, then two bridal showers, another wedding with a full reception and dinner, and an anniversary celebration.

My phone chimed with a text at three o'clock from Luke.

Luke: ***How are you doing today?***
Me: ***Staying busy. Thinking about you.***
Luke: ***Me, too. I have a new case that just came in. I have to do a bunch of reading tonight. Can I take you out tomorrow?***
Me: ***That would be nice. Good luck with your homework.***
Luke: ***:(It never ends.***

Luke and I were building a pattern that I really liked. He had contacted me every day this week and wanted to see me again. Maybe he was finally getting over his hang-up with marriage and was ready to take dating seriously again. My poor heart couldn't take much more drama in the Luke department, so I kept my fingers crossed that he'd keep playing nice and not push me away again.

Every time I thought of my first meeting with Luke, I had a craving for fried pickles. It's weird, but kind of a long story, too. I had been attracted to his tall, muscular frame the first time I saw him. He'd hidden the fact that he was a divorce attorney while we shared fried pickles and made fun of my wedding planning business in the same bite. Still, there was something irresistible about the dimple in his chin and the way his carpenter jeans fit just right. Looks aside, Luke had been there for me through some pretty rough times. I fingered the scar on my chest that had ruined V-neck shirts forever—I couldn't wear them without seeing the pink scar that a previous boyfriend had given me.

Luke had been my rock through that and in Kauai, when the destination wedding I'd planned didn't go at all according to plan. He had a way of looking at a situation and seeing just how I was affected by it. When other people were fooled by my great acting skills, Luke could uncover my true emotions. But for all his goodness, he had a jaded view of marriage and kept people at arm's length, because he knew from experience that it hurt to get too close. I needed him. The thought made me pause, because I was pretty sure that Luke needed me too.

I pulled up his picture on my phone and studied Luke Stetson. He was ruggedly handsome with steel-blue eyes and smile lines around his eyes that hinted at the easy laughter I'd seen more of lately. Maybe my mom was right when she said that my hero was worth fighting for. The thought was a bit scary, but exciting at the same time.

Chapter 6

MASON JAR SEWING DISPLAY

Fill a Mason jar or your favorite glass container with old spools of thread stacked on top of each other. Fill another jar with assorted buttons. Fill a third jar with lace or other sewing notions. The jars make a darling accent to any room, but especially the sewing room.

Courtesy of *www.mashedpotatoesandcrafts.com*

At three thirty that afternoon, Tony walked in the shop and Lorea's face lit up. She hurried over to him, taking his hand and talking excitedly. Her black hair was styled in a pixie cut, and next to Tony dressed in his navy-blue police uniform, she looked like a little fairy flitting about. But Tony stepped away from Lorea and motioned for her to follow him to my desk; he was here on official police business. My palms began to sweat as a sense of foreboding followed Tony through the room.

"Everything just changed with this case," Tony said. "Because Lily didn't die of a heart attack. She was poisoned."

"No." Lorea sat back in a chair, her sewing scissors dangling from her neck.

"There were several things that didn't match up with a heart attack, and the medical examiner picked up on some evidence that isn't consistent. The toxicology report isn't back yet. We have to do some checking, but it looks like foul play."

"Murder?" I asked. "Someone killed Lily?"

Tony nodded. "Off the record, I'll say that I'm certain this was premeditated. We already have a key suspect."

Lorea gasped. "If you have a suspect, then it's likely someone she knew." She looked at me, and I blew out a breath.

"Which means it's someone we all know," I said, finishing her thought.

Tony held up his hands. "I can't say any more, but I did stop by to see if you had any information that might be helpful." He looked at me. "Do you still use those planning binders for your clients?"

I nodded. "Yes. Lily hadn't filled one out yet, but today I've been working on collecting my correspondence with her so that I could put together something for Tim."

Tony's eyes widened. "I'd like to see that, if it's okay."

I hesitated, remembering what had happened to evidence I turned over in the past. "You're not going to confiscate all my stuff again, are you?"

"No, if you need anything, I'll take copies and get it back to you." Tony gave me the look that said, *You'd better not be holding anything back this time.*

I held up my hands. "I created a file that has all of the emails she sent me with pictures and attachments of things she wanted to use in her wedding. It was kind of a lot of work, so give me some credit here." The file was tucked into a drawer in my desk, and as I pulled out the folder, I was comforted by the thought that I could easily print out the entire file again.

I hadn't started taking notes on the papers yet, thank goodness. I hated waiting for the police to sort through my stuff. This was different, but still, if there was something I could do to ease Tim's burden, I wanted to do it sooner rather than later.

I handed Tony the folder. He eyed the stack of papers and flipped through them. "There's quite a bit here. More than I thought."

"I doubt there's anything there that would help, but maybe." I kept my tone even, with no hint of the curiosity I felt about those papers.

"Thanks, Adri." He turned to Lorea and smiled. "I'll probably have a few more questions for both of you later on. Be thinking of anything out of the ordinary. We have very little information at this point."

"Then how are you so certain that it's murder?" I asked.

"How was the poison administered?" Lorea asked.

Tony waved his hand as if to dismiss both of us. "You two, mind your business. But while you're minding it ..." He raised one eyebrow. "Think about your interactions with Lily: was there a time when she acted different? I'd like to know anything that catches your attention, because it could be a clue to her murder."

"Will you let us know more when you can?" Lorea pressed. "I mean, the news is going to catch wind of this soon, so you'd better keep us in the loop."

"I'll do what I can, but don't get any ideas." Tony wagged his finger at both of us. "Just because you've solved a murder before, doesn't mean you should go looking for trouble."

I turned to Lorea. "He wants us to help, but he doesn't want us to help. Is he always this confusing?"

Lorea laughed. "Yes, he wants to kiss me, but then he doesn't 'cause he's wearing this getup." She motioned to his uniform and stage-whispered, "He never takes it off because he's scared of these." She pointed to her lips, and I doubled over laughing when Tony's face went red.

"I'll talk to you later," he said to Lorea, and he headed for the door. She caught his hand before he left and said something that I couldn't hear, but the way he looked at her, I knew he was a goner.

"Hey, I'm thinking that maybe we should schedule a date for another venue." I waggled my eyebrows at Lorea when she returned.

"There's already been one Zubiondo wedding this year, so the pressure's off." Lorea reminded me of her sister Terese's wedding this past February. She fingered the *laburu* cross she wore around her neck—another indicator of her Basque heritage. The silver necklace looked like it was shaped from four commas swirling in a delicate circle. "Besides, what if I wanted to have a traditional Basque wedding in Spain?"

"I'd say I'm up for that. When do you want me to mark off two weeks? November's already getting booked up. How about January?"

"Adri, I'm dating Tony. We're not even close to talking marriage."

"Hmm, I'd say you're closer than you think when you can make a policeman blush."

Lorea giggled. "I've got to get back to work."

"Me, too." I headed straight to my computer to print out the document on Lily again. Now I'd be looking at the information from a different perspective—murder.

Chapter 7

HOMEMADE WHOLESOME AND HEALTHY GRANOLA

1 ½ cups rolled oats, ¼ cup craisins, 1/3 cup slivered almonds, 2 Tbsp honey, 1 Tbsp wheat germ, 1 Tbsp flaxseed, 1 Tbsp Chia seeds, 1 ½ tsp vanilla

Mix all ingredients together. Spread on a cookie sheet and bake at 350 degrees for 4 minutes. Stir and bake an additional 3-5 minutes. Remove from heat and allow granola to cool. Makes 2 ½ cups.

Courtesy of www.mashedpotatoesandcrafts.com

I wouldn't admit it to Tony or Lorea, but I stayed up late sifting through the emails I'd printed out from Lily. On

Friday morning, over a bowl of my favorite homemade granola, I looked through the pages again. It was all wedding related with lots of hearts and smiley face emoticons as she shared about her hopes for the future. My throat tightened and my eyes burned with more tears over her death, which would probably be officially ruled as a murder soon. Lily was only twenty-seven years old—nearly two years younger than me, but close enough to my age that it made it hurt even more. How could her life be cut short when she was on the cusp of a new beginning?

The meager stack of papers in front of me didn't hold any revelations concerning Lily's murder. At least, not to me. Maybe Tony would be able to find a connection that I wasn't seeing. I said a silent prayer for Lily's family and Tim, and then turned my mind to the day ahead of me. My shop officially opened at ten, but I wanted to be there by nine. Jessie would be coming by again sometime that morning, and I wanted to tidy up the shop before she arrived.

Just over an hour later, I'd barely turned the lock on the front door when Officer Hamilton walked through. My fingers tensed. Did he have news about Lily?

"Miss Pyper, I hope you don't mind that I stopped by. I just had a few questions for you," Hamilton said.

"Okay." I tried to keep my voice calm and look like I didn't mind at all that policemen kept frequenting my wedding planning shop.

"Would you mind taking a look at a picture? We're checking to see if this individual might have been involved with the sighting at Everybody's Closet."

"Oh, I'd almost forgotten that after everything that

happened with Lily." I glanced at the manila folder that Hamilton held, and my heart jumped in my throat. The anticipation of seeing the possible suspect was unnerving. What if he turned out to be someone I knew, after all?

Hamilton slid a picture from the folder. "Is this the man you saw?"

The man in the picture had reddish hair, drugged-out eyes, and a shaggy goatee. "No. Definitely not the one." As I said it, the image of the man I'd seen holding a rifle on Tuesday came to mind. "The man I saw didn't have facial hair. His hair was dark brown, not red. And he was short." I couldn't explain why I thought the man in the photo looked tall when it was only of the upper half of his body, but I was confident it wasn't the same man.

"Okay, thank you," Detective Hamilton said. "We wanted to rule out the possibility. This man is estranged from his wife, who lives in the area and frequents that consignment store."

"Hey, Adri, did the shipment for—" Lorea walked out front, but stopped when she saw the policeman next to me. She raised her eyebrows. "What's this about?"

"Miss Pyper witnessed a crime and I'm just following up on it." His tone invited no other questions.

I stopped holding my breath and made my shoulders relax. Officer Hamilton trusted me, and that was a nice feeling. I'd have to fill Lorea in after he left. "So you don't have any other leads?"

"We checked the footage of a security camera on one of the businesses nearby, and we did see a white GMC pickup in that time frame. That has narrowed the search considerably."

He slid the picture back into the manila folder. "We'll find him."

"Sorry I couldn't be more help."

"You've been great. I'll be in contact. Stay safe." He smiled and tucked the folder under his arm as he left.

His admonition was a good one, since I'd been involved with the police department on a rather dangerous case last year. I shivered when I thought of the man holding the rifle. Could he have any connections to Lily's murder?

"So, you didn't tell me anything about witnessing a crime," Lorea said as soon as the door clicked shut behind him. "Does this have something to do with Lily? You aren't investigating on your own again, are you?"

I rolled my eyes. "No, I'm completely innocent. All I was trying to do was visit Everybody's Closet to see the new stuff on Tuesday. I didn't even get to go shopping, because there was some lunatic out front holding a gun."

Lorea leaned back, her brow furrowing. "That's weird. What kind of gun?"

"It was a hunting rifle," I answered. "And he shot it before speeding off." I related the whole incident to Lorea, who listened appropriately and gestured angrily at the danger I might have been in.

"That's so random," she said after I'd finished. "Why would he be in the middle of town firing a rifle?"

I rubbed my temples; the memory of the experience sent stress waves through my body. "Oh, that's right. Tony couldn't tell you about it."

"Yeah, and with everything that happened with Lily, he can't say a word."

I closed my eyes. Neither of us liked to say the word *murder* when describing Lily's death. It jostled my universe on a level that was beyond unacceptable to think of someone killing my sweet neighbor.

"Tony has been pretty chatty, for a cop. He was even talking to Luke yesterday," Lorea said. "It's all official business, though."

"He was? When was that?"

"He was on the phone with him when I went to meet Tony after work." Lorea tucked dark strands of her hair behind her ear. "Anyway, I was hoping my shipment of dress fabric had come in, but it doesn't look like it did."

She had carefully changed the subject, and I let it go, since I wasn't sure if she was supposed to be privy to the fact that Tony had talked to Luke. Of course, now my insides were lit up with curiosity bugs, and I still had a day's work ahead of me. I glanced at my watch. Luke was already in court.

"I'm going to run over to the post office and see if it got hung up there for some reason," Lorea said. "I'll stop by Everybody's Closet on my way back if you want."

"Yes, that'd be great. Tell Necia I'll try to get over there sometime next week."

"Okay. I'm going to see if there's anything that might work for a last-minute gift for Trixie and Derek's dogs." She smirked and headed out the door.

It was just before ten thirty when Jessie came in with her son, Gavin. I had yet to meet her fiancé, but it was fairly common that the men in the relationship weren't all that excited about picking out matching accent shades to the wedding colors, and so on.

"Hi, Jessie. Lorea had to run out for a few minutes, but she should be back soon. I can help you until then."

Jessie nodded, but didn't say anything. It almost looked as if she was trying not to cry.

"Gavin, how would you like to play with these cards for a minute?" I handed him a stack of color chips. He grasped them and smiled. I helped him sit at one of my design desks, and he spread the color chips across the surface and mumbled quietly to himself. Jessie looked like she was in a daze. "How are you doing today?" I asked the only question I could think that wasn't outright prying.

"I'm okay," she answered, but her tone indicated otherwise. "Planning a wedding is tough work."

"Is something else wrong?"

Jessie swallowed, and her eyes filled with tears. "Drago was fired yesterday."

"Oh my goodness," I said. "I'm so sorry. Where did he work?"

"Lost Trails Construction." Jessie hesitated, as if thinking over what to say next. "You know that girl that died, Lily Rowan?"

My throat tightened and I nodded.

"Well, her stepdad, Phil Andrus, owns Lost Trails Construction. There's been some problems with the business, and yesterday Lily's sister, Rose, came in and fired Drago's entire crew."

"But why would she do that? Wouldn't it hurt his company more not to have any workers?" I asked.

"I know. It doesn't make any sense." Jessie twisted her

hands together. "Drago said that some of the guys were talking, saying that Andrus had his own daughter killed for her life insurance money."

I gasped, shaking my head.

Jessie swiped a tear from her cheek. "It sounds terrible, but I guess the policy was for a couple million dollars and Phil has been struggling for months trying to stay afloat." She studied the diamond ring on her left hand. "He even had Drago working some smaller side jobs that they never would have touched before."

"I'm sorry. None of it makes sense." I wanted to ask how anyone would know about a life insurance policy when Lily hadn't even had her funeral, but I bit my tongue.

Jessie stared at Gavin while he played with the color chips, and some of the tension eased from her face. "We're still moving forward with the wedding, but I'm not sure what to do until Drago gets another job."

"I understand. Let me look over your plans and see if I can find some ways to cut back and still give you the atmosphere you want." I closed the planning binder we'd been working on. "Tell you what: I'll bring Lorea up to speed on what's going on, but let's give this a rest for a little bit. Don't worry. I bet Drago will find a new job by next week. The construction business is booming around here, and he sounds very talented."

Jessie squeezed my hand. "Thanks, Adri. You're a really good listener. I'll talk to you in a few days."

I glanced out the front window of my shop after she left. I *was* a good listener, and I'd heard a lot more than what Jessie had said in our conversation. If Andrus's workers knew about the life insurance policy, then the police surely did too. What did Tony think about the allegations?

Maybe Lorea could get some information from Tony … but no, he was too professional. If I wanted to know more details about the case, I'd have to come at it from a different angle. I'd have to find information that Tony needed in return.

Lily's funeral was scheduled for Saturday, but I wondered if it would be postponed with an open murder investigation. It still didn't make sense. And now someone from our own little community might be responsible.

Chapter 8

HOMEMADE DOG TREATS

2/3 cup pumpkin puree, ¼ cup peanut butter, 2 large eggs, 3 cups whole wheat flour.

Beat pumpkin, peanut butter, and eggs until well-combined. Gradually add flour until dough is no longer sticky. Knead dough until it resembles sugar cookie dough. Roll dough to ¼-inch thickness and cut-out with dog-bone cookie cutter or desired shape.

Bake at 350 degrees for 20-25 minutes until edges are golden brown.

Courtesy of www.mashedpotatoesandcrafts.com

My next appointment was one I'd been looking forward to for about two hours. Gladys Tiebold had called in to tell me she was engaged and that she and her fiancé wanted to come and look at some wedding planning suggestions. I didn't know her, but could tell by her voice that she was older. "This will be my fifth marriage, so I've learned a few things, but you're the expert I hear."

"Uh, well, thank you. I'd be happy to meet with you and see how I can help you." I didn't know quite what to say or do to prepare to consult Gladys on her fifth marriage, but I'd do my best. I jotted down a few notes in preparation for her appointment.

"Lorea, I have a lady coming in to plan her fifth wedding later. You might want to get a few catalogs ready for her to look at."

"What?" Lorea asked. "Her fifth?"

I chuckled. "Maybe it's a sign."

"A sign for what?" Lorea put her hand on her hip.

"Oh, nothing."

At two thirty, Gladys arrived and my wedding bells chimed, sounding just the same for her as they did for those who had never been married before. The thought made my lips twitch.

"Good afternoon. I'm Gladys Tiebold, and this is my fiancé, Hank Shaffer." Gladys shook my hand vigorously and then passed me to Hank, who pumped my arm three times before abruptly releasing my hand.

"It's very nice to meet you. I'm Adrielle Pyper; call me Adri. Welcome to my shop."

Gladys and Hank were both over sixty. I suspected that Hank might have even been seventy, but it was hard to tell since his hair was dyed jet black and he kept his face clean shaven. Gladys had smile lines that extended down to her jawline, and her blue eyes twinkled as she spoke. "Hank is a charmer. Just look at this ring." Gladys held out her hand and wiggled her ring finger, adorned with a large fake diamond in a gold setting. Hopefully, she didn't think it was real—but then, most people didn't get to study rings as much as I had.

"That is lovely. What a sweetheart," I replied.

Gladys was thick around the middle, with frizzy salt-and-pepper hair. She wore boot-cut jeans that still had creases from the store shelf, and cowboy boots that also appeared new. I glanced at Hank, noting his well-worn Wranglers and cowboy boots. I wondered if Gladys was a different kind of runaway bride than the one Julia Roberts had played in the hit movie. Maybe Gladys got married to the guy, changed to be who he wanted her to be, and then realized she wasn't really in love.

They held hands, and Hank whispered something in her ear. I hoped for both of their sakes that the marriage would work out.

"I'd like to introduce you to my business partner, Lorea Zubiondo." I stepped back so Lorea could shake hands with our new clients.

"That's a good name," Hank said. "You must be Basque."

Lorea smiled. "I am, thank you."

"I used to work for a man who had more sheep than the rock in the river. Named Etcheverry. He spoke Basque."

"Yes, Euskara is an old language that not many know anymore," Lorea replied.

Ten points for Hank, because Lorea was quite proud of her Basque heritage.

"Lorea does all of our wedding gowns, alterations, and

special requests for the wedding clothing," I said. "Let me know if you're interested in looking over her catalog."

Gladys shook her head. "Oh no, I'm too old for anything fancy. Hank and I are just planning to wear our Sunday best. Although, I might get a new dress and him a matching tie." She elbowed Hank.

He shrugged his shoulders. "I guess. I have enough ties for the army, what's one more going to hurt?"

Gladys gave a loud guffaw that caused Lorea to jump, but she covered it well by pretending to swat at a fly. "I'm going to go finish up the dress I'm working on. Nice to meet you."

Hank nodded. "Well, I'll be back to pick you up in a half hour."

"You can certainly stay if you'd like," I said, motioning to the cozy chairs next to the desk of fabric swatches.

Hank wrinkled his nose as if he'd smelled something bad. "I'll leave those details to the women. Let them do what they do best." He winked and sauntered out the door.

"Thanks, dear," Gladys called after him. When he'd gone, Gladys turned to me and smiled. "He is such a jewel. He treats me so well. I didn't know a woman could find happiness this late in life."

"I'm happy for you both. Would you like to sit right here?" I guided her to the planning desk I had set up and began to go through different color choices and wedding themes.

"So many to choose from," Gladys said. "It sure is hard to decide, but I like purple and red."

I thought I heard Lorea snicker in the back room, probably laughing at the color choice. "Which of the two is your favorite?" I asked, flipping to a page of purples and another page of reds in two color sample books. "Purple and red are both strong colors. I recommend choosing one and then pairing it with accent colors."

Gladys nodded. "Good point. Maybe I could find a color in between those two." She flipped through the books for a few more moments, then sighed. "Such a shame about that young lady, Lily Rowan. I understand she was going to have you plan her wedding. Makes me feel sad, sitting here in a chair where she might have sat."

I mentally jumped to follow her train of thought. Hopefully she wasn't here to pry, but the keen look in her eyes made me wonder. She'd called just this morning to make the appointment. "Yes, I feel so bad for her family," I said cautiously. "Did you know her?"

"I've known the family for ages," Gladys replied. "Lily was the sweetest girl. Everyone loved her. After her mother died, it was just those girls and their stepdad, and he didn't do well with the grieving process. Went off and disappeared for a few months and showed up with a suntan and some Italian girlfriend, but she left a few months later."

"Oh dear, that's terrible." I straightened up in my chair, but then slouched because I didn't want to look too eager.

"I just can't believe that someone murdered her." Gladys closed the color samples and put her hands in her lap. "Hank still thinks it was an accident."

I wasn't sure how to answer. "That would make things a little easier on her family, I'm sure."

"Well, don't be too certain that they didn't have something to do with it." Gladys wagged her finger at me. "Rose has always been a troublemaker, and it's no secret that she and Lily didn't get along."

"What do you mean?"

"Lily was preparing to testify against Rose in the custody case over Jasmine," Gladys said. "Lily believed that Javier should take care of his daughter instead of her own sister."

"I guess every family has their troubles," I said. "I wonder why they didn't get along."

"Some kind of foolishness, I'm sure." Gladys paused and looked out the window. "I do believe that all this planning has tuckered me out. You've given me a lot of ideas, but maybe I could come back another day to do more."

"Sure, that'd be great." I had to blink at the conversational whiplash; Gladys switched topics as fast as she'd flicked through the color samples. "Would you like to schedule a follow-up appointment now?"

"I'd better check with Hank and see what he has going on first." Gladys stood and patted my arm. "We'll be in touch."

I waited until Gladys left before deciding to tidy up the desk, replacing all the fabric swatches she'd pulled from the binders. I couldn't be sure, but Gladys seemed to have changed her mind rather quickly about having a professionally planned wedding. Maybe she and Hank would have a quiet ceremony instead. She wasn't the first bride-to-be who felt overwhelmed by the choices and possibilities of a wedding and subsequent celebration, or the price tag that went along with it.

The lines of my forehead scrunched together as I thought about what Gladys had said. Luke had to have known that Lily was going to testify, which explained why he'd been talking to Tony. It irked me that Luke couldn't confide in me because of privacy regulations, but if he was confiding in Tony then he was making an exception for Tony's cop status.

I squeezed my phone, wondering if a text or a call would be most effective to get Luke's attention.

"Did she choose a wedding package?" Lorea asked as she entered the main room of the shop.

"No, I'm not really sure what her angle is," I said. "She had a bunch of questions about Lily ... or rather wanted to talk about her, I guess."

Lorea tilted her head. "That's odd." She shrugged. "Oh well, I'm still trying to figure out what to get Trixie and Derek for their wedding gift."

For each wedding, I did my best to think of a meaningful gift to present to the newly married couple. I'd put Lorea in charge of this wedding since she was working so closely with the bride and groom and their dogs to create the wedding attire. "There wasn't anything that jumped out at Everybody's Closet? I was hoping you could find something we could repurpose. Trixie seems like someone who would appreciate a unique gift."

Lorea shook her head. "I couldn't find anything that they probably don't already have."

"You know, I have something that I think will work," I said. "My mom just emailed me a recipe she found on Pinterest for homemade dog bones."

Lorea turned up her nose. "I don't want to make dog treats."

I laughed. "I'll take care of it if you'll sew up a canvas bag to put the treats in."

Lorea rolled her eyes. "Ay, okay. That means another trip to the fabric store, you know, 'cause I don't keep canvas around here." She motioned to the clear bags of expensive silks, rayons, and chiffon in her sewing closet.

"Thanks, Lorea," I said. I added one more thing to my to-do list: *Find out more info on Gladys.* I had a feeling there was more to her than I'd originally thought.

Chapter 9

JANEEN'S PERFECT POTATO SALAD

2 pounds whole potatoes (about 6), 2 ribs of celery, chopped, (about 1 cup), 1 medium onion, chopped, (about ½ cup), 4 hard-boiled eggs, chopped

Dressing:

1 1/2 cups mayonnaise or salad dressing, 1 Tbsp vinegar, 1Tbsp mustard, 1 tsp salt, 1/4 tsp pepper

Boil potatoes for 20 minutes, or until fork tender. Carefully drain the cooking water from the potatoes into a sink, and refill the pot with cold water, to cool the potatoes.

While the potatoes cool, in a small bowl, stir together the celery, onion, mayonnaise, vinegar, mustard, salt, and pepper. Set the dressing to cool in the refrigerator.

Peel the cooked potatoes, and chop into ½ inch

cubes. When all of the potatoes are chopped, stir in the dressing. Store the salad in an airtight container in refrigerator.

Courtesy of www.mashedpotatoesandcrafts.com

When my phone started ringing, it startled me. Calming myself, I looked down and smiled at the picture of my mom, Laurel Pyper, on the screen. "Hey, Mom," I answered. "How are you today?"

"I can't believe that we have less than a week to finish everything for the booth!" she said. "I have your dad putting prices on everything and printing up labels, because I decided I should make more of those little crocheted heart garlands."

That was my mom: bursting with life. She usually started a phone call mid-sentence, and today her sentence made my fingers buzz with tension. She was talking about the Ketchum Arts Festival that was scheduled for next weekend on July nineteenth through the twenty-first.

I checked my calendar to be sure that it was still Thursday. "Mom, we have a full week. I know it's nerve-wracking, but I think you'll be fine. You'll have plenty of items to sell."

My mom had been working for over six months to prepare for the Arts Festival. The glorious gathering of artists of all kinds would take place in the Festival Meadows near the Sun Valley Resort next week. With everything that was happening with Lily's death and the weddings I was planning, it hadn't been on my mind like it needed to be this week. My family had attended the past several years, so when I moved back from San Francisco they made it clear that it was one of the events I couldn't miss. And now, somehow, I'd been roped into working a booth with my mom and Lorea.

"But what if we sell out? Or what if some of the things aren't popular enough? I want to make sure we earn a profit," she said.

"Me too. But don't worry. I think we'll do fine, and if not, I can write it off as a business expense because the exposure will pay for itself." I picked up the pamphlet with all the details about the Ketchum Arts Festival and thumbed through it, while my mom continued worrying through the phone.

This year there would be over one hundred and fifty booths. I hoped that all of my mom's hard work would pay off. The fees were steep at nearly four hundred dollars for the booth, but because we were splitting our booth between Mashed Potatoes and Crafts and Adrielle Pyper's Dream Weddings, I felt it was a smart venture. Not that I needed extra business right now—the way this year was headed, I'd have to look at hiring another assistant, because Lorea's dress designs continued to bring new customers and word-of-mouth referrals who wanted the exquisite, specialized dress only her hands could create.

Mom's side of the booth would be filled with creations that she'd worked on with me for several different bridal showers, weddings, and receptions. As if reading my thoughts, my mom paused and asked, "Adri, how many card packets do you have ready?"

"I'm still working on them, so I don't have an exact count, but I promise I'll be ready."

"Oh dear, do you need some help? I just don't know how we're ever going to be ready." I could picture my mom running her hands through the ends of her curly blonde hair, streaked with bits of gray.

"Mom, we'll make it. Just let me get through Trixie's wedding this weekend, and then I'll put my full concentration on it."

"Okay, sorry to bug you. I'll let you get back to work."

"Tell Dad hi and take a deep breath. I think this will be fun," I lied.

After I ended the call, I glanced at my craft table. It never seemed like I had time to craft or make cards like we used to. I flipped through the stack of handmade cards adorned with stamped images, lace, buttons, die-cuts, and ribbon. I loved getting a card in the mail that someone had made just for me. My mom was one of the most thoughtful people I knew, and she was always sending cards to people for any little reason—and the wonderful part of her habit was how much it affected others.

There were twenty-five bundles of cards, each tied with brown twine. Thank goodness; I'd completed them months ago because there probably wouldn't be any more added in the next week. The news of Lily's murder must not have reached my parents yet, but my brother, Wes, would probably hear about it today. Hopefully my mom wouldn't recognize the name of Lily Rowan, because if she remembered that she was my neighbor, Mom would be frantic with worry. After the life-threatening incidents I'd experienced, I guess I couldn't blame her, but I hated to make her worry more than she already did.

The bundles of cards fit neatly into a paper box. All I needed to do was print out a price tag and get all the information and brochures ready to hand out at the festival. When I'd signed up for the booth several months ago, it had seemed so far away. I probably should have listened to my inner worrier when it wondered how I'd be able to juggle a festival booth during the rush of wedding season.

Luke called me at four o'clock, right about the time my mind was wandering back to the revelation I'd heard from Gladys about Lily testifying.

"The judge asked for a recess. This case is almost wrapped up, and I'm ready for it to be over." Luke's voice sounded tired.

"I'm sorry it's been such a messy one."

"Me too. I think everyone was hoping it'd be done before the funeral, but now that it's been postponed, Rose and Javier have found a way to drag the proceedings out a little longer."

"So the funeral has been postponed?"

"Yes. I don't understand why, but Tony assured me it was a good thing for everyone involved."

So he *had* been talking to Tony, but it obviously wasn't a secret if he was able to mention it so casually. "Hmm. I'm not sure what to think of it all."

"Me neither, but that isn't why I called. I was hoping that you could meet me for an impromptu lunch/dinner in Jimmy's park?"

"The one right across from the police station? Sure, my stomach was just complaining that I hadn't fed it."

"I thought that might be the case. I didn't get lunch either." Luke chuckled. "Do you want to meet me inside Atkinson's and we can get something from their deli?"

"That sounds wonderful. I'll leave in five minutes." I hung up the phone, scurried around my shop, and told Lorea I might run a few errands after meeting Luke.

"I'll close up if you aren't back," she said. "How are you and Luke doing, anyway?"

My back was turned to her when she asked the question, so I had a moment to compose my face into something calm and non-twitterpated. "Good. He's been so busy with this case that we haven't been on a real date in quite a while, but he's been calling me. It's kind of nice that he's reaching out."

Lorea arched an eyebrow. "Why are you trying to hide how much you like him?"

I bit the inside of my cheek to keep from smiling. "I do like him, but I want to be careful. You know how he is."

"I do, but I think he's changed. He seems different the last few times I've seen him with you."

"Thanks, but don't get your hopes up, okay?"

"Same to you, little Miss Matchmaker. I saw you looking in the big-and-tall section of the tuxedos for Tony."

"Hey, I was just curious on the availability. It didn't have anything to do with you ... but now that you mention it, why do we even have a big-and-tall catalog?"

Now it was Lorea's turn to blush. Her tawny skin turned pink around her ears. "Weren't you going somewhere?" She pointed at the door.

I laughed all the way to my car. Maybe Tony did have a chance with Lorea—the self-proclaimed skeptic of true love.

It'd be interesting to find out if Luke had noticed anything between the two of them. In my business, I'd become somewhat of an expert at detecting when people were attracted to each other. I'd never admit it to anyone, but me and some of the other associates at my old job used to make bets on how long certain couples would stay together. It was kind of scary how often I'd been right.

It took me ten minutes to drive out of Sun Valley and into the little town of Hailey. There was an Atkinson's grocery store in Ketchum right around the corner from my shop, but the brother store in Hailey had a wider selection and Luke and I both had a weak spot for the delicious food served in the deli. The green-and-red script of the store's name brought back memories of my childhood visits to my grandma's cabin. We loved stopping by Atkinson's for a tub of Häagen-Dazs. The store had recently celebrated its fiftieth anniversary, but it had kept up with the times, offering new and trendy items as well as the standard staples, which thankfully included a mouthwatering supply of rich dark-chocolate bars.

I stepped inside, and the blast of cool air felt good after the ride in my toasty vehicle. I spotted Luke near the deli, checking out the offerings of the day. He straightened when I started walking toward him, turned, and held up one hand in a little wave. I loved that he had sensed my presence. My stomach did a flip that had nothing to do with hunger.

"Afternoon," he said, taking my hand.

"Hey, thanks for the invite. What's on the menu today?"

His hand was cool and firm against mine. "I like the looks of the club sandwich—" He pointed toward the deli. "—with some of this potato salad."

"Hmm, that does look good. The potatoes aren't half-mashed like some salads I've seen." I examined the potato salad—I was picky about that, and since we were in Idaho, I felt that I could be. My aunt Janeen made the best potato salad with medium sized chunks of potatoes, hard-boiled eggs, and just the right amount of sauce so it was neither too soggy nor too dry. "I think I'll try some."

"Are you sure?" Luke teased. "The way you were cross-examining those potatoes, I'm not sure how they'll taste."

"Yes, I'm sure. Hopefully they'll pass muster."

We each scooped up a serving of the potato salad and walked over to the counter to order our sandwiches. Luke ordered a club on wheat, and I ordered a turkey bacon avocado on rye. After we checked out, Luke took my hand and we walked down the street to a tiny grassy area with a few benches. There was an archway of wrought iron that spelled out "Jimmy's Park." I knew the place in passing, but had never taken the time to actually sit down and enjoy the atmosphere. There were strawberry plants bordering a hedge dotted with marigolds and some kind of lily. The park was right across the street from the Blaine County courthouse, which was right next to the old courthouse under construction.

"Thanks for meeting me," Luke said. "I hope you won't give up on me, because I'm planning to take you out on a real date soon."

The wrapper on my sandwich crinkled as I pulled it open. "I'd like that. I won't give up on you, because I understand; it's a busy season for me too. I had a potential client come in just today."

"Oh, that's good if you have room for them." He took a bite of his sandwich and leaned back against the bench as he chewed.

"I don't know if she'll end up hiring me. Her name was Gladys Tiebold, marrying a Hank Shaffer. Do those names ring a bell?" Here was my lead-in to the question I wanted answered about Lily.

Luke shook his head. "Haven't heard of them. Why do you think they won't go with you?"

"They're an older couple, and this is her fifth marriage. I'm not sure she wants to spend as much as I charge."

Luke choked on his sandwich, coughed for a minute, and wiped his eyes. "Did you say fifth marriage?"

"Yes, don't get all prideful about it." I suppressed a laugh.

"What? I didn't perform any of her divorces." He chuckled. "Five times? That's insanity."

"Or expensive, depending how you look at it. But hey, she mentioned that she was a good friend of Lily Rowan and that Lily was preparing to testify in court against Rose in the custody case. Why didn't you tell me about that?"

Luke held out his hand. "Hasn't anyone in this town heard about client-attorney privilege? How did that get out?"

"What do you mean? And I should say beforehand, I wasn't nosing around. This Gladys lady just jumped subjects, started talking about Lily, and then told me that."

Luke shook his head. "Lily hadn't even told Tim she was going to testify because she knew he wouldn't want her to. He thought it was better if she stayed out of it and instead kept up a good relationship with Rose where she could be a good influence in Jasmine's life, or at least that's what Lily told me." He rubbed a hand over his forehead. "I wonder how that lady got that piece of information. Do you think Lily told her?"

I shrugged. "I didn't think to ask that, but I could."

"Man, people need to learn to keep their mouths shut." He set the rest of his sandwich down and pulled out his phone.

"What are you doing?" I asked.

"I'm calling Tony. Don't you see? You may have just uncovered a motive for murder."

The sounds of cars and people around us suddenly grew louder, buzzing in my ears. Had Lily been murdered because of a custody case over a six-year-old? Luke's voice filtered through the noise, and I picked up bits and pieces of his conversation with Tony. I stared at the remains of my sandwich, and wrapped it up for later.

"Sorry about that," Luke said once he ended the call. "Tony has already talked to me about this case and asked if I thought of anything or heard anything to call him immediately. I get the feeling that they're almost ready to make an arrest."

I jerked back. "But who?"

"Rose has a few boyfriends that are unsavory characters, to say the least. She could have put one of them up to it if it meant keeping her daughter."

"But then why not just off her ex?"

"True, but that's pretty obvious, don't you think?"

"I don't think she would kill her own sister just for testifying," I said. Although I wasn't really sure of what anyone would do, based on my own experiences. I had seen people do some pretty crazy things in the past few years.

"Well, Javier's mother, Tina, has been pushing for full custody the entire time. I'm not sure he would have gone for it without her prodding him."

"But she wouldn't want to kill Lily then. That would help her case."

"Unless she didn't know which side Lily would be testifying for."

I swallowed. The way Luke said it, several people could have been out to murder Lily. His statement hung in the air, and I wondered who had the most to gain by her death.

Chapter 10

BATH SALTS BY GLADYS

2 cups Epsom salts, ½ cup baking soda, ¼ cup sea salt, 25 drops lavender essential oil, 10 drops of your favorite essential oil. Try lemongrass, bergamot, or peppermint.

Mix all ingredients in a medium size bowl. Store in an air-tight jar and use ¼ cup per bath.

Courtesy of www.mashedpotatoesandcrafts.com

Friday morning was a time for me to get all the last-minute details done before the weekend. Lorea and I usually had orders to put in for a variety of items that we'd need for the weddings in coming days, and for some reason there were always several things that came up just before the weekend.

I had just hung up the phone with the caterer when Gladys breezed in the doorway. She wore a purple muumuu with red hibiscus flowers. I guess red and purple do work together sometimes—at least the outfit suited Gladys.

"Good morning," I said.

"It is a wonderful morning," Gladys replied. "I've just stopped by to invite you to my wedding. I can't believe I'm getting married today!"

"Oh?" I tried to get the right intonation of surprise to show up in my voice. I was definitely surprised, but it looked like Gladys wanted me to be happily surprised, and excited for her.

"Yes. Hank and I are just so in love, we decided, why wait?" She spread her arms out, and the purple muumuu fluttered with the movement.

"Well, that's wonderful. Where will you be married?"

"At Hank's place. He lives just outside of Hailey and his yard is lovely."

"Oh, backyard weddings are perfect this time of year." I struggled to come up with something to say and quiet my inner wedding- planner voice from chanting what I'd learned while working at Bellissima, the premier wedding design boutique in San Francisco, California. *Don't be hasty with your dreams. Design your future in detail.*

"We're inviting just a few close friends and family, but I wanted you to come since you gave us so many wonderful ideas."

I choked on the credit she'd given me. Hopefully word wouldn't spread too far that I had helped with this impromptu wedding. "That's very kind of you."

"So you'll come?"

"Uh, what time did you say?" Now to decide if I should go to the wedding or hope that I already had something planned. Luke would probably bail me out if I begged, but the eager look on Gladys's face was hard to turn down. I also needed to find a way to ask Gladys a little question about the information she'd shared with me yesterday.

"It'll be at six-thirty. I'm so glad you can come. Make sure you bring a date." She took both my hands in hers and gave them a little squeeze. "Here's the address." She handed me a purple index card with the details handwritten on the lines.

I lifted my cheeks into an uber-fake smile. "I wouldn't miss it. And, uh, I wondered if you could help me with something for Lily's fiancé?"

Gladys's expression changed, and the keen look returned to her eye. She was a gossip; I could almost see her antennae go up. "Yes, that poor dear. I'd do anything to help."

I bit my bottom lip. Now how could I phrase the question so it wouldn't look like I was the gossip? "Well, I'm trying not to step on any toes, but I wondered, when did you hear that Lily would be testifying in the custody case?"

Gladys scrunched her brows together, probably wondering how her answer would help Tim. "It was just the other day. I took her over a bag of my homemade bath salts to congratulate her on her engagement." She looked at me expectantly.

"Oh, that was nice of you. Homemade gifts are the best."

"Yes, well, this bath salt recipe would work great on that Idaho-potatoes-and-crafts website you have." Gladys put her hand to the side of her mouth. "It's my own secret combination. Works like a charm every time and leaves you feeling delightfully refreshed."

I couldn't be surprised anymore by Gladys. Not only was she having a shotgun wedding at the age of sixty-something, but she seemed savvy enough to understand the workings of my Mashed Potatoes and Crafts website. How in the world did she even find out about the site?

Before I could think of a response, Gladys was handing me another index card, this one pale yellow. "Here's the recipe. If you'd like to post it, I have the pictures ready, and maybe you could link it to my Etsy shop?"

"Well, that would be wonderful, I think," I stammered.

"Make sure you remember the combination of essential oils is what makes this recipe stand out." She placed the card in my hand with a smile.

"Okay, I'll definitely try this out," I tucked the card into my back pocket. "Now, you were saying you took the bath salts to Lily and that's when she told you about testifying?"

"Well, she was just so upset." Gladys waved a hand in the air. "And I would be too, having to go against my own family, but it was the right thing for Jasmine, I suppose."

"And did she say for certain that her testimony would be *against* Rose?"

"Hmm. Well, I thought that was why she was all worked up, but now that you mention it, I can't be one hundred percent certain on that." Gladys tapped her chin. "There was so much going on that day. I'd filled ten orders for my bath salts already. You might want to carry some in your store. Brides always need a little pampering." She winked.

"Thank you. Let's start with this recipe. And I'll plan on being to your wedding tonight," I added before she could push any more of her wares on me or my store.

"Wonderful! Oh, and I'll be at the Ketchum Arts Festival too, booth number twenty-eight. You ought to stop by." Gladys scurried out the door, her muumuu trailing behind her like some hideous nightmare, before I had a chance to tell her I'd be working my own booth.

The wedding would definitely be interesting. Time to call Luke and invite him to yet another wedding, and give him the scoop on Gladys. Although the conversation had been so disjointed, I still didn't know how Gladys had discovered Lily was testifying. Luckily, Luke had been promising me another date, so I was pretty certain he'd try his best to make it.

I heard the door open and shut in the back of the store and poked my head around the corner to greet Lorea. "We have to make sure that everything is ready for the wedding tomorrow, because I've been invited to Gladys and Hank's tonight."

"What? Where's my invite?" Lorea put a hand over her heart as if she'd been wounded.

I waved the purple index card at her. "I'm sure this would work for you, too."

"Ahem, what was I saying? Oh yes, I'm ready to check off every detail for Sadie's wedding tomorrow."

"You mean Trixie, right? 'Cause the dogs aren't actually getting married." I felt the distinction was important to bring up, since Lorea kept mixing up Trixie's dog with the bride.

Lorea burst out laughing. "Please help me if I make that mistake again tomorrow. I don't know why I can't keep it straight. I'll go get to work right now. Mike should be here for his final fitting soon."

Twenty minutes later, Mike, Trixie, and Derek showed up for the final fittings.

"I can't wait for tomorrow. It's going to be the best day, and guess what?" Trixie clapped her hands together as she spoke. "My mom found a basket that can clip to Sadie's collar. We're going to fill it with rose petals and the rings and let her bring them to us."

"Oh, that will be a nice touch," I said, because Lorea was speechless as usual. I elbowed her, and she coughed.

"Um, let's try these on and get you on your way. I just went over the checklist, and I have to say, this is one of Adri's most well-planned events. Everything has been arranged far enough in advance that we didn't have to do a rush on anything."

"So you think it's okay that we skipped the rehearsal dinner?" Derek asked. He was of average height with a wiry build and he wore his dark hair trimmed severely. It made his ears seem to jut out a bit, but the bushy sideburns he sported evened things out.

"Definitely," Lorea answered. "It's your wedding; you get to choose."

Derek patted Mike's head. "I don't think that would have fit well with the dogs, anyway. Thanks for helping us come up with ideas to keep things running smoothly."

I nodded. The dog wedding wasn't over yet, so I only hoped that things would run smoothly.

Lorea helped Mike into the tux, and I think the boxer might have stolen her heart, she looked so proud when he strutted around in his tux. Lorea scratched behind his ears and patted his head. "That's a good boy."

Trixie and Derek loaded Mike into the car. I'd only met Sadie once, because Trixie left her home after she'd knocked over my display of antique wedding invitations. Trixie said that Sadie was too excited for small spaces. Hopefully she would behave for the wedding tomorrow night.

Chapter 11

ANTIQUE WEDDING CARD RECIPE

Fold 5 ½" x 8 ½" piece of ivory cardstock in half to make 4 ¼" x 5 ½" card base.

Rip 1/8" from the outer edge of the card to create a distressed look. Using a sponge, press on a brown ink pad and then gently sponge the ripped edge of the card.

Stamp desired image on coordinating colored cardstock scrap and rip the edges of the cardstock, sponging again with ink.

Glue lace or ribbon across card and glue stamped image over the lace.

Stamp a quote or write a wedding day message on the card below the image.

Example: Forever and Forever Starts Today

Courtesy of www.mashedpotatoesandcrafts.com

I clicked send on another order of paper doilies and heard Lorea's phone buzz with several texts in a row. Two seconds later, she ran past me and toggled my mouse to open another screen. "That was my sister. She said that there's breaking news regarding Lily's murder investigation."

"How'd she find out?"

"Terese was watching TV and it said to stay tuned for the headline news at noon." Lorea typed in the local news station website, and Lily's face alongside a picture of Tim's animal clinic came on screen. Within a few seconds, a video began with a reporter standing outside Tim's clinic.

"Tim Esplin was brought in for questioning in connection to the murder of his fiancée, Lily Rowan, today," the reporter said. "It's alleged that Lily died of poisoning with chemicals similar to those found in the euthanizing injections for animals. As a veterinarian, Tim is the prime suspect, and it's rumored that the euthanizing agent may have come from his office. Toxicology reports will confirm the substance."

Lorea and I both gasped at the same time. "No, he couldn't have," Lorea said.

"There's no way," I said. "Someone must have set him up."

The reporter continued. "There are strict guidelines regarding the use of euthanasia by the Board of Veterinary Medicine. It must be purchased and acquired through a veterinary license. All solutions have to be kept locked up, and only the vet and his assistant have access to the substance. Because there has been a rise in suicides recently from euthanizing agents, the rules are very specific about how it can be handled and administered.

"All dosages are recorded, dated, and witnessed.

Detective Anthony Ford from the Ketchum Police Department stated that arrests are not made without substantial evidence. Hopefully this will lead to full resolution of the murder case of Lily Rowan. Reporting live from Hailey, Idaho, this is Tracy Harper."

The video stopped, and Lorea scrolled through the website to see if she could find any more information on the case. "Do you think Tony can share any more info with us?" I asked.

Lorea shrugged. "Only one way to find out." She pulled out her phone and sent him a text.

"Tim loved Lily. What reason would he have to kill her?" I asked, more to myself than Lorea.

"If the evidence stacks up so neatly, the police will know it's a frame job," Lorea said. "I'm sure Tony is already looking at other angles."

We both tried to work, but it was hard to concentrate with so many unknown questions circling around us. Half an hour later, Tony texted Lorea back to tell her that he couldn't share more info at this point, but Tim would be okay.

"Hopefully that means he thinks that Tim isn't guilty," Lorea said.

"Yes, but the damage will already be done to his clinic," I pointed out. "Can you imagine how many patients he lost today?" I clenched my fists when I thought about how bad publicity affected businesses like his and mine. Of course, I wouldn't blame people for not wanting to bring their cat or dog in to see a potential murderer, but after the fact, when Tim was proven innocent, those people weren't likely to return. "He didn't kill her, did he?"

Lorea shook her head slowly. "I don't know."

I kept seeing Tim's face from the news flash across my mind, and then I'd remember things about Lily—how she was always so sweet. She had brought me a plate of cookies when I'd first moved in, and we'd talked on the porch for twenty minutes. She fed my cat, Tux, when I visited my hometown of Rupert every few months. I had given her several hollyhock starts from my mom's garden, and she'd cultivated them in her own little plot on the side of her condo. The mystery of her murder was too big for me to solve, and I told myself that I'd stay out of it.

Luke picked me up at six o'clock and we headed out to Hank's place west of Hailey. On the way, we discussed the murder investigation. "Tim didn't kill her," I said.

"What makes you say that?" Luke asked. "The police must think he did it, or they wouldn't have arrested him."

"Maybe they needed to make a move to appease the public or Lily's father-in-law." I had heard murmurs from a few different people that Phil Andrus was upset at the way the police were handling the investigation. Someone said he'd even hired his own private investigator to search for the truth.

Luke rubbed his right thumb along the steering wheel. "I don't know Tim well, but I heard some things that have me siding with the police on this one."

"What kind of things?"

"Something about a life insurance policy he had on her."

"But, wait. How could Tim have a life insurance policy on her?" I asked. "And how come I keep hearing about life insurance? How do people even know these things?"

"Well, I heard it had something to do with the policy that Phil had. Something like they were both beneficiaries." Luke turned slowly onto a gravel drive that led up to Hank's house.

"Before they were even married? That seems kind of morbid." I stared out the window as we approached. "None of it sounds right."

"Let's try to think of something else for a little while so you can enjoy your wedding." Luke turned the car off.

"Oh no, this is not one of *my* weddings," I insisted.

Luke chuckled as he helped me from the car. "If you say so."

"I do," I hissed, but it was loud enough that a woman looked askance at me as we walked around the back of the house.

Luke's smile broadened, and he squeezed my hand. "I do, too," he whispered.

We passed a handwritten sign on cardboard that had been tacked onto one of the trees. It had a big red arrow pointing toward the backyard, and the words declared, *Hank & Gladys Forever.* We had to duck under a wire clothesline that was draped with purple and red crepe paper. There were a few long white tables flanking the side of a sagging barn, and various folding chairs, rocking chairs, and large stumps dotted the yard, where a makeshift altar was set up near the horse trough.

We stopped and signed in at the guest book, and I set the handmade wedding card I'd brought in a vellum envelope on the table. The design was one of my favorites, because the one edge of the card was torn and then brushed with ink to make it look old—almost like the antique wedding cards I collected.

We wove through the obstacle course of mismatched furniture toward the middle of the yard. My eyes bulged when a cow came over near the fence and nearly ate some crepe paper before someone shooed it away. Luke's shoulders moved in quiet laughter, and I tugged on his hand. He looked at me, and the mirth in his eyes made me laugh, but I wasn't so good at the silent laughter.

Luke led me back to a pair of rickety folding chairs, and we sat underneath an ancient willow tree. "This is nice," he murmured.

"Now, you stop," I whispered. "It's not every day you get married for the fifth time."

Luke laughed so hard he snorted, and he stopped abruptly and sat up straight in his chair. The music started then: it was the traditional wedding march, the tinny quality coming from an old tape player that was plugged into an extension cord coming from the barn. Everyone quieted, but then the music stopped and we heard someone say, "False alarm. The bride ain't ready yet."

"Maybe they are waiting on a few more guests," I said. "By the way, I forgot to tell you that I asked Gladys about Lily testifying. She wasn't sure if it was against Rose or not."

"That makes me feel a little bit better, but I still don't know why Lily would tell her," Luke said.

"I'm not so sure that she did. Gladys is extremely flighty, and it was hard to keep her on topic. I don't know if she was deliberately changing the subject, but maybe she overheard something instead of actually being told."

Luke nodded and turned his head to glance down the path behind us. He stiffened, and I turned to see who had arrived. A woman wearing a sleek red dress, holding the hand of a little Latina girl in a frilly yellow dress, stopped at the guest book. She flipped one of her dark brown curls across her shoulder and bent to sign the book.

"Rose and Jasmine?" I whispered.

Luke nodded, his lips turning down in a frown.

I reached over and pretended to smooth his mouth upwards into a smile. "Relax. It's a public setting." But even I knew that attorneys didn't like to be seen in public with the opposing side of the courtroom.

I held my breath as she walked past us and to the other side of the yard. She took a seat, settled Jasmine in beside her, and looked up. Her eyes widened when she saw Luke.

I quickly averted my own gaze, murmuring quietly to Luke and motioning to the refreshment table set up near us. "Hey, pretend you're really interested in these refreshments while Rose checks us out and decides if we're a threat or not."

Luke leaned his head toward mine. "You watch too many detective shows. You know that, don't you?"

"Only *Castle*," I retorted. "I'm too busy to watch anything else." Well, I did sneak in a few home remodeling shows on HGTV sometimes, but I doubted Luke would be interested in those.

He smiled. "Thanks for inviting me, even if I do know what you're scheming."

"What?" I whispered.

"You got me to attend this so I can recognize what an expert you are when I come to one of your weddings."

I nudged him with my elbow. "Not my scheme at all."

Luke put his arm around me and pulled me toward him. "Well, I can tell the difference. You do great work, Adri."

His words made me feel all wobbly inside, and I might've glanced at his lips and wondered how it would feel to kiss them. Instead, I leaned my head on his shoulder. "Thank you."

The music started again, and Gladys arrived. She walked along the grass in low heels, watching Hank as she approached. She wore a peach-colored jacket over a bright-purple skirt. Her wardrobe suited her well, and as she stood next to Hank in what looked to be a new pair of Wranglers and a snap cowboy shirt with a bolo tie, it didn't really matter that they hadn't spent a fortune on their wedding.

The preacher gave a few words of advice and then asked Gladys if she would have Hank as her husband.

She nodded vigorously. "I do, I surely do." I could see her squeezing Hank's hand.

The preached then turned to Hank. "Mr. Hank Shaffer, do you take this woman to be your lawful wedded wife?"

The audience collectively leaned forward for the crowning moment of the evening. Then, out of nowhere, I thought I heard an old Chris LeDeux song called "8 Second Ride" start to play. I looked at Luke and he scrunched his eyebrows, turning an ear toward the sound which seemed to be coming from Hank's back pocket.

"I do," Hank said. The song grew louder and he jolted, then grabbed the phone from his pocket. And answered it. "Hello?" He held the phone close to his ear and took one step away from Gladys.

I tugged on Luke's hand and mouthed, "What?!"

He subtly shook his head and grinned. Gladys didn't seem perturbed; she lifted up her bouquet of daisies and sniffed them daintily. The preacher's face was stoic and his concentration was focused on Hank, who was still on the phone. The preacher checked his watch and then said, "I now pronounce you man and wife. Congratulations."

Hank held one finger up and then said, "Well, Earl, I'll have to get back with you on that. I'm just gettin' hitched right now." There was a pause. "No, not my horse, to my wife."

Everyone laughed, and then Hank ended the call. I kept laughing because Luke was laughing and trying to hold it in, but the craziness of it all was leaking out the corners of his eyes.

"Thank you all for coming," Gladys said. "Please enjoy the refreshments." She hugged Hank.

"Luke, I can't believe it. He forgot to kiss the bride," I sputtered.

"I guess you're right. Oh well, that's just a technicality, right?"

I looked up toward the sky. "I've never."

Luke put his face right next to mine. "What are we looking at? Are they releasing doves?"

"Quit making me laugh. My sides hurt already." I poked him and he moved over, but I could still feel the stubble on his cheek against mine and smell the hint of pine in his cologne.

He stood and held out his hand. "Would you care for some refreshments?"

"I'd love that."

We walked over to the long tables graced with red and purple tablecloths and decorated with paper plates of E.L.

Fudge cookies, Oreos, and bowls of M&M's. There were also cups of homemade root beer and ... I wasn't sure, but maybe some cups of moonshine. Luke and I steered clear of the unknown and stuck with E.L. Fudge.

We sat back down, and I surveyed the guests. It was a motley crowd, some dressed nicely in skirts or suits and several dressed casual. There were even a few younger relations wearing stained tank tops and sporting mullets, ball caps, and shorts. Guests were starting to exit the backyard, some carrying plates full of Oreos and M&M's, when a new visitor arrived: a Latino with close-cropped black hair, wearing tan cargo pants and the skimpy white tank tops we used to call wife-beaters, charged in through the back gate. Luke didn't just flinch; he jumped out of his chair, dropping his paper plate of M&M's, and headed for the man I assumed to be Javier Benavidez.

"What are you doing bringing my daughter here?" The man stomped over to Rose and pointed at Jasmine.

"She's my daughter too!" Rose stood. "This is uncalled for. You weren't invited to this wedding."

"I told you I don't want you taking Jasmine anywhere without letting me know first."

"Hi, Daddy," Jasmine said.

The little girl stepped forward, but Rose pulled her back and stomped her foot. "This is a wedding, you—"

"Javier," Luke interrupted. "Talk to me for a minute." He pulled Javier aside, and Luke spoke softly while Javier muttered angrily.

"Mr. Luke, what seems to be the problem here?" The preacher addressed Luke and watched Javier warily.

"I think we've about got it settled," Luke said. "I apologize for the outburst." He turned to Javier and said something I couldn't hear. Javier gestured to Rose and Jasmine several times, and then left.

Luke didn't say anything to Rose. He headed straight for me and held out his hand. "Is it okay if we go now?"

"Sure." I took his hand and let him help me to my feet. He kept hold of my hand as we exited the yard.

"I can't believe he did that," Luke spat. "He completely disregarded all the warnings and guidance I gave him. He's not supposed to talk to Rose except through an attorney because of how heated things have been in the courtroom. He may have just sabotaged his own case."

"I'm sorry. That was really bad," I said. "I saw a couple people pull out their phones. They might have snapped a picture."

"Or called the police," Luke grumbled. He walked me to the car and unlocked the door.

"Well, nothing really happened," I replied. "Javier just yelled, but he didn't touch Rose or Jasmine. It was good that you were there to break up the fight before it got ugly."

Luke groaned. "All of those witnesses."

"And don't forget the preacher, Mr. Luke."

That cracked a smile, and Luke pulled me close. "Thanks for letting me rant."

"Anytime. You've listened to me plenty," I said.

"Not really. I need to work on that–listening to you." He put his hand on my cheek. "You're good for me, you know?"

He stroked my cheek with his thumb and forefinger, and it was like a match striking the box and bursting into flame.

He leaned toward me, and I almost closed my eyes; the moment sparkled with anticipation. Luke kissed my cheek and then my forehead before pulling me into his arms.

"You're good for me too," I murmured. And I meant it.

Chapter 12

"MR. RIGHT" AND "MRS. ALWAYS RIGHT" PILLOWS

This pillow set is the perfect gift for an older couple. Embroider, applique, or stencil the words "Mr. Right" onto one decorative pillow. Next put the words "Mrs. Always Right" on the second pillow. You could also screen print the words onto a matching set of pillowcases.

Courtesy of www.mashedpotatoesandcrafts.com

I awoke the next morning, drowsy from dreams of red and purple crepe paper monsters and Javier yelling and chasing them through the barn. Shaking off the convoluted nightmare, I decided to focus on that magical moment when Luke had told me I was good for him. My insides warmed with the spark that I'd felt between us when he'd kissed my cheek—almost my lips.

The pleasant butterflies floating in my belly thinking of almost-kissing Luke were replaced with angry hornets when I saw the Saturday morning news recap headlining the arrest of Tim Esplin in the murder of Lily Rowan. The police had decided to arrest him after all, and bail was set for one million dollars. I ground my teeth together. "He didn't do it," I murmured.

There was plenty to do in preparation for Trixie and Derek's wedding, but I stopped by the Ketchum police station on my way to the shop. Tony was in his office, surrounded by stacks of files. "Tony, can I talk to you for a minute?"

There was a clear space on his desk where he leaned his forearms and surveyed my stance. "Shoot."

"Why did you arrest Tim? You know he didn't kill Lily."

Tony huffed. "Evidence is what puts things in motion. I couldn't stop the amount of evidence or its veracity from implicating Tim. I'm sorry, Adri, but I don't think he's innocent."

"But what about the motive that Luke talked to you about? I saw Rose last night with her daughter, and she seemed fiercely protective of her."

"That was kind of a long shot. We went out and talked to Gladys, and she couldn't remember where she'd heard that information," Tony said. "Have a seat." He gestured at the hard plastic chair in front of his desk, and I sat on the edge.

"That's kind of odd, don't you think?" Although I wasn't surprised that Gladys couldn't pinpoint where she'd "heard" the information, I kind of hoped that the police would be able to get more out of her.

Tony tapped his finger on the desk. "Murder and everything related to it is odd. That's why you need detectives to figure things out." He said the last part pointedly and I felt the jab, but I wasn't ready to give up.

"Did you at least question Rose?"

"Rose has a solid alibi for the entire day of Lily's murder. She wasn't even in town." Tony stacked another file folder.

"Where was she, then?" I asked.

"She was at a design conference in Boise and she was seen by several of the associates there," Tony replied. "I talked to them myself and one of them faxed me her business card with a note she'd written on it about a bid."

The backs of my legs felt tight from all the nervous tension I held there. I rolled my ankle, hearing it pop several times. "Tim is innocent. You've got to look at someone else, or tell me who to look at. If it's not Rose, then why isn't Phil behind bars?"

"I can't go over all the details of the case with you," Tony said. "We don't make an arrest unless we have evidence. The euthanizing agent came from Tim's clinic. He doesn't have an alibi, and he has motive."

I shook my head. "What motive?"

"There's more to this than you can see." Tony stood and walked around the desk. "You'll have to trust me on this one."

"Can I talk to Tim?"

Tony's lips folded into a frown. "I'll let you know."

"Wait, I heard on the news that only Tim and his assistant have access to the euthanizing agent. That's probably Vickie, isn't it? What about her?"

"Adri," Tony's voice was stern.

I pushed on anyway with my line of questioning. "She could totally have something to do with this. Have you met her? The woman couldn't even smile at my cat."

Tony chuckled. "Yes, I've met her and she also has a very good alibi."

I groaned. "How good?"

"She was getting her hair done," Tony said. "The salon verified her appointment."

My shoulders slumped. "Okay. Thanks for answering my questions. I'm really not trying to be a pain."

"I know." He patted my shoulder, and I heard the unspoken ending to his sentence: *But you are one*. Or maybe I just imagined that's what my older brother's best friend would have said to the younger sister who always found a way to tag along.

The police station was largely quiet for a Saturday morning. I knew which hallway led to the jail, but now wasn't the time to try to talk to Tim. That was a request that I'd have to follow up on my own. I was pretty sure that Tony wouldn't let me know if I could talk to his prime murder suspect. What was I missing, and what kind of motive could Tim have to murder Lily before they were married? I shook my head. There wasn't time to investigate now. I had Sadie—er, Trixie's wedding that evening.

I stopped by the pet store to get a new set of food dishes for Sadie and Mike to go along with their homemade dog treats. I planned to take them to the shop and wrap a white bow around each of them. On my way out of the store, I saw Jessie. Her eyes were puffy and red, and Gavin wasn't by her side. I'd never seen her without her son, so my first thought was that something must be wrong with him.

"Jessie, what's wrong? Where's Gavin?"

She jolted, and eyed me warily before taking a breath. "He's at the babysitter's."

"Oh. Can I help you with anything?"

Tears leaked out the sides of her eyes and trickled down her high cheekbones. "It's Drago. They've accused him of embezzling from Lost Trails Construction."

I sucked in a breath. I still hadn't met Drago, but Jessie was so sweet and down to earth, I couldn't imagine that she'd get mixed up with someone pulling something illegal ... although, as soon as the thought crossed my mind, I thought of Gavin and of how Jessie had admitted she was young and naive and too trusting. But she'd grown up, hadn't she?

I rummaged through my purse for a tissue and handed it over. "Are you worried that he might have done something?" I asked as gently as I could.

Jessie shook her head. "Never. Drago loves America. He tells me all the time about how lucky we are to have grown up with this kind of independence and privileges. He never had that in Croatia. Drago would never break laws that would jeopardize his freedom."

"So this Lost Trails Construction, are they going to go bankrupt?"

Jessie shrugged. "I'm not sure. I know things are really bad. They've suspended several projects that were supposed to start this week. Drago actually picked up a few of the customers they've dropped and we thought things were going to work out, but now Phil Andrus has decided to take legal action. His daughter, Rose, has some fancy lawyer who is encouraging them to sue."

"But they'd need proof to open any kind of case against Drago," I said.

"They have loads of proof. There are tons of documents that Drago signed as things passed through. He said he stopped paying attention—there just wasn't time to analyze every piece of paper that went through company channels."

"Oh no. Jessie, there's got to be something we can do to help him."

"I've tried calling a few lawyers to get an idea of what his best move is, but they're all so expensive and they don't really want to give a free consultation." Jessie wiped her eyes with the tissue again.

"I actually have a good friend who is a lawyer. He mostly does family law, but he might be able to give Drago some advice."

Jessie dropped the tissue and grabbed my hands. "Really? Oh, that would be a lifesaver."

"I'll give him a call and see if he has any time in the next few days. Why don't you give me Drago's information and I'll pass it along to him."

"Yes, thank you," Jessie said.

"No promises, but we'll try."

Jessie gave the info, and then hugged me before she left. My heart broke for her. It was unfair that all of this was being dumped on her and Drago when they were trying to plan their wedding. Wasn't it enough that his family was against their union?

The mid-July heat was stifling so I cranked on the air

conditioner in my Mercury Mountaineer. The leather seats were a plus in the summertime once the air conditioner hit its stride. I dialed Luke's number, and it rang several times before he answered.

"Hey, you enjoying the heat?" I asked.

"Just wishing you weren't so busy, 'cause today is the perfect day to go cruising up the mountain," he replied.

"Don't tempt me." Sitting on the back of the Harley with my arms around his middle and the cool mountain air rushing past us was exactly where I wanted to be at the moment.

"Maybe next Saturday?"

"No, it's the art festival. The one my family's all coming to."

"Oh, that's right. Well, I wondered if you'd like to go to church with me tomorrow?"

Wow. He was asking me to church? That would open up the floodgates for questions if he was a regular parishioner. "Sure. What time?" I answered before I had a chance to second-guess myself.

"Starts at ten, so I can pick you up at a quarter 'til, if that works."

"Yes, that'd be nice. Hey, uh, I called not just to get you to take me on another date—although I'm really glad I called now—but I need a favor." I was rambling, but since he'd just asked me on two dates in the same phone call, my brain was jumbled with twitterpated birds singing songs of love.

"Okay, I'm considering." I heard a smile in his voice and wished I could be having this conversation in real time.

"Would you be willing to do a free consultation for a

friend of mine?" I paused, but decided to just dump the info before he had to answer. "It's Jessie Wilder. Her fiancé Drago has been accused of embezzling from Lost Trails Construction. They fired him last week and now they're pressing charges against him. I'm planning their wedding, they've already put money down, and Jessie has a little boy. I feel so bad for her." I sucked in a breath and waited for him to answer.

"And you're sure that this guy is innocent?"

I hesitated. "I really don't know. I haven't met him, but I'd like to take you over to meet him."

"Well that's not really my area of expertise, but I'd be willing to give him some ideas about what he can do," Luke said. "Sounds like you're pretty booked today and tomorrow. What about Monday before nine?"

"Yep, that'll work," I said. "Thanks. I'd better run before I'm late to my own wedding."

Luke laughed at the joke that I always used while working on weddings I planned. "See you later."

Chapter 13

PAPIER MÂCHE BALLOONS

Inflate over-sized balloons. Dip crepe paper, strips of colored paper, and/or lace in mixture of 1 part flour to 2 parts water and affix paper to balloon until it is completely covered. Allow to dry for 24 hours. Add another layer if desired for stability. Pop balloon and cut a small hole in the bottom to insert battery-operated tea light. Tape the tea light in place. Tape over the hole. Thread string, twine, or ribbon through globes and hang from trees or backdrops for mood lighting.

Courtesy of www.mashedpotatoesandcrafts.com

The harp was set under the shade of a green ash tree; the music was light and ethereal, nothing that would stir up the excitement of the pets in attendance at the wedding. Lorea was the leash checker, as I had insisted that all dogs be on a leash. There were a few cats, but leashes didn't work as well for cats, so I told Lorea to keep an eye on those felines. One guest had brought his iguana, and the hideous-looking thing sat on a chair next to him, enjoying the sun. It was still too hot at seven thirty on that July night, but Trixie and Derek wanted their reception to be at sunset. I had checked, and sunset would be at 9:18 p.m., hopefully the heat and end of day would encourage the animals to rest during the ceremony.

Trixie had been a pleasure to work with despite the special canine circumstances, because she had a great eye for unique beauty. She and Derek had made two dozen papier-mâché balloons and hung them from the trees. The hanging orbs were black, white, yellow, and green to match Trixie's wedding colors. They looked like giant ornaments, and I happened to know that they each had a small battery-operated tea light inside that would provide mood lighting during the reception.

The guests were all settled, and I was about to give the signal to Lorea to prepare Mike to walk Trixie down the aisle, when one of the canine guests started howling. Everyone looked toward the mournful sound of the bluetick coonhound seated near the back of the audience. There was a man standing near the coonhound with a yippy poodle on a neon-green leash. He must have just arrived and somehow set off a chain reaction, because now several dogs were howling. My heart rate increased as the animals began squirming and straining at their leashes. The iguana slithered off his chair and into the grass at his owner's feet. A cat growled, and that's when Sadie decided it was time to get the party started.

I'd only met Sadie briefly, because Trixie hadn't brought her by the shop after the first incident. Sadie was much too excited about life to go in stores with breakable items. I was grateful for that, but at the same time a worry had been gnawing at my gut ever since. If Sadie couldn't behave herself in a store, then how could she behave herself at a wedding attended by more than a dozen other animals?

Derek tightened Sadie's leash as she jumped forward barking at the man in the back, who must have been wearing bad cologne.

"Sadie, no!" Derek cried as the dog lunged forward, pulling him away from the pastor, who held his Bible close to his chest and retreated to the side of the tree he stood under.

Sadie kept straining, and rose petals bounced around in the basket attached to her collar. Hopefully the wedding rings weren't already in Sadie's basket; I could just imagine Sadie running after some cat and sending the rings flying. I cringed and looked back at the bluetick and the now-snarling poodle next to the man who was talking to Lorea. She was pointing toward the parking lot and he was shaking his head.

"I can't believe this," I mumbled. I didn't run toward him, but I hurried as quickly as I could with my wedge sandals. I had chosen the less speedy pair of shoes because heels would sink into the grass. As I approached, the man's features came into focus. He looked familiar. It wasn't until I was within earshot of his and Lorea's conversation that I recognized him as Lily's father, Phil Andrus.

"Sir, all I'm asking is that you walk your dog around the parking lot for a few minutes while we get things settled here," Lorea said.

"But I just got here," Phil answered. "I walked Otis here so he wouldn't be hyper."

Lorea gritted her teeth and looked in my direction.

I held out my hand. "Hi, I'm Adrielle Pyper, the wedding planner for Trixie and Derek."

He shook my hand and bobbed his chin. "Phil Andrus."

"Yes, I remember seeing you over at Lily's house. I'm her neighbor—er, was—I'm so sorry for your loss. So, so sorry," I blabbered. I grabbed onto his arm and pulled him away from the group.

He swallowed, and his eyes tightened. "It's been terrible."

"Lily was so excited about her upcoming marriage. I was helping her get started on the details." Right after I said the words, I saw Phil stiffen and realized that I'd said the wrong thing. Before my brain could catch up to my mouth, I said, "Tim didn't do it. There's no way he could kill Lily."

Phil stopped and turned almost robotically toward me. "People are capable of many things that we could never imagine."

I took a step back, involuntarily shaking my head. "I know, but—"

"I hope he's innocent," Phil interrupted. "But I trust the police, and they must have evidence if they've arrested him."

"But you don't really believe Tim did it," I protested. "Do you?"

"Tim is a fine man and I was happy to support Lily, but I'm not sure they would have made a great match. The years change us."

"Adri, I think we're ready now." Lorea approached from behind and motioned to the guests, who may as well have been sitting in a petting zoo. From this angle, the bushy tail of a raccoon stuck out from the side of the fifth row.

"If we make it through this wedding, it will be a miracle," I hissed. I pasted on a smile and followed Lorea to the mass of whimpering, barking, yowling guests of Trixie and Derek's wedding.

During the ceremony, I kept glancing at Phil. He sat in the back, stoic, next to Otis, who was very well behaved. I thought about what he'd said, about what people were capable of. I knew it was true, but I still didn't want to believe it of Tim.

Thankfully everyone, pets included, survived Trixie and Derek's wedding. My nerves felt frayed and my back was stiff from holding in the stress that at any time someone would start howling again. By the time the wedding was over and cleaned up, even if I'd had the energy to visit Tim, visiting hours at the jail were closed. I tucked away the questions for Tim that were burning in the back of my brain, and made plans for the next day.

I took a few minutes to sort through the folder of emails that I'd compiled from my correspondence with Lily. Things had kept me so busy that I hadn't had much time to examine the notes after I'd turned the first folder over to Tony.

After I read through all of the emails, I slumped in my chair. There wasn't anything remotely significant. I'd made a few notes of possible questions for my own suspects: Phil, Rose, the mystery gunman, Tim (even though it couldn't be him), Javier, maybe his mother Tina, and even Vickie, the grouchy assistant from Tim's vet clinic. If Tony saw my notes, he would laugh and he wouldn't try to hide how ridiculous my ideas were.

My chair squeaked as I leaned back against it and stared at the ceiling. Then I remembered something that had me sitting up straight and scrambling for my phone: Lily and I had texted back and forth a few times. Maybe there was some clue in the short bursts of messages on my phone.

I scrolled through my texts until I found Lily Rowan's name. The picture next to her name made it hard to swallow. My finger hovered above her smiling face before tapping into the messages. There were about a dozen, so I pulled out a spiral notebook and began writing down information that Lily had sent. Nothing seemed out of the ordinary.

Scrolling back through the texts, I paused on one from last Friday, just four days before Lily died. I had asked her if she could come to my shop and meet, and she hadn't replied for several hours.

Lily: ***Let's try for next Tuesday. There are some things at work that are stressing me out and I can't concentrate on my HEA right now.***
Me: ***No problem. I'll bring some ideas to go over with you.***
Lily: ***It'd be nice if we never had to worry about money, right?***
Me: ***For sure!***

I frowned at Lily's mention of her HEA, or Happily Ever After—that chance had been stolen from her. I studied the conversation again. The turn in the conversation to money seemed a little out of place when I read through it now. Lily hadn't mentioned money before. She seemed sensible, and hadn't spoken of anything that extraordinary in costs. Besides, her stepdad Phil was footing the bill for her wedding, and anything he wouldn't have covered could easily be paid for by Tim. He did very well with his animal clinic.

I slid my finger back and forth over the conversation. Was I making more of this than there really was? I wrote a note and a few questions about the conversation in my notebook. It was an account of information that I would give to Tony—after I asked Tim what he thought it meant. Maybe it would mean something to Tim, and if not, I'd ask Tony if he thought the text sounded abnormal.

With the faces of my suspects dangling on the edge of my consciousness, I finally dropped off to sleep.

At six-thirty Sunday morning, I dragged myself out of bed and hurried to get ready for church with Luke. My plan was to visit Tim right at nine when visiting hours opened and then speed back to my condo in time for Luke to pick me up. It wasn't much time, but I couldn't wait another day and the visiting hours were extended on Sunday, so I needed to take advantage of the chance to do my own investigating. I didn't tell Luke or Tony, because I knew they would discourage me, but both of them would find out. I would tell Luke later, and Tony would hear about it when he came into the station on Monday morning.

I drove to Hailey and passed through the security checkpoints to enter the Blaine County detention center. After I retrieved my wallet, notebook, and pen, I was led to a room with a screen connected to Tim's cell. Inmates were allowed only two twenty-minute visits per day by video, so I was grateful when Tim agreed to my visit.

The fluorescent lights in the room were an unnatural bluish color, and one of the bulbs flickered accompanied by a low hum. In the quiet of the room, the buzz seemed to increase while I waited for Tim to show up on the screen. With a flicker, Tim came into view. The cell was all white walls with a steel bunk frame and a blue mattress.

Tim wore a faded orange jumpsuit and had shackles on his wrists. My stomach clenched as I took in the pallor of his skin. It might have just been the lights, but it appeared as if part of his life had been sucked from him—and in a way, it had. I still felt certain that he didn't kill Lily.

As Tim lifted his head to view the screen, one corner of his mouth pulled upwards in what might have been a half smile, but the hollow look in his eyes just made him appear like a wounded animal. He studied me for a moment, probably wondering if I was there to accuse him like everyone else.

I couldn't smile, not when he was dressed in a jumpsuit, but I tried to convey with my eyes that I believed he was innocent. I opened my mouth to say so, but he spoke first.

"Hey, Adri. Sorry you had to come here."

"It's no problem." I cleared my throat. "Listen, Tim, I know you didn't kill Lily."

He leaned forward, and the first bit of life ignited in his eyes. "You do?"

The poor man. It was hard to imagine the pain he must be feeling, losing his fiancée and then getting arrested for her murder. I glanced to the side, where an armed officer stood nearby—a reminder that nothing on the video visitation would be private. "I wanted to talk to you because ... well, I thought maybe if we worked together, we might remember some detail that would help your case."

"My lawyer has advised me not to talk to anyone without him present," Tim said.

"I think that's wise," I said. "But I'm not just anyone. I know you. I knew Lily. I want to help you."

Tim stared at me through the screen for a moment. Then he leaned back and blew out a breath. "I've thought and thought. No alibi, no witnesses, all evidence pointing to me." He held up his hands. "I can't see any way that I'm ever gonna be free."

I narrowed my eyes. "Unless we figure out who really killed Lily."

Tim's lower lip trembled; he coughed, and rolled his shoulders back. "The police said they have no other suspects. They're not even looking at anyone else."

"I wouldn't be too sure of that," I said. "I happen to know that some people on the force don't believe you did it." I leaned forward and tapped the table with one of my chipped blue fingernails. Maybe I was fudging the truth just a little, because Tony hadn't said what he really believed about Tim. "I know that maybe this seems like a long shot, but I wanted to ask you a few questions. And even if you've answered them before, I still want to know."

Tim nodded. "Sure. This beats sitting here staring at the wall."

I flipped open my trusty spiral notebook, at the same time clicking my ballpoint pen open. "Tell me about the night Lily died."

"I wasn't at the office. I'd planned to take off early to be with Lily, but I was called out to treat a horse with colic. The owner had another emergency with one of his kids while I was treating the horse, so they left before I was done." Tim sat as still as a statue in front of the video screen. "After that, no one can attest to where I was. I finished with the horse after five, maybe five thirty, and then headed back to my place to shower and change. Lily was supposed to come over to my house for dinner. I'd been working on a little surprise for her, to celebrate our engagement." Tim stopped and wiped his mouth with his hand.

"I'm so sorry." There was nothing else to say. Nothing that would bring Lily back or help with Tim's pain. I knew something of what he felt. After my best friend was murdered, there was an empty space inside that echoed with memories of all the times we'd shared. Every time I thought I was doing better, something would knock up against that empty space and the hollow ringing of my sorrow would start all over again. There weren't very many words that helped me then. "What evidence specifically do the police have against you?"

Tim clenched his fists. "It's such an obvious plant, but even I can't figure out how someone got the euthanizing agent."

"Why? Is it that hard to break into your office?"

"We have a security system, but no cameras. The euthanizing agent is locked up—with a double lock system." He glanced at his hands and unclenched his fists.

"Meaning two separate locks have to be opened to get the poison?" I leaned forward in my chair.

"Yes. Vickie and I are the only ones who have access to

the poison," he said. "And there is only one second key. Vickie can't open the locks without me."

"What about Vickie? Is she capable of something like this?" I still didn't want to let go of my suspicion of the grouchy assistant.

Tim scoffed and shook his head. "She can be ornery sometimes, but no. And she has a solid alibi."

"I still don't see how that's enough evidence," I said. "It all seems circumstantial."

"Except for the part where the murderer left the empty bottle of poison from my office in a trash can near the murder scene." He paused. "Handy that my fingerprints were the only ones on the bottle."

I gasped. "But how?"

Tim shrugged. "It's all Houdini to me now."

I stopped and jotted down a few notes. The evidence was definitely incriminating, but I had the sense that Tim was speaking with me carefully, perhaps holding something back. I tapped my pen against my notepad. "Can you think of anything that was strange around that time? Anything at all?"

I was thinking of the text Lily had sent me that was only slightly out of the ordinary. I sat on the edge of my seat, hoping Tim would remember something that would tie in to the text she'd sent me.

"Well, I already told the police that there was this foreign guy at the construction place that was giving her a hard time. They questioned him and he had an alibi—he was at a bar with several friends. I guess he mostly had a crush on her, and the language barrier made some things come across as inappropriate."

I straightened, thinking of the foreign person I knew who worked at Lost Trails Construction—Drago Kovacevic. "Do you remember his name?"

"Uh, I think it was Boris something? But I asked around and found out he's just a harmless kid. I worried that I was trying too hard to find someone to blame, so maybe I saw more than there was."

I relaxed. "Well, I'm sure they're keeping an eye on him anyway."

Tim nodded. "That's what Detective Ford told me. But that was the only thing I could think of. Lily was as open and honest as they come, and everyone knew she wore her heart on her sleeve. She didn't have secrets."

"What about money issues? Did she ever talk about that?"

Tim rubbed a thumb across his lips and rested his chin in his hand. "No, Lily was great with money. She had a knack for figures. She did the books for the construction company, and they were meticulous. Sometimes she got stressed if things didn't balance correctly. She'd go at those figures like a hound after a coon until she got things right." He stopped, and his eyes widened. "You know, I just remembered something."

My heart pounded against my ribs. "Yes?"

"Last week Lily was going on about an issue with the expense sheets at Lost Trails. She was on the hunt again." Tim paused; his eyes held a faraway look, and a hint of a smile tugged at the corner of his mouth.

I sat expectantly, watching him. He turned his hazel eyes back to me, and I saw again the heartache he was suffering.

He rubbed a hand over his face and sighed. "I guess I forgot because it was kind of a normal thing for Lily to get excited about bank statements and accounts and stuff, but, well, she just didn't look as satisfied as she usually does when she finds the source of the problem."

"So she figured out what the problem was?"

"Yeah, I'm pretty sure that's what she said."

"Do you remember what she said, exactly?"

"She said she'd found the error but it hadn't solved any problems." Tim hesitated then tapped his chin. "I remember now: she said once she found the error and fixed it, all the other accounts started having problems. To be honest, I'm not good with numbers, so I'm not sure I understood what she meant."

I wrote down what he said in my notebook and clicked my pen back and forth. "I heard that there were some problems with Lost Trails Construction. Do you know anything about that?"

"You mean about Phil losing his head in that imported tile business?"

I nodded.

"Yes, but I thought that had been taken care of several months ago."

"Did you ever hear Lily mention other names of people who might have been involved?"

"No, she liked pretty much everyone she worked with, and Lily was quiet. A lot of times she went into the office early so she could work uninterrupted. She wasn't there for socializing. She was there for the numbers."

"She was a sweet girl." I decided not to mention the

embezzling accusations against Drago just yet. But there was one question that I did need to ask. "Tim, who do you think killed Lily?"

Tim licked his lips. "I really don't know. Phil is cousins with criminals, if you know what I mean, so for some people it's easy to imagine him in this. But I don't see it."

"What about the life insurance money?"

Tim sat back, and his face lost some of its color. "What life insurance money?"

"Everyone's talking about how Phil had a two-million-dollar policy on Lily."

Tim's Adam's apple moved up and down three times, and he cleared his throat. "Is he the sole beneficiary?"

I shrugged. "I have no idea. But why would he have a policy like that on his stepdaughter?"

"Phil used to sell insurance, or his brother did, or something like that. Anyway, he's big into life insurance. When Lily and I started getting serious, he told me I should get a policy. It was a little strange, but once he gave me his pep talk, it made sense. He's pretty gung-ho about taking care of the family." Tim was talking faster and not making eye contact with me. Maybe he did suspect Phil but didn't want to voice it in the presence of the police officer.

I glanced at my watch and hurriedly closed my notebook. "I've got to go. I'm sorry if I upset you."

"No, it's just a lot to process," Tim said. "But you've given me a few things to think about."

"I'd like to talk to you again soon. Do you think you'll be able to make bail?"

"My dad flew in from Florida, and he's working on

getting a loan against my vet clinic. He put a mortgage on his home and liquidated his savings. Hopefully only one more day, but I don't know."

"I'm so sorry. I wish there was something I could do to help."

Tim sat up straight and blew out a breath. "The fact that you believe me is a great help. Maybe someone else does, too."

"Keep thinking. Maybe there's something, some little clue that could help you." I gave him a weak smile. "Thanks for your time."

"I'll do that. Thanks for the visit." Tim waved, and the screen went dark.

After I left the station, I drove as fast as I dared to get to my condo before Luke arrived. The car was silent and the roads were moderately quiet, leaving me to mull over my conversation with Tim. He had seemed surprised about the life insurance policy, but now that I thought about it again, maybe it was more worry than surprise. He hadn't seemed surprised about the amount. I thought about Tim's question of the life insurance beneficiaries. Would the police be privy to that information? And why did that matter to Tim?

Chapter 14

ZESTY CHICKEN ENCHILADAS

1 chopped onion, 1 can cream of chicken soup, 1 can mushrooms, 1 cup chicken broth, 1 can green chilis, 1 pkg corn or flour tortillas, ½ lb. grated pepper jack cheese, 1 lb cooked, shredded chicken. Extra Zesty, add 1 seeded jalapeño

Brown onion, add soup, broth, chilis, mushrooms, and chicken. Mix well. Fill each tortilla with about 3 Tbsp filling and sprinkle with cheese. Roll up tortilla and set in 9 x 13 baking pan. Sprinkle cheese over entire pan. Bake at 350 degrees for 30 minutes.

Serve with rice and chopped lettuce. 6-8 Servings

Courtesy of www.mashedpotatoesandcrafts.com

I pulled into my parking lot and breathed a sigh of relief

that Luke wasn't early. I didn't want to tell him about my visit to Tim until after church. I had just enough time to park in my single-car garage, dash in through the side door, and check the mirror before I saw Luke arrive in his dark blue Dodge pickup. He approached the door, looking relaxed and unruffled, a slight smile on his clean-shaven face. I opened the door before he could knock.

"Good morning," I said.

"It is a beautiful morning, and you look nice in that color." He indicated the light-yellow blouse I wore with a white skirt. He reached out and took my hand. "Are you ready?"

I nodded, feeling the tingles zing up my arm. Holding Luke's hand felt natural, and I loved how something so simple brought happy butterflies to life in my stomach. "Yes, thanks for the invite. I've been looking forward to this."

Luke squeezed my hand. "I'm glad."

I locked my front door and walked with Luke to his pickup. He wore a short-sleeved button-up dress shirt in a light blue that brought out the color of his eyes. The silver rimless glasses he wore hid a few tired lines around his eyes. "I'm sorry you've had to work so hard lately." I touched his cheek. "You look a little short on sleep."

Luke turned toward me, and some emotion that I didn't recognize flickered through his eyes. But the way he smiled, it must have been a good feeling. "When I'm done with this case, we need to celebrate."

A thrill passed through me. "I would love that. Fried pickles or ice cream?"

Luke chuckled. "Something better. I'll think about it."

"Something better than fried pickles and ice cream? I'm game."

The church was less than two miles from my condo, so we arrived a few minutes early and took a seat in a pew about halfway back. Luke greeted several people, and I also found a couple parishioners that I knew. After the publicity from my attempted murder last year, I'd stopped attending for a while to avoid awkward questions and well-meaning do-gooders, but with Luke at my side I felt safe. Enough time had passed that I could probably become a regular attendee of the services again.

When the preacher took the stand, I grinned because it was the same preacher who had married Gladys and Hank. Now I understood why he knew "Mr. Luke." I elbowed Luke, and he winked at me before sliding his arm around me and resting his hand on my shoulder with a gentle squeeze. His nearness made everything a little fuzzy, like I was looking into the sun as it set. The warmth of Luke's arm around me was definitely something I could get used to.

"Good morning. I'm Preacher Dan, for those of you who are visiting. I'm glad you could come out this morning, and I hope you will leave uplifted and with a closer connection to Christ."

The sermon was a good one with an emphasis on the importance of family. I especially liked it when Preacher Dan quoted a scripture about a man cleaving unto his wife. Luke didn't flinch, and it set my mind to thinking about the possibilities that might be in our future. It was forbidden territory; I had banned myself from going there because Luke had first introduced himself as someone against marriage. But I knew him better now. I could see him for the hurt and grieving widower he was and how hard he was trying to do well with living.

After the service, Luke took my hand and walked with me to his pickup. "Would you like to come over to my place for lunch? I made a little something in the hopes you were hungry."

"Oh?" I smiled up at him. "That sounds like a great idea." And hopefully there would be an opportunity for me to confess that I'd gone to visit Tim before church that morning.

When we arrived at Luke's two-story house just a few blocks off Main Street in Ketchum, he opened the front door for me with a flourish. "Welcome."

"I haven't been in your house before. This is really nice." I examined the dark hardwood flooring and the white staircase that swept up to the left of the entryway. "Did you remodel it?"

"I did some of it. Hired out most of it," he said. "It was in pretty sad shape when I moved in."

He led me into the kitchen, where I admired the white cabinets and gray granite countertops. "This is gorgeous." I ran a hand over the cool surface.

"I made a pan of chicken enchiladas and even set the timer on my oven to cook them while we were gone."

"Hey, it smells like it worked." I noticed the spicy and sweet aromas wafting through the air. "I'm impressed."

"Wait until you taste them." Luke held up his hands with fingers crossed.

I laughed, liking the feeling of closeness Luke and I

were sharing. It was the relaxed version of us that I'd been hunting for ever since I found out he was "the hottie" who loved to run the trails of Sun Valley. I would never admit that I'd ogled his shirtless abs for months before discovering who the man behind the sunglasses and ball cap really was. Even in a dress shirt and tie, Luke's body held a strength and definition that made my heart quiver.

He leaned over the oven and pulled out the pan of steaming enchiladas. "Did I let it cook too long?" he asked as he set the pan on a cooling rack.

"It looks perfect." The edges of the white sauce were crisp and dark brown, the tortillas a golden-toasted mass of cheese, and the green chiles mouthwatering.

My stomach grumbled loud enough for Luke to hear. He smiled. "Let's eat."

Sitting next to Luke at his round dining table felt different, in a good way. It was like we'd walked from dating stage one, right into dating stage three. While we were busy fighting over marriage, divorce, solving mysteries, and whatever else sparked our fires, we'd grown closer than either of us realized. I took another bite and caught Luke watching me. The side of my mouth quirked up, but I didn't drop my gaze. The look he gave me was deeper—intimate. My mouth grew warm from the spiciness of the enchiladas; at least, that's what I told myself as the heat sizzled right through my middle.

"Wow, this is delicious," I finally said. "I didn't know you could cook like this."

"I'm glad you like it. Not too hot?" Luke asked with what seemed like a knowing smile.

"I like it with a little zing." I wondered if my cheeks were turning pink, because we were definitely full-blown flirting.

Luke leaned forward and took my hand. "Thanks for coming over today."

"Thanks for the invite." I found myself leaning toward him. "Maybe I can make you dinner sometime."

"I'd like that," Luke said and his voice sounded husky.

His mouth looked so kissable. I pulled my eyes back up to his, certain he'd seen me just check out his lips. I swallowed. What was I doing? I wanted Luke Stetson to kiss me, but not with enchilada breath.

I pulled back and cleared my throat. "So, I have a little confession to make," I ventured, and immediately kicked myself for dousing the heat building between us.

Luke raised his eyebrows. "I'm listening." He picked up his fork and took one last bite of enchilada.

"I went to visit Tim Esplin today at the jail."

"You what?" Luke coughed and started choking. He swigged his lemonade and wiped his mouth with a napkin.

I took the opportunity to explain before he could say anything else. "It was all on the up and up," I said. "I went during normal visiting hours. There was an officer there. I just asked Tim a few questions."

"Adri, I thought Tony told you no more detective work." Luke's voice was even, but I could tell by the tightness in his eyes that he was upset.

I bristled. "Look, I didn't even have to tell you, but I figured you'd probably hear about it anyway since you and Tony are so tight these days." I leaned back and folded my arms. My jaw was tight with annoyance; I didn't understand why Luke was so upset.

Luke blew out a breath of frustration. "Tony is doing his job. Why can't you just let things be?"

"Because. I'm involved whether I want to be or not." I raised my voice to match his authoritative tone. "Tony asked me to go through all of my notes and conversations with Lily. I did that and I gave him everything I had, but I had a few questions that I wanted to ask Tim myself."

"Tony would ask any question you needed if you're helping him in an investigation." Luke put his fork down and placed his palms on the table. "Why are you so determined to put yourself in danger?"

"I'm not putting myself in danger. Tim is not a murderer, and if he was, then I was in just as much danger when I took Tux into his clinic last week. I needed some answers. Lily was my friend too." My voice cracked, and I hung my head, blinking back the tears that had abruptly appeared.

I heard Luke's chair slide across the floor and he was at my side. "I'm sorry." He touched my arms, but I pulled away. "I just don't want you to get hurt. Don't you understand how I feel about you?"

My anger immediately dissipated. In two sentences we'd gone from fighting to somehow having a define-the-relationship chat. I pressed my lips together and took a slow breath in through my nose. If I turned the situation around, it made sense that Luke was worried about my sleuthing. He'd helped me out of two pretty scary situations. I couldn't think of anything to say. I didn't understand for certain how he felt about me, because Luke was always sending out contradictory signals. One minute he was holding my hand, and the next he was making fun of people getting married. But I had to admit that there was something between us that lately, he hadn't been denying.

"Speechless, huh?" Luke's voice was low and appealing. I looked at him out of the corner of my eye, and my cheeks twitched from holding in a smile. Luke took my hand and pulled me up to a standing position beside him. "Adri, it's really scary when something happens to someone you care about. I've seen you almost die twice now. I don't ever want to see that again. I hate feeling helpless, like there's nothing I can do to save you."

His words pierced the armor I had built up around my heart. Luke did care about me. I knew that, but I found every reason to doubt the authenticity of his feelings.

Luke stepped forward and put his arms around me, and I let him pull me into a hug, wrapping my arms around his waist. "I'm not trying to get into any trouble," I said. "I promise I haven't tried any investigating work until this morning. I found some text messages from Lily that I wanted to ask him about."

"But what are your plans now that you've talked to Tim?" Luke asked. His breath near my ear sent sparks up my spine.

I tilted my head to look at him and carefully crossed my fingers, which were behind his back. "Three weddings, a possible family reunion, and an appointment with you tomorrow."

Luke studied me, as if he could see how I'd dodged his question. He narrowed his eyes slightly and then shrugged, stepping back from the embrace. "What was the appointment for again? One of your friends?"

"It's for one of my brides," I said. I liked the way Luke's arms wrapped around my waist so easily, and maybe I wished he hadn't let go so soon. Turning my thoughts back to safer territory, I told Luke a little about Jessie and her son. "Jessie's fiancé is in some trouble with Lost Trails Construction. I thought I'd come along with you to meet him, since I haven't had the chance yet."

"Well, hopefully I can give him some information that might help," Luke said. "I don't think we'll have enough time in the morning. Do you mind going later? I'll be done with court at three tomorrow."

"Great! I'll pick you up at the courthouse."

Luke laced his fingers through mine. "Promise me you'll be a good girl."

"Always." I knew what he wanted me to say—that I wouldn't even think about Lily's murder case or how Tim was innocent or what I might be able to find to prove his innocence, or ... But I was never a very good liar, so I just smiled.

Chapter 15

CLEVER TIPS TO FIND A COLOR SELECTION FOR YOUR EVENT

Visit https://coolors.co/ to access a free color schemes generator with the actual color codes your designer needs. Browse until you find your favorite main color. Next choose two accent colors, keeping in mind that an accent color should not overpower the primary selection, it should enhance, not detract from it.

Courtesy of www.mashedpotatoesandcrafts.com

Every time I thought about Luke, my mouth warmed like I was eating his spicy enchiladas. We'd covered new relationship territory yesterday at his house, and I couldn't wait to see him again. My insides were lit up like a Christmas tree—the kind with twinkling lights. All morning long he kept visiting my thoughts, and I may have imagined more than once what it would feel like to kiss him.

"Adri, are you going to tell me why you're smiling like it's your birthday?" Lorea asked, startling me from my Luke fantasies.

I recovered and widened my smile. "I'm glad you're back from lunch. I have four cartons of color swatches, pictures, and layouts I need to go through before our next appointment."

Lorea frowned. "*Gidariaren esklabo*," she grumbled in Basque. "I don't see anything wrong with the old color swatch booklets."

"You know how it is. New season, fresh colors. The brides want the latest and greatest patterns and selections and it's our job to give it to them. And quit calling me a slave driver. It's Monday."

"Hmm, maybe I have too many alterations to help you right now. Unless . . ." Lorea's eyes danced with mischief. Nothing got by her. She noticed my moods and was always there to cheer me up, tease, laugh, or swear in her native tongue. I was surprised she couldn't read Luke all over my face, but maybe she was being cautious and letting me dish on our favorite lawyer. One way or another, Lorea would find out.

"All right," I huffed. "Luke and I are sort of moving past the 'just friends' phase."

Lorea squealed and clapped her hands. "I knew it! You have that dreamy look in your eyes—not that I've seen it this clearly before."

"Oh, pshaw." I leaned over to open a box. "I've fully admitted that I like Luke. He's a good guy, but he's also a big pain."

"He's not so much of a *tontua* anymore. I kind of like him, too."

I rolled my eyes because for a while Lorea definitely thought Luke was stupid, among other things. "The only reason you can see anything here—" I waved my hand in front of my face. "—is because it's a mirror image of you."

Lorea laughed. "I think you're right. And yes, I just said that."

"Really?" Now it was my turn to squeal. "You and Tony are getting serious?"

Lorea tilted her head to the side with a shy smile. "Well, we're talking about things, and everything is perfect when I'm with him. I'm kind of a wreck because I think about him all day."

I nodded. She'd just described me, but Luke and I hadn't even kissed yet. There'd been so many ups and downs in our friendship that I was kept on the edge of my seat, wondering what might happen next.

"What's that look?" Lorea asked. "That's not dreamland. What are you worried about?"

I looked down at my hands, clasping the new swatch binder that had just arrived. "I'm scared he's going to push me away again. Every time he's opened a door for me, he ends up pushing me out the back door a few days later. What if he never recovers from losing Dana?"

"Oh, girl," Lorea said. "He won't, not really, but that's why he's a keeper. When he loves someone, he does it with his whole heart. And I bet he's pretty scared to put a piece of himself out there again."

I rolled my tongue over my teeth, trying to think how to phrase my next question. Finally I blurted out, "Do you love Tony?"

Lorea's eyes brightened. "Yep, and it's a pretty fantastic feeling."

I hugged her, barely maintaining a cheer for my friend who had once been nearly as cynical about romance as Luke. "It's happening! I couldn't have picked a better guy. Tony is rock solid."

Lorea hugged me back. "Thank you."

We both busied ourselves with unpacking boxes and sorting materials while old-fashioned love songs played over the sound system of my little bridal shop.

Luke was waiting for me at the courthouse when I pulled up, and my stomach flipped like an Olympic gymnast. I put a hand across my middle and told myself to settle down.

"Hey, thanks for the ride," Luke said as he hopped in the passenger side of my SUV. "How's your day been?"

"Nothing too exciting. Just a regular Monday, sorting the new color styles and patterns for the next wedding season. What about you?"

"Oh, you know. Two divorces, one prenup, and a will." He leaned back against the seat and closed his eyes. "All in a day's work."

I fought down the urge to reach over and touch the shadow of stubble on his cheek. He hadn't shaved this morning, and his hair was tousled. "You tired?"

He cracked open one eye. "This custody case with Rose and Javier is kind of wearing me down."

"I'm sorry," I said. "Anything you can talk about?"

"It's just ..." He paused. "I feel so bad for that little girl. Both sides lose in this case. There is no winner."

My heart melted, and any doubts I'd had from earlier fled the scene. Luke was rock solid too, and I wanted him the way Lorea wanted Tony. I mentally shook myself from my high-speed train of thoughts. "I can't imagine how that would be. The poor little girl." I reached my hand over and placed it on top of Luke's.

He grabbed onto it and laced our fingers together. The summer sun bounced off the silver edges of Luke's glasses. I felt like one of those sunbeams, bursting with light every time he touched me. Luke sighed, and I made myself breathe normally, which was hard because he smelled so dang good—like hiking in secret meadows up the canyon.

Maybe the heat was getting to me. I kicked the air conditioner up another notch.

Luke opened his eyes. "Would you rather have a normal day, or a day with someone like the bridezilla?"

I laughed. "I'll take paperwork over Sylvia any day of the year." Luke still liked to tease me about one of my almost-brides, an almost celebrity (if you counted the daytime soap opera that was canceled) and almost turned-criminal client who was now a reality TV star, Sylvia Rockfort.

"Me too," Luke said.

"But sometimes it's nice to have an ordinary day. Today was a great day, because Lorea confessed that she and Tony are getting serious."

"I know."

"What do you mean, you know?"

Luke chuckled and held up his other hand. "You know, you can just tell when people are neck-deep in it. Tony mentioned something that made me think that's where he was headed."

"Neck-deep, huh?" I chose not to take offense at his comment, for once.

"I'm happy for them. They make a great couple."

I softened. "Me, too. I really never thought I'd see Lorea like this—she's acting like all the brides she used to make fun of."

That brought another smile from Luke. "Any bets on when the big day will be?"

"Hmm. Maybe they'll surprise us, but I think Lorea won't want to drag things out. Once she puts her mind to something, she wants to get it done."

"Sounds like someone I know." Luke raised his eyebrows up and down. "No wonder you two are best friends."

I nodded, thinking of that term. *Best friends*. It had been a few years since I'd been called anyone's best friend—ever since Briette died. Driving down the sunny street from Hailey, it struck me that the sharp pain surrounding Briette's murder was gone. There would always be sort of a dull ache, but I realized that I'd been holding myself back from friendships and relationships because of the hurt. My shoulders relaxed, and I took a deep breath.

"Quarter for your thoughts?" Luke asked. "'Cause it looks like you have more than a penny's worth going on."

I gave his hand a squeeze. "Just thinking that I'm doing better lately, here." I moved my other hand from the steering wheel and motioned to my heart.

"Me too." Luke's voice was soft. I let the moment roll over me, content to ride with Luke's quiet companionship.

We drove over to Bellevue, a skip on the map next to Hailey, to meet Jessie's fiancé, Drago, at one of his work sites. When we pulled up to the stacks of tile, a man raised his head at our approach, and my heart seized in my chest. "Wait, that's him." I grabbed Luke's arm and pointed at the man in front of us. "That's the guy with the rifle."

"Who has a rifle?" Luke jerked his head forward.

The man looked over at us, and I dropped my hand. "Not right now. The guy at the consignment shop who was shooting a rifle," I said.

"Are you sure it's the same guy?"

"Yes." If my head wasn't sure, my pounding heart recognized the short, stocky man with dark brown hair that I'd described to the police. I peeked out the windshield, but the man had walked away. "Should we call the police?"

"I don't know. Looks like he's working, and I don't see any guns," Luke said. "Maybe we should ask Drago who he is."

I let out a disjointed breath. "Okay, you lead the way."

Luke hopped out of my car and hurried around to help me out. I appreciated his chivalry, especially at the moment, because my heart was hammering like a steel drum and it wasn't playing a calypso tune. Luke took my hand, and we walked toward the office building.

Another man rounded the building, and I stopped walking, yanking on Luke's hand. The man was short with a barrel chest and huge biceps, and he looked almost identical to the mystery gunman sorting tile. The only difference was his neatly trimmed mustache and goatee.

"Hello. Are you Adri, the wedding lady?" He spoke with a foreign accent.

"Yes, hello." I extended my hand. "Adri Pyper, and this is Luke Stetson, my attorney friend."

"Drago Kovacevic." He shook my hand and Luke's. "Thank you for helping me." The edge to his words reminded me again of German, or maybe Russian, but I remembered now that Jessie said Drago was from Croatia.

The man by the tile hollered something at Drago in another language, and he answered and shrugged his shoulders. Luke and I looked at each other, and I swallowed hard. "Uh, so how do you know that man?"

Drago chuckled, shouted something at the man, and motioned for him to come toward us. My hands were sweating, but I didn't want to let go of Luke as the man approached us.

"This is my brother, Borislav," Drago said, patting the man's shoulder. "You can call him Boris. His English is a little rusty. He emigrated here only six months ago from Croatia."

My eyes widened. "Your brother?"

"Sure, sure," Drago said. Boris started to say something, drawing his attention. "Give me a minute." Drago said it like "me-noot" and held up one finger.

My phone was like a hot brick in my pocket, urging me to call Tony and tell him about the man in front of me. Drago spoke in a different language, most likely Croatian, to Boris, and motioned to the boxes of tile behind us. I recognized the sounds as those that Boris had spoken that day in the parking lot. Boris said something, looked at me, cocked his head, and began speaking rapidly.

Drago shook his head, pointed at me, and said something else. His voice took on a tone that indicated Boris was in big trouble. He waved both of his hands, and Boris stepped closer and lowered his voice. Drago turned to me with a desperate look in his eyes. "Boris says he saw you last week in town when he was shooting magpies. I just told him that he can't shoot his gun near businesses or in the city limits. He said he's really sorry if he scared you."

"Oh," was all I could think to say.

"Did you report him to the police?" Drago asked.

I cringed, and my voice came out in a squeak. "Yes."

Drago lifted his head to the sky and muttered something in Croatian.

"I'm sorry. He didn't look like he was hunting birds. He looked disturbed."

"Well, he is my younger brother." Drago pointed to Boris and rattled off something else in Croatian. Boris said something back and waved at me.

Drago shook his head. "He says that he's really very sorry, but magpies are dirty birds." Drago motioned to Boris and said something else. Boris smiled at Luke and me, then returned to his job of unpacking boxes. He looked harmless today. Not like some crazed gunman that had grown to a dangerous threat in my nightmares over the past week.

Drago watched him for a moment. "It's been tough on him. Everything's different: the culture, the land, the laws. He keeps making mistakes, but he's a good kid." Drago studied him with a look reserved especially for younger brothers. "Could you explain to the police what you found out?"

"Yes," I said. "But I'm sure they'll probably give him a citation, since he did fire the gun next to the store."

Drago put his head in his hands. "This doesn't help my case."

Luke cleared his throat. "You're right, it doesn't, but Adri has a detective friend that might be able to keep things quiet."

I glanced at Boris and then made eye contact with Drago. "I'll call Tony and tell him what you told me. They'll come and ask Boris questions, and I'm sure they'll be firm, but fair."

"Thank you. You're very kind to help my family." Drago rolled back his shoulders. "But I have not made the mistake that Lost Trails says I have." His voice took on an edge, and his accent became more pronounced as he spoke. "They think that because I'm not native that I'm stupid. But I see things. Whoever took the money wants me to take the blame."

Drago continued to tell us about the accusations against him and the evidence that pointed at him for the financial chaos in the accounting department.

"You're right," Luke said. "I think you were framed. There's too much evidence against you that was too easily found. Don't let anyone threaten you into taking a plea bargain. As long as you plead not guilty, no matter what happens, there is the possibility of appeals."

"Do you think they'll arrest him?" I couldn't keep the tone of disbelief out of my voice.

Luke rubbed his hand over his chin. "I wouldn't be surprised if they show up today."

Drago stiffened, but then heaved a sigh. "I should have been more careful."

"What do you mean?" I asked.

"Lily tried to warn me." He glanced around to be sure no

one could hear. "She said that things weren't adding up right and I needed to check all of my ledgers, but I've been so busy."

Luke arched an eyebrow in my direction. "Did she give any idea as to who might be causing the problems?"

"No, and I asked her about it, but she said she couldn't say until she did some more checking." Drago shoved his hands in his pockets and looked at the ground. "I worried when I heard Lily had died, and then when people started saying it was murder . . . well, I wondered if it had something to do with what was going on here."

Drago's words hung in the air. Luke's eyes widened, and so did mine. "Have you told the police any of this?" I asked.

"No. I didn't have anything, you know, facts about what she said."

Luke studied Drago for a moment. "What about texts? Did she send you anything that could prove she thought you were innocent?"

Drago shook his head. "Nope. It was just when I took some paperwork into the office. Lily never texted me."

"I still think you should talk to the police and tell them what you told us," I said.

"Yes, it would help their investigation into Lily's death as well as give them something to look into regarding your innocence in the embezzlement claims," Luke added.

Drago frowned. "But what if they think I'm just saying stuff to make myself look innocent?"

"I'm going to call Detective Ford right now," I said. "He'll listen to you and take everything under consideration. But Drago, if what you're saying is true, then it might be a lead on her murder investigation."

Drago spat in the dirt. "I didn't think Phil had it in him, but I heard he's going to collect on a huge life insurance policy that'll probably save his company."

My stomach rolled every time I thought of the implications. Could her stepfather have arranged something so heinous? Someone in Phil's business must have known something was amiss if Lily was voicing her worries out loud to Drago. "I'll go and make that call now. Then you can meet with Tony as soon as you're off work here," I said.

"Let's go over a few things while Adri makes that call," Luke said.

"Sure, I've got the copies of the paperwork in my truck." Drago motioned toward a white two-door Ford pickup.

I shook my head. Poor Boris. I wished that I didn't have to call Tony, but it was better than someone recognizing Boris from the description I'd given and the police chasing him down. Luke followed Drago and I dialed Tony's number, thinking that maybe I should just assign him to one of the speed dial settings in my phone.

After making my report, which had Tony grumbling in what sounded like a good-natured way, I slipped my phone into my back pocket. Luke and Drago were talking beside his pickup. I couldn't be certain, but Drago seemed a little more relaxed. Maybe Luke had discovered something that would help Drago's case.

I looked past them to the beautiful Sawtooth Mountain Range rising up to meet the sun, which smoldered above us. My thoughts circled around the events of the past week. Even though Tony and Luke had warned me off sleuthing, I didn't think a visit to Lost Trails Construction absolutely qualified as amateur detective work.

I pulled out my phone again and searched for the address to the office. It was about a ten-minute drive from my shop. After I dropped Luke off in Hailey, I might have time to stop by before they closed at five. My stomach filled with jitters and little warning bells, but now that two of my brides were involved with the mystery, it was my duty to investigate.

Chapter 16

KEEP SEWING NEEDLES SHARP

Do you have a tomato pincushion with a little strawberry attached? That strawberry is filled with emery sand to keep your needles and pins sharp. You can make your own sharpening pin cushion by filling it with emery sand. In the meantime, don't leave that strawberry dangling, fill it with needles!

Courtesy of *www.mashedpotatoesandcrafts.com*

I ended up getting a call from another potential client on the way back from meeting Drago. Luke was understanding, and blew me a kiss when I dropped him off at the Hailey Courthouse while still talking to the exuberant new bride-to-be. Even his innocent air-kiss made my stomach flutter. I didn't hide my smile, which helped me to cope with the chatty Zara Lowry, who was describing in great detail how she had fallen in love.

Usually I enjoyed hearing how my brides met their grooms, but something about the way Zara spoke in a too-sensual voice made my ears itch. She talked nonstop, and I did my best to interject with a few questions. By the time I got off the phone, I'd been sitting in my car in the parking lot for fifteen minutes. I huffed, because I'd burned up the time I needed to visit Lost Trails Construction. Zara would be coming in tomorrow for a consultation. I needed to prepare, but maybe if Lorea helped me there would still be time to make it to the construction office before it closed.

Grabbing the crumpled receipt where I'd scrawled Zara's info, I slipped in through the back door of my shop. "Did you hear?" Lorea asked as soon as I entered.

"Uh, no?"

"Tim's out on bail," she stage-whispered. "I'm not really supposed to know that, but I figured it out from hearing one side of Tony's conversation."

"Lorea, don't get him in trouble."

She smiled. "Never. I may have made a phone call to someone who is always in the know."

"Your sister? What is she, a reporter?"

Lorea nodded. "Terese got a job with the *Idaho Mountain Express* newspaper. She didn't tell anyone at first because she wanted to make sure it was the right thing for her. It's been a few months, and she's trying to get a piece that will break into the Associated Press."

"So Terese already knew about Tim?"

"Not on the record, but apparently when there's any movement on this kind of a case, it's pretty hard to keep things quiet." Lorea stacked up a few spools of thread and put away her sewing scissors. "Anyway, I thought that was good news. Maybe something will come up to clear Tim's name."

"I wonder if they're looking very hard at anyone else."

Lorea shrugged. "Not sure, but Terese did say that Tim hired a pretty good lawyer."

"I guess I need to talk to your sister," I said. "I feel like I live under a rock." My mind spun with the new information. Maybe there was a chance for Tim after all. The fact that he was out on bail was at least one minor triumph in the tragedy.

"Not a rock, just a big, fat wedding planning book," Lorea teased.

"Speaking of which, I just talked to another new bride." I pulled out the crumpled receipt and started transferring information to my computer.

"When's the date?"

"She's thinking about mid-January," I said.

"Well, that gives us plenty of time. When is she coming in?"

"I set up an appointment with her for tomorrow afternoon," I said. "She sounded a little ... intense."

"Ah, so maybe the appointment will be a pre-screening?"

I traced the embossed border of the wedding planning binder. "I think maybe our schedule is getting full, so we'll have to be selective, but let's see how it goes."

Lorea nodded. "Do you want to see the new gown I'm working on?" she asked with a lilt to her voice.

"You've already started on it?" She'd shown me several

sketches a couple weeks ago and ordered some special beaded silk that was extremely expensive, but I hadn't seen anything else.

I followed Lorea to her dress bodice, which was now sheathed with the base layer of the gown. The beaded silk was pinned to the scoop neckline of the dress, and it sparkled under the overhead lights.

"I didn't know it had a shimmer to it." I carefully ran my fingers over a section of the silk.

"Isn't it pretty? And I'm using this rayon blend for the bow in the back."

I walked around the dress bodice and noted the unique design of a bow from Lorea's sketch just below the shoulder blades. The tails of the bow were large enough that they swooped down to create a smaller train on the dress. "This is going to be magnificent," I said. "Are you going to enter it in the design contest for Country Bride?"

Lorea chewed on the end of her thumbnail. "I'm thinking about it."

"I think you should."

"I'm going to add a panel of the silk beading on the front of the skirt." Lorea began stitching the silk with a fine gossamer thread.

"I'm thinking of the love story that will go along with this dress." I paused and studied Lorea. "Have you designed your own dress yet?"

Lorea chuckled. "You are funny, you know that?" She didn't include the usual accusatory tone that came with the subject. Tony was slowly breaking down all of her barriers—at least, the twitch of a smile at the corner of Lorea's mouth indicated as much.

"Hmm, maybe not as funny as I used to be."

"What's that supposed to mean?" Lorea asked, her voice light.

I smiled and headed to the front of the shop to finish my work, glancing at the clock as I went. If I left in the next ten minutes, I could make it to Lost Trails Construction by four thirty.

The office for Lost Trails Construction was decorated in sleek, modern lines and definitely made a statement of opulence. With granite countertops, a vintage-style chandelier overhead, and a beautiful picture window overlooking a patio out back, it was obvious that they knew design. White custom cabinets lined the walls, and the floor was hardwood with tile surround in a spectacular display.

"May I help you?" The receptionist smiled from her large cherrywood desk with a nameplate that said "Savannah."

"Yes, I wondered if anyone could help me with some questions on remodeling."

"You've come to the right place," Savannah said. "Let me see if Rose is free."

She walked down the hallway, and I took the moment to try to compose myself: I knew she was referring to the same Rose Benavidez involved in a court case with Luke as the opposing attorney. I hadn't expected to meet with Rose. If Luke found out, there might be another murder investigation. And what would happen if Rose recognized me from Gladys's wedding?

Savannah returned and waved her hand with a little flourish. "Right this way."

"Thanks," I managed as I followed her down the hall, which had several beautiful pieces of artwork adorning the walls. She led me to an office that was equally as beautiful as the front entryway.

"Good afternoon," Rose stood and walked around the large black desk with a white marble top. Her light-brown hair was pulled back into a messy bun and she wore a green linen skirt with a white-and-blue blouse. Her posture was straight, and "professional" was written all over her. She offered her hand, and I shook it firmly. "Rose Benavidez."

"Adrielle Pyper." I watched her face for any flicker of recognition, but saw none. "Thanks for seeing me," I said. "It's nothing urgent, just a few questions that have come up with my remodeling ideas." I stopped and took a breath because my words had come out in a rush, stumbling over each other. Why was I so nervous?

"Sure. Have a seat and I'll see what I can do. I'm here until five thirty today." Rose sat behind her desk, and I sat in one of the leather armchairs flanking the desk.

Now that I was here, seated in front of Lily's sister, my mind was a jumbled mess of nerves. Everything I'd heard about her divorce and custody battle swirled through my thoughts. She seemed nice enough, definitely not the type to neglect her own child. I swallowed and thought through my approach. "Well, I've been thinking about remodeling a room in my, uh—office," I stuttered. If I mentioned my wedding shop, she'd probably be able to connect the dots. But then I thought of an idea that might help. My lip trembled. "Lily was one of my clients, and she always spoke so highly of the work her father did."

"Her stepfather," Rose corrected with a note of malice, though she smoothed it over with a smile. Her lipstick was a deep red, and she wiped the corner of one lip with her manicured nails. "But yes, we do extraordinary work here. How did you say you knew Lily?"

I didn't, I wanted to say, but instead I took a breath. "I was helping her plan her wedding." I hesitated, tamping down the emotions that were flaring up as I thought about Lily. I wasn't acting. It was hard for me to think about what had happened to her, but if my show of emotions would help me get information from Rose, I wouldn't hold back. I blinked several times and looked at Rose.

Her own eyes had filled with tears. "The whole thing is such a waste," Rose said. "Lily was brilliant and fantastic at anything she put her mind to. I don't like my stepfather, but he didn't kill her. Just because he had a life insurance policy isn't motive for murder."

"I've heard mention of the life insurance policy," I said, sniffling. It seemed everyone in town had heard of it, and there were several different amounts rumored. I wondered if Rose knew how much the policy was for. "Do you know if anyone else would have been listed as a beneficiary?"

Rose narrowed her eyes. "Why do you ask?"

"Because there's usually more than one sole beneficiary on those kinds of policies, especially one that large." I'd done a little research before asking my questions, and this one was well placed.

"I wouldn't be surprised if it's one of Phil's girlfriends. Show that man some leg and he loses his mind." She lifted one shoulder in a half shrug, but didn't contradict my statement about the policy being large. "It doesn't really matter to me anymore. I'm leaving soon. There's nothing left for me in this town."

"Oh? What about—" I barely stopped myself from asking about her divorce case. I conjured up a fake cough and held up my finger for one moment while my mind spun through possible acceptable endings to my sentence. "What about your job?"

"I've got that taken care of, but thanks for asking." Her tone indicated that she didn't appreciate my asking. She checked her watch. "Perhaps you'd like to make an appointment with a designer who can help you long term?"

I had to try one more tactic. "If Phil didn't kill Lily, then who do you think did?"

Rose stiffened, likely taken aback by my direct question. She pursed her lips and huffed. "Tim Esplin, whom I'm sure you're familiar with." She paused, assessing my reaction, but I didn't say anything. "Lily was having second thoughts about marrying him. She had even mentioned breaking up with him before he proposed to her. He was controlling, possessive, and manipulative. If he couldn't have Lily, then no one could. I think it will be only a matter of time before the police catch on."

My jaw hung open. I knew Tim. I'd seen the love in his eyes when he talked about marrying Lily. But how well did anyone know a person?

"See, you're surprised too," Rose said in a satisfied tone. She sat back in her chair and eyed me carefully, as if deciding what she wanted to say. "Everyone thinks Tim could do no wrong, but they probably haven't seen him when he's angry."

"I—uh, I didn't know," I stammered. "Lily seemed so happy and excited about her engagement."

Rose pursed her lips. "I think she was at first, but then she found out some things about Tim—the way he ran his clinic, the things he hid from everyone."

My stomach clenched. I didn't want to believe anything that Rose said, but her hatred of Tim was convincing. "What do you mean, how he ran his clinic?"

"Financially. Maybe you've heard how smart Lily was with numbers? She could assess any business quickly and see the problems. She said something about Tim's clinic—that it wasn't as financially sound as she first thought."

"Oh dear," I said. "That's too bad."

"It doesn't matter now," Rose said. "He mortgaged his clinic and everything else to get out on bail. He won't have anything left, but he'll be behind bars anyway. It's more than he deserves."

The venom in her voice had a razor edge, and I wondered what Tim had done to get on her bad side. "I'm sorry. Are they going to let you have the funeral?"

"Yes, it's tomorrow. We've tried to get word out since it had to be postponed." She leaned her head forward and massaged her temples. "It's at ten o'clock."

"I'm so glad you told me, because I hadn't heard. I'll be there." I stood to leave; my trail of questions had the air charged with so many emotions that I needed some fresh air. "Thank you again for your time."

"You can make an appointment with one of our other design directors with the secretary." Rose stood and led me to the door.

"Thanks." I left the office quickly, hoping Rose didn't notice that I didn't make a return appointment.

Once I got back to my car, I sat there for a moment and let the cool breeze from my air conditioning take the heat out of Rose's words. Did Lily really have second thoughts about marrying Tim? As I thought about it, I remembered that day in the vet office. Tim had blamed Lily's potential cold feet on Rose's divorce, but maybe there was more to the story. With a sigh, I backed out of the parking lot, mulling over the measly crumbs of information I'd gathered from Rose.

Every time I asked questions about Lily's murder, I didn't find answers, only more questions. My gut didn't feel so certain anymore when it came to Tim's innocence. I asked myself again if I could be wrong about Tim. I'd been wrong before, but that was in a different time of my life, before I learned to trust my instincts. There weren't any warning signals sounding in my head or my heart. I wanted to trust Tim. Rose and Javier were still on my list of suspects, but Tim was lingering on the edges. I needed to find out what Lily might have been referring to when she said Tim's clinic wasn't financially sound.

Chapter 17

FUNERAL POTATOES

Peel, then boil 6 potatoes until tender. Drain water and replace with cold water. Grate potatoes into a pan (Use disposable gloves so you don't burn your hands.)

Pour a mixture of 2 cups grated cheddar cheese, ½ cube melted butter, 1 can cream of chicken soup, and 1 cup sour cream over the potatoes. Stir the sauce into the potatoes. Add ½ cup buttered breadcrumbs or crushed cornflakes over the top.

Bake at 350 degrees for 45 minutes or until bubbly on top.

Courtesy of www.mashedpotatoesandcrafts.com

The funeral home was packed for Lily's service that Tuesday morning. I had to park my car on the other side of the street, and I noticed several others doing the same thing. Lorea was already inside, saving me a seat beside her and

Tony. Luke had offered to come with me, but he didn't know Lily, and it was obvious that it was hard for him to offer to attend the funeral. He'd looked relieved when I'd told him to get his work done so we could go to lunch later.

My heart felt pinched when I thought about what it must have been like for him to attend his own wife's funeral. It made his offer mean even more. Luke was stepping out on the ledge with me. I smiled as a little thrill went through me at the thought of jumping off that ledge, with Luke holding my hand. Before entering the funeral home, I tucked my smile away, holding that secret hope for later.

Tears welled up in my eyes and my breath caught as I stepped inside the chapel. There were dozens of lilies in every color decorating Lily's coffin and placed around the room. Only one week ago, Lily had been alive. I had called and talked to her on the phone to reschedule her appointment. Part of me couldn't believe how much things had changed in one week. It seemed like my little town had been turned upside down with murder allegations, rumors, and the investigation into Lily's cause of death. I blinked until my eyes cleared, and swiped a finger underneath my lashes.

Phil sat in the front row next to a woman I hadn't seen before, and Rose sat on the other end of the bench next to Jasmine. I scanned the crowd until I found Javier, neatly dressed in a suit, near the back. Lorea caught my eye and nodded her head toward the empty space next to her. Inwardly, I cringed when I recognized Vickie from the vet clinic sitting right in front of Lorea and Tony.

Edging my way through the throng of people, I brushed up against someone and murmured, "Excuse me."

"It's no problem," the man said in a familiar accent. He pronounced "it's" like "eats." I jerked my head up to make eye contact with Boris Kovacevic. His eyes were red and puffy, and he held a handkerchief in one hand.

I nodded and moved past him to my seat. Lily had so many people who loved her, but what about her enemies?

When Tim walked in through a side door and sat on the second row, every single one of my murder suspects was in the room. I heard a few people murmuring and I noticed a man and a woman pointing in Tim's direction, their faces pinched in anger. Tim kept his head down. My chest filled with sadness at the situation. I leaned back against the padded chair and listened to the prelude music.

Lorea gave me a hug, her eyes tight with emotion. "Poor Lily. I hope she knew how much she was loved before she left this earth."

I nodded. "It's still hard to believe she's gone."

Tony reached across Lorea and patted my hand. "At least Tim could be here for the funeral," he whispered in a voice so low I barely caught the words.

Before I could reply, the services started. The program was shorter than I expected, but maybe that was because the life sketch that Lily's cousin gave was short—her life was cut short when there was so much more she could have done. My eyes kept wandering to different people in the crowd—mainly those in the category of suspects. Each person seemed to be grieving in their own way. Tim's was the most obvious display of grief: he didn't hide the trails of tears running down his cheeks, dripping onto his suit coat. An older woman, possibly his mother, handed him a handkerchief, but Tim just clutched it tightly in his hands, staring ahead at Lily's casket.

During the final hymn, I wondered over a disturbing question. Would the murderer be sad because Lily had died, or because they had killed her? Or worse, was one of these people acting, portraying grief to broadcast their supposed innocence to those watching?

After the funeral and graveside service, we returned to a church, where I helped set up casseroles and pans of funeral potatoes. It always felt weird to me, having a luncheon after a funeral, mostly because it was odd that no matter what happened in life, eventually we would be hungry again. I peeled the tinfoil off one of the steaming pans of potatoes sprinkled with cheese and crushed corn flakes. The grated potatoes bubbled in creamy sauce as I put a serving spoon in each pan.

Lily's family wasn't very big, but there were still about sixty people at the luncheon. Lorea stayed to help with the serving as well. Once the meal was underway, we shared a plate of food in the kitchen. The funeral potatoes were delicious. As I savored the perfect combination of cheese, potatoes, and crunch in the casserole, I decided that maybe hunger stuck around to keep our minds from dwelling on grief.

My wedding shop felt especially subdued and gloomy after Lorea and I returned from Lily's funeral. We both went through the motions of work, setting up appointments, paying bills, and calling clients, but there was a hollow feeling to the work that day. Lorea hummed "Abide with Me," the hymn sung at the end of Lily's funeral, while she stitched more of the fine beaded-silk wedding gown.

When a customer entered at one fifteen, I realized that

I'd completely forgotten about Zara's appointment. I pasted on a smile and went to greet the bleached blonde wearing gold high heels, a red leather miniskirt, and some kind of sheer gold fabric that could loosely be defined as a blouse. If it wasn't Zara, then I was completely losing my touch.

"Oh, hi! You must be Adri," she said as soon as she saw me. "I'm Zara Lowry, and your shop is just darling." She held out her hand, bedecked with bangle bracelets, a gold watch, and several rings.

I shook it, and smiled. "Yes, it's nice to meet you. Let's have a seat right over here at my design table." I motioned to the table set up with binders of fabric and color swatches. "I have a questionnaire you can fill out."

Zara scooted past me and plopped down into my office chair, which faced the window. I usually sat there so I could keep an eye on the comings and goings in my shop, and because I had things organized to work efficiently in each appointment. I mentally shrugged and sat in the other chair.

"So, I want my wedding to be glam—like the ring Maddox gave me." She flashed a gaudy diamond on her ring finger that looked a lot like cubic zirconium, and continued, "Like I want my old boyfriends to see what they're missing." Zara leaned over the desk, and her push-up bra strained at the sheer fabric of her shirt.

I swallowed my cringe and rolled my shoulders back, ready to tell her just how busy we were, but before I could say anything Zara popped open one of my wedding planners and began flicking through the pages. She pulled out a questionnaire and started filling out the top line.

"I can bring you a picture of the type of wedding gown I

want," she said. "It's straight from the red carpet. I want a V-neckline—" She pointed somewhere near her belly button. "—and Maddox loves the high-cut slits that show a little leg."

She batted her ultra-fake eyelashes, and I gulped in a breath. "Well, the thing is, my schedule is much busier than—"

"Oh, hang on a minute." Zara slipped the diamond ring off her finger and dropped it into her purse. She smoothed back her hair and, if possible, looked even perkier.

"What are you doing? Is there something wrong?" I asked. At the same time, the bell above my door chimed.

"Him," Zara said. She stood and grabbed her purse. "Be right back," she whispered as she walked past me.

I turned around and my jaw went slack as Zara made a beeline for Luke. Luke's eyes caught mine with a question as Zara approached him. There wasn't time for me to relay even a facial tic, let alone an explanation for what was about to happen.

Zara sidled up to him. "Hi there, handsome." She took his left hand and squealed. "Oh, he's single, too!"

Luke pulled his hand away from Zara. "Excuse me, but I'm here to—"

"Oh, I know honey." Zara put her hand on his arm and slid it up to his bicep. "It's love, right?" She gripped his muscle, stood on her tiptoes, and whispered something in his ear.

Luke's face turned crimson, and he shrugged out of her grasp. "I'm here for Adri." He practically sprinted to my side. "I'm taking her out on a date." He reached down and grabbed my hand, squeezing it three times.

Zara studied Luke and then leveled her gaze at me. She sniffed, then shrugged. "Dang, he was a fine one," she murmured as she dug through her purse until she found her ring. She slid it back on her finger and walked toward us.

I felt Luke stiffen, and I squeezed his hand this time.

"Sorry for running late for my appointment," Zara said. "Maybe we can go over more details next time?"

I opened my mouth, strained to think of something to say, and closed it again.

"Actually," Lorea spoke up from behind me. She stood next to me with her arms folded. "This was just a pre-screening. Adri has a big client load right now, so she meets with people to help them find the right wedding coordinator. We won't be able to fit you in, but we wish you the best of luck."

Zara frowned. "But then why the questionnaire?"

I wanted to say, *You mean the one you took out of a binder without asking?* But instead I said, "I like to see if there's anything I can do to help you, but I really am overscheduled." I snatched the form off the table. "Here's your form. I think it'll come in handy with the rest of your planning." Zara had only filled out the top two lines.

"Well, that was a waste of time," Zara spat. "It's not like wedding planners grow on trees around here."

"I'm sure you'll be able to find someone who can accommodate your schedule," I said.

"You should have told me you were full before I sat here for half an hour."

"Actually," Lorea cut in again, "She was about to tell you right before you started flirting with her boyfriend."

Zara stiffened. Her eyes cut to Luke and back to me. "Is he really your boyfriend?"

I nodded, not daring to look sideways at Luke.

Zara's lip curled, and she glared at Lorea. "I understand." She turned and stomped out of the shop.

"What in the world was that?" Luke finally said, once the door closed.

"That was a crazy *txori buru*," Lorea said.

"Isn't there a better word in Basque to describe her?" I asked. "Because calling her a birdbrain sounds too nice."

Lorea tapped her cheek with her index finger. "How about *beldurgarri*. Scary. As in restraining-order scary."

"I agree," Luke said. "What's her name, so I can file one tomorrow?"

Lorea burst out laughing, I started laughing, and then we couldn't stop. Tears ran down my cheeks, and even Luke's shoulders shook with laughter.

"Why do I attract the crazies?" I said.

"It's because you're so sweet," Luke said. He touched my cheek and a zing went right through me, killing the laughter and replacing it with butterflies.

"Thanks for saving me there, Lorea," I said. "At first, I wasn't sure what to say to her."

"Anytime," Lorea said. "I knew exactly what I wanted to say to her, but I didn't say any of that."

"Are you about ready to go?" Luke asked. "If I wasn't worried before about being in a wedding planner shop, I definitely am now."

Lorea and I laughed. "Yes," I told him. "Let me just put this away."

"I'll get it," Lorea said. "You go, and you'd better hold on tight to Luke. Zara might be out there waiting for him." Lorea waggled her eyebrows.

Even though she was teasing, I saw Luke scanning the area as we walked to his car.

Luke had picked up sandwiches before he came to get me, and we ate under a large fir tree, not too far from the Sun Valley lodge. Even though I'd had a portion of potatoes at the funeral, I was still hungry. The bacon-and-salami slammer Luke offered me made my mouth water.

"So, how was the funeral?" Luke asked.

"It was very nice. Sad. I noticed Tim had a hard time." I pulled up a bunch of grass and let it fall through my fingers.

"I'm sure it was tough for him." Luke watched the grass catch the breeze with a faraway expression.

I decided to change the subject. "This is a perfect day for a picnic. I haven't been able to spend as much time outside this summer. Too much work."

"I agree." Luke refocused on me, and his eyes lit up. "I do have one tomato plant in my garden box and some kind of squash."

"Volunteers?"

Luke nodded and took another bite of his sandwich.

"My mom grows enough vegetables in her garden for half the county, which is good since I don't have any place for a garden."

"Nothing like fresh tomatoes." Luke bit into a tomato hanging from his sandwich.

"Or cucumbers with salt and vinegar." We smiled at each other. "Hey, sorry again for earlier at the shop. How are you doing?"

Luke grimaced. "Well, it took my mind off work for a minute. I don't know if a distraction like that is what I need, though."

"That case still dragging on?"

"Yes," Luke said. "I'm really worried about this custody hearing tomorrow."

"It's the real deal, isn't it?"

"The judge has made his decision, and he'll let us know tomorrow afternoon."

"Stomach all tied up in knots?"

"Yep." Luke put a hand on his stomach and looked almost physically ill. "Javier wants to win, but he also wants to be part of his daughter's life in whatever way he can."

"So what do you think will happen?"

"I think he has a good chance. Rose has made a lot of mistakes, and there have been several documented incidents of neglect."

I shuddered. "It's hard to believe that someone could treat their child like that."

Luke wiped his mouth with a napkin. "I keep hoping it will turn out all right, but mostly I just want it to be over with."

"Will you call me when you find out?"

"Yeah, I can do that."

I touched his cheek. "I like spending time with you."

He covered my hand with his. "Me too. Can we do this again, maybe tomorrow?"

"I think I have an opening in my schedule," I said with a wink.

Luke kissed the tips of my fingers, and my insides

sparkled with unseen fireworks. He leaned forward and pulled me close to him, so close that I could see the gray flecks in his blue eyes. He smiled and brushed his lips against mine softly.

Right about the time I closed my eyes, we were knocked over by something large, furry, and wet.

"Mike! No, no! Bad dog!" Trixie yelled from across the park.

I felt Mike's tongue on my cheek and pushed the dog off me. "Get off, Mike!"

Luke jumped up and pulled me to a standing position beside him. Mike yipped and pushed against Luke's leg. "You know this dog?"

"Yes, this is the dog that walked the bride down the aisle," I said. "And there's the bride."

Trixie jogged up next to us, with Sadie tagging along on a leash. "I'm so sorry. Mike got away from me. He's a sneaky fellow, aren't you, Mike?" She patted his head and picked up the blue leash dangling from his collar. Trixie gripped both leashes in her hand and smoothed back her purple-streaked hair. "I really am sorry about that."

"It's no problem," Luke said.

I wanted to say that actually it was a problem, because Mike had interrupted my first kiss with Luke. Instead, I nodded. "No problem. Good to see you. How's Derek doing?"

"He's great. We're great. Summer is keeping us busy, but we're planning to take the kids camping next week," Trixie said. "We're going to be honeymooning all summer."

"That'll be fun. Well, take care of yourselves." I waved as she jogged off with the dogs.

Luke furrowed his brow and whispered, "I thought you said they just got married. Did they have kids from a previous marriage?"

I laughed. "No, they refer to their dogs as their kids."

"Oh, I get it," Luke said. "Well, I guess we better get this cleaned up." He bent over and picked up the wrappers that Mike had scattered. I shook out the blanket, all the while feeling like I got cheated out of my birthday party. My lips felt warm from Luke's interrupted kiss.

When we'd loaded everything into the car, Luke pulled me in for another hug. "Thanks for taking a break with me. Maybe tomorrow we can celebrate."

"Yes, let's do that." I checked my emotions. A celebratory first kiss would be the best kind after how hard Luke had worked on this case. And this time, I'd make sure there were no dogs in the area.

Chapter 18

FRESH COCONUT LOTION

½ cup olive oil

¼ cup coconut oil

¼ cup beeswax

Optional: 2 Tbsp Cocoa Butter

Your favorite Essential Oil, try lemongrass, chamomile, mint

Directions:

Combine ingredients in a glass jar, mason & pickle jars work well. Fill medium saucepan with a couple inches water over medium heat. Put a lid on the jar loosely and place in the pan with the water. As the water heats, the ingredients will start to melt. Shake occasionally to incorporate. When melted, pour mixture into a half-pint jar or tin for storage. Use within 6 months for best results.

Courtesy of www.mashedpotatoesandcrafts.com

PROPOSALS AND POISON

Luke dropped me off at the shop and headed back to his office to work. He often worked later in the evening, when there were no interruptions. It would have been nice if we could have extended our date, but I needed to finish up a few things before we closed.

It was almost three o'clock when I returned to find Lorea scanning the news online. She looked mildly guilty when I came up behind her.

"Something I should be worried about?" I asked.

Lorea shook her head. "Just checking to see if there's anything new on Lily. I imagine there will be some articles tomorrow about who was at the funeral."

"It's such a shame." I paused. "I hate to think it, but the murderer was definitely at the funeral today."

"I know." Lorea blew out a breath. "Tony has been working nonstop on this murder investigation. I know they're going to find out who did this." Lorea put her hand on my forearm and tilted her head to catch my eye. "And I have a confession."

I perked up. "About what?"

She fingered the *laburu* cross around her neck. "I might have been doing a little investigating of my own."

"Wait. What?" I grabbed Lorea's other hand. "Did you find something? You found something about Lily, didn't you?"

"Easy." She pulled her hand free. "Don't get me in trouble with Tony."

"How does that get you in trouble with Tony?"

"He specifically told me, 'Don't encourage Adri in any

way to look into this case. The police are handling it, and I don't want her to get hurt.'"

"Hmph." I sniffed. "Poor sport." Just because I'd helped solve a few murders and might have endangered my life a few times, he thought that he could boss me around? I hadn't done anything to jeopardize the case, or even asked that many questions. Lorea, on the other hand … I studied my friend. Her short dark hair flipped at the ends, adding to the spunk that resonated in every interaction I'd had with her over the past two and a half years. Lorea was smart, resourceful, genuine, and now she had an in with the best detective in the Sun Valley area.

"I'm going to tell you, as long as you promise to stay calm. Don't go off on some hunt for the bad guy, okay?"

I held up both of my hands. "I don't go looking for trouble, remember?"

"I know, I know." She pointed at me. "Trouble finds you no matter where you hide."

"Something like that. Now, what is it?"

"Well, remember how my sister, Terese, has been working for the newspaper?"

"Oh, so that's your angle. You want me to get involved so you can give Terese the big scoop."

Lorea swatted at me. "That's a great idea, but no, that's not my angle." She put a hand on her hip. "I know you've been really upset that Tim was arrested. At first, I didn't give it a second thought, but I know you and your gut, and it's not often wrong—even if you don't always listen to it."

"That's fair." Her reference to one of my former boyfriends was well documented, so I kept listening even though thinking of him still made the hair on the back of my neck stand on end.

"Anyway, this may be something, or maybe not," Lorea hedged.

"Just tell me already." I stomped my foot.

"I really don't know if I should. Maybe you should ask me some questions so I can honestly tell Tony that I didn't encourage you." Lorea scooted back in her chair.

"Lorea! That's not fair," I protested, but she just folded her arms, prepared to wait me out. She leaned around my desk and opened the jar of fresh coconut lotion Jenna had made for me. Lorea scooped out a dab of the coconut oil mixture and rubbed it on a dry spot on her upper arm.

I had plenty of questions, but I wasn't sure what kind of information she thought she'd found. The lemongrass essential oil in the lotion reminded me of Jessie's request to diffuse the same oil at their wedding. Then I remembered Drago and Boris. "Did Drago get arrested? Or maybe his brother Boris?"

Lorea shook her head. "No, that I can tell you. Tony cited Boris, and he'll be fine. It sounded like Drago had some pretty important information about Lily's case. Tony got all excited and started flipping through his notepad when he told me that Drago hopefully wouldn't get arrested anytime soon."

"Well, that's a relief. I'm glad that they listened to Drago. Poor Jessie has had to deal with so much stress lately. I was afraid if they arrested Drago, she'd fall apart."

"I know. I think Drago will be okay. It was good of Luke to go and talk to him so that he wouldn't be afraid to talk to the police."

"I'll have to tell Luke. That'll brighten his day." I thought about how Luke had taken time out of his overloaded schedule to go and help someone he didn't even know. He'd done that for me. Little goose bumps erupted on my arms. Because of Luke, Jessie and Drago could move forward with their wedding plans. There could still be a snag in their future, but hopefully the threat of Lost Trails had diminished enough to allow them peace of mind.

"That wasn't the right question," Lorea stage-whispered.

I realized that I'd completely gotten off track with Lorea's guessing game. "Okay, it has something to do with the news because you mentioned Terese. Wait a minute." I snapped my fingers. "What news story is about to come out relating to Lily's murder?"

"Aha!" Lorea leaned forward. "Now that is a good question."

I clapped my hands together. "What's the answer?"

"Well, most of my information came from Terese. She said the reporters get together and brainstorm ideas for articles—"

"Wait, they brainstorm ideas on news articles?" I interrupted. "I thought Terese wanted to work in the current news department—as in breaking news."

"Well, that's the thing. I guess sometimes news happens with a little coaxing."

My eyebrows rose up into my hairline. "Is someone doing something illegal?"

Lorea pressed her lips together and hesitated. "I talked to Tony about it, and he said the department has their eye on someone. He didn't say who, but he seemed interested when I mentioned a few of the freelancers' names."

"Is someone blackmailing to make news happen?"

"I'm not sure how it works, but Terese said that several things have been pushed into motion by a few key individuals. Politics plays the biggest role, of course, but as they say, money talks."

"Okay, my head is kind of spinning. How does all of this relate to Lily's murder and Tim's arrest?" I sat next to Lorea and stared at the computer screen.

"Sorry, it's convoluted, but I'm hoping you can make sense of it. There has to be a connection. I just can't see it yet." Lorea glanced at a notepad where she'd scribbled something down. She put her hand over the words and looked back at me.

"You have my attention. I promise. Now tell me what's going on," I almost pleaded.

Lorea blew out a breath. "Tim's brother somehow leaked the info about the second life insurance policy."

"Wait, did you say second policy?"

Lorea nodded. "Yep, and it's worth almost as much as the first one. And get this: Tim is the sole beneficiary."

I thought of Tim in the orange jumpsuit; Tim at the funeral, crying for Lily; and Tim raking in a huge sum of money from her death. It didn't match up. "But why would his brother ever do that? And how do we know it's true?"

"I'm betting it was inadvertent. He probably never really divulged the info but said something to someone, and that someone gave a guess that drew the bluff."

"Surely he's smarter than that. And how did someone at the newspaper get this info?"

Lorea rubbed her fingers together. "My sister says, money talks, money takes, and money kills."

I shivered. "Maybe your sister should write detective novels."

Lorea laughed. "Yes, she could just write your life story, right?"

I rolled my eyes. "But where do all these cryptic hints get us if you've already told Tony?"

"Someone is definitely trying to frame Tim Esplin. We just need to find out who."

"But why would Tim even have a policy on Lily? They weren't even married yet."

The bell on the front door of my shop chimed, and I walked out to greet my patron, leaving the question hanging in the air. Lorea had uncovered a new angle to the murder—an angle that someone in my little town had murdered Lily Rowan for. And they were still walking the streets.

Chapter 19

Marriage Advice: Keep your eyes wide open before marriage, and half-shut afterwards. - Benjamin Franklin

Courtesy of www.mashedpotatoesandcrafts.com

Wednesday morning, I drove to Tim's animal clinic before I went to work. I didn't tell anyone what I was doing, because they would have all told me to stay away from the possible murder suspect. But I was too angry to care. If what Lorea said was true, then Tim had deliberately hidden the fact that he had a life insurance policy on Lily. No wonder he had paled when I'd brought up the rumor of the life insurance; he thought no one knew about it. I clenched my fist and banged the steering wheel. If Tim wasn't truthful, the police wouldn't be able to help him, and he would look even guiltier. The more I learned about Tim's part in all this, the more I worried that he could be more than a suspect—he could be guilty.

I pulled into the front parking lot, which was noticeably empty at nine in the morning. There were three vehicles parked at the side of the building, so I felt safe enough to go inside. I marched into the waiting area. "I need to speak with Tim for a few minutes. Tell him it's Adri Pyper and it's an emergency."

The secretary's eyes widened, but thankfully she didn't ask questions. She scurried through a door to the exam rooms. I folded my arms across my chest and tapped my fingers against my upper arm.

A couple minutes later, the secretary returned through a different door. "He can see you now." She held the door open for me, and I followed her down the too-bright hallway to an office with a beat-up metal desk. The faint smell of dog lingered in the air around us; I wrinkled my nose, because it wasn't a freshly shampooed dog smell. "Have a seat. He'll be right in."

I sat down, studying the name placard: Dr. Timothy Esplin.

"Hi, Adri," Tim said as he entered the office. "What can I do for you? Is Tux okay?" He sat at his desk and leaned toward me.

"Yes, he's fine, thank you." I waved my hand to dismiss his question. "I'm here because I want to know why you lied to me when I was trying to help you."

Tim leaned back. "What do you mean?"

"The life insurance policy that you have on Lily." I kept my tone even and my words clipped.

Tim sighed and shook his head. "I still don't understand how the press got wind of that. My brother is too trusting."

"So it's true? You had a life insurance policy on Lily before you were married?"

"Yes. I know it sounds ... well, terrible. I've talked to the police about it, and I'm trying to lie low."

"I can understand that. But wouldn't it have been better to tell the police before they found out from someone else?"

"I'm sorry that I didn't say anything before," Tim said. "My lawyer cautioned me not to reveal anything incriminating to anyone, so I didn't tell the police. You really scared me when you brought up the other life insurance policy. I never imagined that someone would find out about that."

He still hadn't answered my question, so I decided to be bold. "Why did you have a policy on Lily?"

Tim seemed to shrink in his seat. He pressed his lips together. "This part hasn't leaked out. Can I trust you?"

"Of course," I said.

"Lily's mother died of renal cancer when Lily was fourteen. Cancer of the kidneys was also the cause of death for her paternal grandmother. That type of cancer can be hereditary. A few years ago, Lily found out that there could be a very good chance that she carried the same genetic markers that upped her chances of getting cancer significantly."

"Oh dear."

"That was one of the reasons she was so hesitant to get married," Tim continued. "Lily wanted to be a mother, but she didn't want to leave her children alone. I finally convinced her to take a chance on life instead of living in fear."

Tim gripped the side of the table and pressed his lips together. "My brother does insurance. He helped us get a good deal on a life insurance policy for five hundred thousand dollars. Lily set it up and set up each of the beneficiaries. I know she listed me as one of them, but honestly, I hadn't thought about any of this until the police arrested me." He scratched his head. "Everyone knows the euthanizing chemical came from my office. I don't know what proof the detectives found on how it was administered, but they're using that as the main motive for murder."

"But can't they see what an obvious setup that is? I mean, couldn't someone have broken into your office and stolen the injection?"

Tim took a deep breath. "There wasn't any evidence of tampering with the safe. Either the person had a key, or they are a professional thief."

"Everything seems so neatly stacked against you." I clenched my hands into fists and picked through the questions I'd prepared. Rose's allegations seemed weak when I was sitting across from Tim's innocent face, but I had to ask. "Can you tell me about your experience with Rose?"

Tim furrowed his brow. "Rose is a selfish, spoiled brat who doesn't want anyone to be happy, because she isn't. She sabotaged the last relationship Lily was in, and when it didn't work with me, she came at me with a vengeance."

"Sabotaged?"

"Rose tried to seduce me out at the house." Tim stared down at his desk, where he rolled a pencil back and forth. "She had it all planned, except for the part that I called Lily and put it on speaker phone when Rose wasn't looking."

I put a hand over my mouth and gasped.

"Yeah, Rose pretty much hated me after that. And I have to say that Lily didn't hold much love for her, either. She looked up her old boyfriend and found out that Rose had instigated that affair as well."

"She sounds disturbed. Do you think she could have killed Lily?"

Tim gripped the pencil and looked up. "It would make sense, but no. Even though Rose was crazy, she loved Lily, because her sister was all she had. And Rose never came to this clinic. She hates animals."

"That explains a lot."

"Agreed." Tim actually smiled.

"I'm sorry that word leaked out about the life insurance," I said. "I wish there was something we could find to help you out."

"Me too," Tim said. "It's strange, but I could have sworn that I remembered Lily saying something about there being a stipulation that we would have to be married at the time of her death in order for me to get the money. It was a slap in the face at the time, but she said she'd seen enough divorce that she wasn't going to chance her future children's welfare."

"And what about if you were married, but she died before there were any children? Did the stipulation change?"

"I'd have to ask my brother on those details. My lawyer is doing a lot of research to show that the motives the police thought I had are weak. That's why he recommended that I mortgage my practice to get out on a bond."

"I'm glad that you don't have to be in jail. Definitely ask your lawyer to look into beneficiary clauses on your life insurance. I'm sure Tony would want to know if there were other beneficiaries."

"I'll do that," Tim said.

"I have one more question."

"Go ahead."

"Well, before you had to mortgage your clinic, how were your finances?" I held my breath, because my question went beyond prying.

Tim tipped his head slightly as if wondering where the question came from, but he leaned forward to answer. "I've been very successful here. I make all of my payments, and I was able to purchase some new equipment for the office last year. Why do you ask?"

"It's just that ... Did Lily think that you were financially stable?"

Tim pulled back as if I'd slapped him.

"I'm sorry. That was harsh. I'm only asking because I'd like to refute some statements that others have made." It was my turn to squirm under his gaze.

After a moment, he deflated with a sigh. "Lily didn't like it when I did work for free. She thought people were taking advantage of me, and that I should at least set up a payment plan with them." He licked his lips. "I did with some patients, but I love animals. That's why I became a vet—not for the money, for the work."

"And Lily hadn't caught that vision?"

Tim looked down at his desk. "She was catching it. I think she was finally starting to see the wisdom of how I ran my business. It didn't make sense on paper sometimes, but I know from experience that a good deed doesn't go unrewarded. I've never had to worry about paying my bills, until now."

My eyes burned with moisture, and the room grew very quiet. Tim's words echoed in the stillness, and I felt a confidence that I hadn't that morning on my drive over. Tim didn't kill Lily. He was a kind and gentle man. I didn't want to be wrong about that. It felt impossible to think otherwise.

"I'm so sorry, Tim. For what it's worth, I believe that you would never harm Lily."

"Thanks, Adri. That means a lot."

He walked me out to the empty waiting area and I waved goodbye. Before I could leave the building, Vickie approached me from the other side of the waiting area. I hadn't seen her before, and now I wished I'd hurried out before she could talk to me, because she didn't look happy.

"Why are you here?" Her tone was neither gentle nor encouraging.

I hesitated, taken aback by her curt question. "I came to talk to Tim."

"You should leave him alone. It's upsetting to him, talking to all these people with nosy questions. It's none of your business," she spat.

I'm sure she saw my eyes widen, because there was no way I could hide how surprised I was at her attack. "Hey, I know it's upsetting," I said, trying to be non-confrontational. "The whole thing is terrible. I'm only here to help Tim."

"You're not helping him. You're hurting him. Just stop asking so many questions and go take care of your cat." She pointed at the door.

My brow furrowed. "I don't appreciate your tone or your

attitude. If Tim doesn't want to talk to me, he'll let me know," I snapped. Maybe I should have held my tongue, but Vickie had a personality problem that needed adjusting. "He's under a lot of stress, so I won't tell him right now about this conversation, but in the future you would do well to remember that I am one of Tim's customers."

Vickie glared at me. I stared her down until her eyes dropped to the floor, and then I hurried outside before she could say anything else.

As I pulled away, I noticed the parking lot was still empty except my car. How many people had canceled their appointments when Tim was arrested? Maybe Vickie was scaring off just as many. I shrugged off her verbal assault and took five cleansing breaths to rid myself of her toxic influence.

With that, I went to work and did my best to concentrate on the weddings I had coming up, but everything seemed dark and gloomy with all the questions and accusations circling in my head.

Chapter 20

DEEP BREATHING FOR STRESS RELIEF

Take in a deep breath through the nose and when lungs are filled, pack in another breath. Hold for three seconds and exhale slowly. At the end of the exhale, push air out from the lungs three times. Repeat this process 20 times for rejuvenation and stress relief.

Courtesy of *www.mashedpotatoesandcrafts.com*

"Hey, Lorea, can you pick up some posters I ordered for the art festival at the copy shop?"

"Sure. You look like you have a lot on your mind."

"Yeah, I can't get my mind off Lily." I didn't tell her about my run-in with Vickie at Tim's office, but my mind was on that as well.

Lorea leaned forward. "I know what you mean. I was

talking to Tony the other night, and he said something that got me to thinking. Don't worry, it wasn't anything about the case," she reassured me. "But it made a light bulb go off in my brain."

"What did he say already? You're killing me here."

"He said sometimes the best clues are like geodes. On the outside they look like a rock, but crack them open—" She snapped her fingers. "—and you find the real treasure. The inside of the geode is like the details that line the most obvious clues. You know the flashy suspicions. The first hunch or jump to a conclusion. Tony said that he solves cases by looking inside those clues, deep inside, and then tearing them apart and putting them back together."

I drummed my fingers on the countertop, considering her metaphor. "And this led to what great revelation?"

"I think Tim and Phil are both involved in Lily's murder."

"Not Tim." I shook my head. "I already told you, there's no way he's involved."

"Adri, I'm going to tread on thin ice for a minute." Lorea lowered her voice. "We both know people from our past who were incredibly talented at hiding the truth. People who appeared to be completely different than what they really were. Dangerous people."

I held up my hands. "Okay. I get what you're saying." I blew out a breath. "I've been wrong in the past. We've all been wrong. But I'm not wrong this time. It's not Tim."

"Prove it."

I raised my eyebrows. "Maybe I will." I nearly told her right then about my visit to Tim's clinic, but I held back. She was determined to have her opinions, and I had mine. The only way to change her mind was to uncover a clue that pointed away from Tim.

About thirty minutes later, Lorea came stomping out from the back room. "Why do you think you're the only one who can figure things out?" Lorea snapped.

I felt like she'd just stepped on my toes hard—or maybe I'd stepped on hers. "I don't."

"You're so sure that Tim didn't have anything to do with this that you're willing to undermine Tony's investigation to prove your point."

"Hey, that's not true," I protested, holding my hands up. "Where is all this coming from?"

"It's coming from a place where I trust the police to do their job. Tony just texted me and said that he got a complaint from the animal clinic that you've been bothering Tim. Did you go there today?"

I rolled my eyes. "Let me guess, was the complaint from someone named Vickie?"

"I don't know, but Adri did you go talk to Tim today?"

I chewed on my bottom lip. "Yes. I just asked him why he didn't tell me about the second life insurance policy when I talked to him before. And just so you know, his assistant is a witch. She all but threatened me for talking to him. I can't believe that she called the police. Why would she do that?"

"You talked to him before?" Lorea threw up her hands. "Adri, he's a murder suspect."

"But he didn't kill Lily."

Lorea was usually even-keeled, but now she was fuming. "You shouldn't be talking to Tim—definitely not going to his clinic! The police arrested Tim for good reason, and now, just because he has a great lawyer, he thinks he can get away with it."

"I'm sorry, but I can't believe it." I was starting to sound like a recording, but every time I defended Tim, it felt right. He didn't kill Lily. I couldn't be wrong again, not on this one. I'd thought Lorea agreed with me on that hunch, but something had changed her mind.

Lorea pulled out her phone and sent a text. "I'm asking Tony about that Vickie person."

"I promise that Tim didn't mind at all. He thanked me for helping him."

Lorea waved her hand at me and sent another text.

"Have you ever wondered if it was some kind of mistake?" I asked. "What if Lily wasn't supposed to die? Maybe there was some kind of mix-up and this is bigger than anyone's thought of?"

Lorea scoffed. "She had a needle full of poison injected into her body. I don't see how anyone could make that big of a mistake."

I lifted one shoulder and let it drop. "There are just lots of things that don't make sense in this case."

"Only if you're trying to make things more difficult than they really are. Tim and Phil colluded to murder Lily for almost three million dollars of life insurance money. That makes sense."

I shook my head. "It's too easy. Fits together like a puzzle. Murder is messy."

Lorea ran her fingertips through the hair at the nape of her neck. "Just let Tony do his job."

"I am." It was all I could do to keep my tone even. I

hadn't even snooped around that much with this case. Tony was a great detective, so I decided to let it go. Lorea was obviously in love; there was no other way to explain her strange behavior.

As the day went on, I still felt uneasy about the semi-argument Lorea had instigated about Tim and Phil's guilt. What was the driving force behind her certainty that they had killed Lily? She'd mentioned some kind of clue, but nothing I'd heard or thought of was so clear cut.

At ten minutes to five, I got a text from Luke.

Luke: ***Bad news. Lost the Benavidez case.***

Me: ***Oh, I'm so sorry. Really, that is terrible news.***

Luke: ***Sucks to lose.***

Me: ***What can I do for you? Can I make you dinner?***

Luke: ***I'm thinking of wallowing in my sorrow, but I got two new cases today and I'll be up until midnight working.***

Me: ***Sorry! :(Maybe tomorrow?***

Luke: ***Yes.***

Me: ***My place at six for dinner?***

Luke: ***I'll be there.***

"Well, this day just went from bad to worse," I muttered as I swept up in the back room.

"What happened?" Lorea put down her needle and thread and looked up at me.

"Luke lost the case against Rose Benavidez."

"Oh no! He's been working his guts out on that case, hasn't he?"

"Yes, and it really dragged on because of the delays with Lily's funeral." I put the broom in the closet and leaned against the door. "I feel so bad for Luke."

"What will happen with the dad?"

"I'm not sure, but I think it means they'll have shared custody. Or maybe not? I wasn't clear on that."

There was an ache right in the lining of my heart whenever I thought of little Jasmine Benavidez and the fierce custody battle her parents had fought. Luke lost, which meant Jasmine would still spend time with her mother, Rose. I couldn't decide if that was a good thing or not. Poor Luke. I had no doubt that he would stay up late working, but part of me wondered if he was burying himself and his pride in his work.

I made up my mind to do something for him. He'd shown me he cared in lots of little ways. It was my turn. "Hey, Lorea. I'm closing up early so I can run to the store," I said. "See you in the morning?"

"Wait. I'm sorry about earlier." Lorea stood next to the desk with her hands behind her back. "I shouldn't have snapped at you."

"It's okay. You're right. We both need to be careful and let the police do their job." I ducked my head. "I know Tony is an excellent detective."

"Thanks, Adri. Sounds like you have something planned for Luke. Good luck."

I smiled. She was good at reading me, but I hoped she wouldn't blow up again if something about this mystery sidelined me on my way home from work. I flipped the sign to "Closed," turned off the showroom lights, and waved at Lorea on my way out.

I was almost to my car when I remembered I needed to check the drip system on the hanging plants I'd ordered earlier that summer. They hung in front of my shop, and when I'd looked out the window earlier, I'd noticed they appeared a bit wilted. In the dry desert heat of Sun Valley, they would shrivel up within a couple days if not tended to.

Dark purple petunias cascaded over the side of one of the hanging plants, accompanied by a scattering of white alyssum, purple asters, and bright-blue Salvia. It made me happy to see the flowers blooming so beautifully in the chosen array of my company's design colors. They were a nice accent to the flowing script on my shop window—*Adrielle Pyper's Dream Weddings, Where Happily Ever After is Your Destination.*

I poked my finger into the soil and found it to be slightly damp, but a bit too dry to combat the July heat, so I fiddled with the nozzle of the drip system to allow more water to slowly irrigate the flowers. With one more look at the front of my shop, I wiped my hands on my pants and headed for my car.

I walked around the corner and ran into Tony, coming out of Walter Mayfield's ring shop. "Oh, hi. Coming to see Lorea?" I teased.

To my surprise, Tony blushed. "Uh, no. Actually I was just, uh—meeting with Walter—er, going over some details on a case." He stopped and moved his hand behind his back, but not before I saw a clear bag with "Mayfield Jeweler's" printed on the front. And inside the bag was a velvet green ring box.

I gaped. "Is that a ring—"

"No," Tony interrupted me. "Walter didn't want anyone to know about this, so please don't say anything. It should be an open-and-shut case."

I eyed the sack, then Tony. "... Okay?"

"Not a word to anyone, Adrielle Pyper. I can arrest you for interfering with a police investigation." His voice was stern, but I detected a hint of nervousness behind his police bravado.

"Got it." I patted him on the shoulder, noting that he was dressed casually—not on duty. "Good luck. I'll talk to you later." He was up to something, and I wasn't sure it actually was police business, but I'd give him his space—at least until I found out otherwise. I bit the edge of my cheek so he wouldn't see the grin begging to be released.

He hurried on his way, and I waited until I was in my car to let out a giggle. Police business? I didn't think so. I'd missed a chance to grill him about the investigation or share anything that I might have learned, but Tony had been very preoccupied. Maybe I could try to catch him tomorrow.

Chapter 21

SPINACH SALAD WITH HONEY MAPLE DRESSING

Toss 3 cups spinach, 1 cup shredded red cabbage, ½ cup chopped celery, 2 sliced carrots, 2 diced tomatoes, ¼ cup golden raisins, and ¼ cup pumpkin seeds in a large salad bowl.

Dressing:

2 Tbsp real maple syrup

2 Tbsp olive oil

2 Tbsp red wine vinegar

1 clove garlic

Blend ingredients and incorporate into salad mixture. Serves 6.

Courtesy of www.mashedpotatoesandcrafts.com

As I started my car, my thoughts returned to Luke and what might lift his spirits on a day where the sun beat down, intent on melting everything and everyone. The asphalt shimmered with heat as I pulled out of the parking lot and drove to my condo. My fingers had a smudge of dirt on them, which gave me an idea. I remembered over a year ago, finding Luke with a hose, nearly killing the flowers in his front yard. I'd given him a lesson on how to care for the plants, and since then he'd tried hard to keep his yard looking nice.

My mother had been born with a green thumb—her garden was one of the best in Rupert—and she'd taught me everything I knew about keeping flowers alive in the sandy desert soil. It was time I used some of my hard-earned skills. Luke's flowerbed would probably be the perfect place to perform an act of service.

First, I needed sustenance. My stomach gurgled with hunger, so I opened the fridge, trying to decide what I could eat that was both quick and refreshing. A summer salad was my go-to meal, so I made myself a spinach salad with chopped apples, walnuts, and my favorite honey maple dressing.

The crunch of the apples and the tangy sweetness of the dressing against the walnuts were delicious. While I chewed, I mentally reviewed my list of suspects, crossing off Tim and moving Rose up a notch, if for no other reason than she seemed to be a very troubled individual. But then I thought of Phil's business at Lost Trails Construction. Losing that company would be worth millions because of all the potential business he could have had. The company was his livelihood, and he had a beautiful mansion to maintain. I could imagine someone doing some desperate things to keep the lifestyle they were used to. I crossed Boris off my list as well, but wondered if there could be another worker from Lost Trails involved with the embezzling scheme that had been pinned on Drago.

Then I remembered Vickie. She had access to the animal clinic every day. It wasn't far-fetched to think that she had something to do with the euthanizing agent, but what would her motive be? I chomped hard on the next few bites, wishing that I could ask Tony if the police considered her a suspect despite her alibi. I would have to trust that they'd investigated every angle before making their arrest, but that didn't mean that I would cross Vickie off my list.

I finished my salad with more suspects on my list than when I started. I decided I probably should take a break from analyzing the case and focus on the preparations for the art festival, which was now only one day away. With a groan, I pulled out my checklist and spent a few minutes gathering my thoughts regarding the booth and everything we'd need to make the experience successful, then busied myself in arranging a few more bundles of greeting cards and affixing prices to everything.

When the clock chimed seven, I hurried to tidy up my kitchen and change my clothes to gardening digs. As I walked through the kitchen, I noted my stack of greeting cards that were prepped to sell at the festival. I sat down, pulled one from the stack, and wrote a note to Luke. Hopefully it would help lift his spirits. I tucked an old pair of gardening gloves in my sun hat, patted Tux on the head, and locked the door.

I drove to Luke's house and spent the next hour in the waning heat of the day tending to his flowers and plants, which were strategically placed along the front walk of his house and in the flowerbeds. There wasn't much traffic by his house, but every time I heard a car approaching, my heart jumped and it was all I could do to keep from whipping my head around to see if it might be Luke. Part of me felt silly, working in the dirt on his flowers. What if he didn't think my idea was so great after all?

The more I thought about it, the more anxious I grew with the sound of every car driving down the street. I needn't have worried, though, because I finished, swept the walk, and threw the weeds away, and still there was no sign of Luke. The card I had written earlier burned in the back of my pocket.

Luke,

I'm really sorry how things turned out with your case, but I want you to know that I admire you for working so hard. I care about you and I've really enjoyed spending time with you lately. Thanks for making time for me, and making this summer special.

Adri

I put a little heart by my name. It was definitely a forward move for me, but I placed the card in his mailbox. With one last glance at the freshly cultivated flowerbed, I walked toward the street.

A gray Silverado pickup pulled up behind me just as I was opening my car door; I turned to see Javier Benavidez hop down from the driver's seat. Goose bumps raced across my arms, and I resisted the urge to look to see if anyone else was around.

He noticed me and glanced towards Luke's house, and then back at me.

"Hi, Javier." I decided to be bold and let him know that I knew his name.

He scrunched his eyebrows. "Is Luke at home?"

"No, he's not." I didn't tell him that Luke was working late at the office, because I really hoped that he would show up. For some reason, Javier made me nervous. I recalled how angry he'd been at Gladys and Hank's wedding, and I held tighter to the door of my car. The way he stared at me made him move up a couple slots on my mental suspect list.

"I was hoping to talk to him for a minute." His consonants sounded clipped, and I detected a slight Spanish accent as he continued to speak. "Do you know when he'll be back?"

I shook my head. "I thought he'd be here by now, but I was just dropping something off for him. Why don't you try calling him?"

Javier looked down at the street. "I, uh, did already."

"He's probably in the middle of something," I said. "Can it wait until tomorrow?"

"*No importa*," Javier muttered. He pushed a hand through his black hair and looked at me again, as if seeing me for the first time. "Are you Luke's girl?" His eyes ran down the length of my body and then back up to my face, which I felt heating up under his scrutiny.

My heart was thumping in my chest, and my feet itched to run, but I held perfectly still and raised my chin a couple inches. "What kind of question is that?"

Javier arched one eyebrow. "You seem to know a lot about Luke. You're very pretty, but you're not with him."

"Luke and I are dating," I said. "Have a nice night." I turned to get in my Mountaineer.

Javier was instantly at my side. He gripped my arm and leaned in close to my ear. "I've seen you around, asking too many questions. Luke should be more careful with you, because questions are dangerous."

"Let go of me." I yanked my arm free and stepped back against the open door of my vehicle.

Javier stepped back and held his hands in the air. "Sorry. I didn't mean to scare you." His voice became softer, more soothing. "People know you, Adri the wedding planner. They know you're trouble."

I scowled at him. "I am not *trouble*. What people are you talking about?" My voice wobbled a little, even though I was trying to sound like I wasn't scared at all.

"That murderer, the vet. I saw him watching you in the park the other day."

"What day?" Cold chills ran down my spine. The evening sun was beating down on my back, and I felt a trickle of sweat run between my shoulder blades.

Javier backed up a couple more steps. "I shouldn't have said anything. I'll just go now." He turned and jumped into his pickup.

"Wait! When did you see Tim?" I yelled, but he started up his pickup and peeled away from Luke's house. I watched him drive away, the sun glinting off the chrome.

With a shiver, I got into my car and locked the doors. I dialed Luke's number, but there was no answer. My body was on high alert, and my hands were shaking as I gripped the steering wheel and began easing out into the street.

When a horn honked, I screamed and looked in my rearview mirror. I turned to my left and saw Tony in his cruiser, almost even with my car. He smiled and waved, but his face lengthened with a worried look when he met my gaze. He parked his car right in the middle of the street and jumped out. A mixture of relief and nervousness sped through me as he approached. I put my car in park and rolled down the window.

"Are you okay?" he asked as he leaned against my door. "You look kind of pale."

"I'm always pale," I said. Before answering his question, I ran through about ten scenarios in my mind. All of them ended with Tony lecturing me about staying out of police business. If I told him what Javier had just said, it would look bad for Tim. I hadn't noticed Tim anywhere outside of the animal clinic. And why was Javier acting so strangely? I thought about the custody case he'd just lost. Javier hadn't mentioned anything about that, but surely that's why he wanted to talk to Luke. My heart climbed up my throat with a new worry. What if Javier was angry with Luke? If he blamed him, would he be willing to harm Luke?

I sighed, knowing I would have to confide in Tony. As I turned off my car and opened the door, Tony stepped aside with a questioning look on his face. He might have looked contrite, too. Maybe he felt bad for threatening me earlier when I saw him with a ring box outside of Mayfield Jeweler's.

"It's a long story," I warned him. "Do you have a minute?"

"Sure. This is Luke's house, isn't it?"

I nodded. "Yes, and I wondered if you could check on some things for me?"

"About Luke?"

"No, about Javier Benavidez, who just stopped by here looking for him and sort of threatened me."

"What do you mean, sort of?" Tony stood up straighter. "What did he say?"

I repeated the conversation, reluctantly adding the part where Javier said he'd seen Tim watching me.

Tony scuffed his boot on the asphalt. "That's kind of strange. And you didn't see Tim?"

"No, and I'm worried that Javier is too upset about losing the case. He seemed intent on talking to Luke, but what if he didn't want to talk?"

"I'll drive by Luke's office and see if I can talk to him. At the same time, I'll keep a lookout for Javier," Tony said. "Will you be okay?"

"Yeah, the whole thing was just weird. I think I'm a little tired, and the stress of everything is getting to me."

"Be sure to look around before you go into your house, and call me if you see anything suspicious." Tony turned toward his car.

"Gee, now I'll be able to sleep just fine," I said.

Tony chuckled. "I'll keep an eye out for you." He tapped his badge.

"Thanks, Tony." Part of me wanted to let Tony leave without addressing the issues I'd discovered today while interviewing Tim, but if I wanted Tim to have a fighting chance, I needed to step deeper into the mud. "Hey, I'm sorry about earlier with Vickie from the animal clinic," I ventured.

Tony made a clicking noise with his tongue. "I'm not even going to say it."

"I know: can't stay out of trouble." I held up my hands.

"Was there anything you wanted to tell me about that visit?" Tony asked.

"Actually, there was. I'm more certain than ever that Tim isn't your guy."

"And what proof did you find that led you to that conclusion?"

Dang. Tony had called me out before I could even speculate. I ventured further into the metaphorical pool of mystery anyway. "Tim told me about the second life insurance policy, but that it wasn't in effect until he and Lily were married. He didn't know who the other beneficiaries were. I think that could be key to your investigation."

"It's probably Phil, since he's the one that helped set them up."

"No, Tim said his brother helped set this one up."

Tony rubbed his chin with his hand. "Why didn't Tim tell us that when we questioned him earlier?"

"It seemed like he just remembered it when he was talking to me. I can understand that, with the stress the poor man has been under."

"Well, you do have a point there," Tony said. "I'll definitely look into it. We'd have to get a court order and that could take another day, but I'll put things in motion."

"Thanks, Tony. So maybe I did something right for once?"

"Maybe." Tony grinned. "Now go home."

"I'm heading there now."

I jumped in my Mountaineer and headed to my condo, knowing that Tony would probably put my area on someone's detail tonight. It was nice having someone in law enforcement to look after me, since even when I was trying to do a good deed I stumbled into trouble. I shivered when I thought of Javier. When Luke had talked about Javier previously, I'd had the sense that he thought Javier was a good guy, but the man I'd just met didn't seem like a suitable father for a little girl.

I tried calling Luke again, with no answer. I wondered if he was really busy or if he was burying himself in his work to hide from the frustration of reality. Losing the case had to be hard on him. It would be interesting to see how he reacted to the situation. He was a successful attorney, but I was certain he'd lost cases before.

My cell phone sat next to my bed, hopefully waiting for a text or call from Luke, but I fell asleep without hearing anything from him.

Chapter 22

PINCUSHION ROUNDUP

For a great selection of tutorials on how to make your own pincushions, visit our website or pinterest page at MashedCrafts.

Courtesy of www.mashedpotatoesandcrafts.com

The battery on my phone went dead during the night, so I plugged it in first thing Thursday morning. My phone buzzed with several incoming texts and missed calls as soon as it powered up. The first was a text from Luke early that morning:

Luke: *Hey, thanks for the card! And I think something happened to my front walkway. :)*

He'd either stayed up all night or was up early again despite his late hours. I was grateful he'd noticed his flowerbeds. I texted back while I ate breakfast.

Me: ***Glad you noticed. I've been thinking of you!***
Luke: ***I missed you.***
Me: ***Me too. Today will be a better day!***
Luke: ***It can only go up from here. Let's try to get together tonight.***
Me: ***Okay. Talk to you later?***
Luke: ***Sure.***

The sun was already working overtime with temperatures reaching eighty degrees by the time I drove to work at nine that morning. Thinking about the simple text from Luke brought a smile to my face. It also made tingles go up and down my arms. I cared about him, and I felt okay to admit that. It looked like he was okay with it too.

Work today would be all about prepping for the Ketchum Arts Festival, which began at ten tomorrow morning. Lorea and I would set up the booth at seven o'clock, and my entire family was arriving shortly after. My parents planned to be there by eight, and Wes and Jenna would bring their kids after Wes finished with work. Normally I looked forward to family get-togethers, but today I felt unprepared because of all the mental energy I'd exerted on Lily's murder investigation. I resolved to give that a rest so I could focus on the festival. All I'd done was apparently stir up more trouble, questions, and antagonism from the local citizens of Sun Valley.

PROPOSALS AND POISON

"Hi, Lorea," I said as I entered the shop. "You beat me here again. I thought I was early today."

Lorea waved a pincushion at me. "I'm addicted to this gown. Isn't it going to be incredible?" She turned the bodice she was working on.

I nodded. "I love your style. The way your gowns are simple, yet elegant." I walked forward and admired the shirring that Lorea had painstakingly created along the sides of the bodice. The fitted look was a great contrast to the flowing train decorated with the silk beading. "You've come a long way on this already."

"I might be able to finish it next week and start getting pictures ready for my portfolio." Lorea bent her head over the dress and continued pinning.

"Are we all ready for the festival tomorrow?"

"Yep. I got my work done early, unlike some people I know," she teased.

"Hey, I made some cards and gave my mom advice on what else to make." I sighed. "Okay, I fully admit that I'm lame and should not have agreed to do a booth."

"Whatever, your mom loves making crafts. You gave her permission to pursue something that makes her happy. And I bet she's going to sell a ton of those darling pincushions she loves to make."

"Thanks for saying that. I'll try to feel a little less guilty." My mom had sewn the pincushion Lorea was using that morning with polka-dot fabric and stuffed it tight with birdseed. I ran my hand along the tight seams, which formed a hexagon. "These are a fun shape."

"Yes, that's what I love about it. It doesn't roll off the

table, and it's not too big to carry in my apron pocket." She motioned to the sewing apron she wore, the pockets filled with all kinds of sewing notions. "There's my box of stuff." Lorea pointed to the corner, and I crouched down to pull out the portfolio she'd created for the booth.

The photo book of her gowns was beautifully put together. She'd written some notes about her style, along with price guides for alterations and other items. Bringing a full wedding gown to the festival was too risky according to Lorea, and I had to agree with her. Too many hands would want to reach out and touch the silky fabrics and pearl beadings Lorea loved to use. Instead, she had an assortment of ring pillows she'd made with sample fabrics. Lorea had adopted her own logo, a Z-shaped design.

I wanted her to be successful, but the selfish part of me worried that she might leave if she became *too* successful. Catching myself, I reprimanded myself for my weak thoughts. Lorea wouldn't leave Sun Valley—Tony was here and they were looking at building a life together, maybe.

I'd seen Walter across the street when I came in that morning, and he looked happy. I doubted very much that Tony was investigating anything when I ran into him.

I was grinning when I heard Lorea tsk beside me. "What is that dopey smile about? Did Luke finally kiss you?"

"I wish. We've had some close calls, but we've both been so busy that our dates have all been in public places with lots of opportunities for interruptions."

"Hey, you didn't deny that you want to kiss him." Lorea stepped forward and put her hand on my head. "Are you feeling okay?"

I pushed her hand away. "You stop. This is all your fault. Cupid shot you and then you pointed me out as his next target."

Lorea laughed and put her arm around me. "I'm excited for us. It feels good to be in love."

"Love? I didn't say anything about love."

"Yes, you did. You're the one who brought up Cupid. That guy's all about love."

"And who are you and what did you do with my best friend?"

"Don't worry. I'm not getting married or anything."

"We'll see about that."

"Quit changing the subject and admit that you're in love with Luke," she demanded with mock ferocity.

I set her portfolio back in the box and then stood. "I meant that I might want to be in love with Luke. Just not sure yet if I'm there."

"It's okay," Lorea whispered. "I won't tell anyone, but don't worry. Luke is totally in love with you."

"How do you know?"

"Tony said so."

I groaned. "Man, those guys are thick as thieves lately. What's the deal?"

"Tony has had to talk to Luke several times during this case with Lily. I guess they're kind of friends now." Lorea shrugged. "At least it means it won't be awkward to go do something together as couples, right?"

I wasn't paying attention to what she was saying because I was still analyzing her earlier statement. "What did he say that made Tony think Luke was in love with me?"

"Not sure if it was an exact statement," she admitted. "Maybe more of the vibe that he got from Luke."

"I'll remember to keep Tony on my good side," I said. "Now, I need to get ready for my appointment with Jessie. She'll be here any minute."

"Sounds good. Let me know if you need any help."

The folders and wedding planning book were already prepped for Jessie's meeting, but I double-checked just in case I'd forgotten something. It was hard to concentrate with Lorea's words buzzing in my brain. Did Luke really love me? He'd definitely been on his best behavior lately. He'd only made teasing remarks about marriage, and I had noticed how he made an effort to call or see me every day.

I gazed out the window of my shop to the beautiful tree-lined streets. The sun shimmered on the green leaves and reflected off the cars parked on the side of the road. A couple walked by holding hands, smiling at each other, and I found my own lips turning up in a smile. The world seemed to shift as I recognized the change that others had noticed in Luke. Maybe he really was falling in love with me.

The bigger question was, Did I love him?

The door chimed before I could ponder that thought any more. Jessie walked in, half-dragging Gavin, who was crying about a donut.

I stood and hurried to help her. "Hi, Gavin. How are you today?" I crouched in front of him, but he turned in toward his mother's leg.

"Sorry." Jessie sighed. "He had a rough morning and didn't eat his breakfast. I tried offering him other stuff and he refused, but of course, now he's hungry."

"I have a granola bar I can give him, and I don't mind if he eats at the design table with us." It was bending my normal policy a bit.

Jessie's features softened. "Thank you. That would be perfect."

I noticed that Gavin had stopped crying and was now looking at me intently. "Can you be a good boy and I'll get you that granola bar?"

He nodded and followed Jessie to sit down. I rummaged through my purse and found a chocolate-chip peanut-butter granola bar. When I handed it to Gavin, he smiled and held it out to his mom; she unwrapped it halfway and handed it back to him. The interchange looked familiar between mother and son. Jessie had done a good job in raising Gavin on her own. It made that little biological clock of mine tick harder when I thought about the possibilities of having my own family someday. A little dark-haired girl with Luke's blue eyes flitted across my vision.

I blinked. All Lorea's talk about love had my daydreams running wild. I tucked my hair behind my ear and focused on Jessie. "What do you want to discuss first?"

"Drago quit his job," Jessie announced. "He decided to follow Luke's advice and distance himself from everything to do with Lost Trails Construction. He'll be working out of town for the next few months."

"I'm sorry about how it all turned out," I said.

"We're trying to keep moving forward and hope for the best."

"Are they still talking about pressing charges?"

Jessie adjusted Gavin's wrapper one more time. "They

haven't said any more; maybe they're too busy worrying about their own court cases. Did you hear that Rose might be taking her stepdad to court?"

"What?" I leaned back. "On what charges?"

"Something about misappropriation of funds?" Her statement was more like a question.

"Like Phil was embezzling from his own company, or what?"

Jessie shrugged. "I don't really understand how that works, but Drago heard that something weird was going on from one of the other workers there. One of his friends said he'd try to find out anything he could to help Drago."

"That is interesting." I tucked the thought away as something else to add to my list of questions.

"No, Gavin. Please don't touch anything. Here's your Kindle." Jessie tapped the screen, and a game with bright colors and circus music played. She turned back to me. "Sorry, he's a little out of sorts today."

"I understand. I have a niece close to his age." I thought of Bryn, my darling little four-year-old niece who lived in Rupert. She'd been so cute over the fourth of July, lugging her baby brother around. Ethan was already seven months old. My arms longed to hold him close again and smell that sweet baby smell. For some reason, Luke popped into my mind again and everything blurred. I shook my head. "I apologize, what was that?"

Jessie lifted an eyebrow. "Who has your head in the clouds?"

I smiled. "Hey, I'm supposed to be asking the questions here." I neatly sidestepped her question and flipped to a page in the binder where we had planned out several of the wedding activities. "My mom and dad said they would make the cornhole boards and paint them to match your colors." I made a note to send my mom the paint chips for the creamy yellow and dark gray colors Jessie had selected.

"That'll be great. What about the fish pond? Do you think that'll still work?" Jessie tapped the edge of the paper, where I'd put a question mark next to that item. Running a fishing booth, just like those at a carnival, meant we'd need at least three people manning the booth at all times. Maybe I could get some of Lorea's nieces and nephews to help out.

"You may get quite a lineup, but I think if we set up each activity so they're streamlined, the kids should be able to rotate through easily." I crossed out the question mark. The activities were important to Jessie; she wanted this wedding to be about Gavin too, something to make the day stand out in his mind as a special time. Jessie was a kind and unselfish person, and I planned to do my best to make her wedding celebration memorable.

"I'm going to order the prizes online," Jessie said. "I found some whistles, and plastic dinosaurs that I'm sure any kid would love."

"It might be fun to order a few dozen personalized keychains, and we can invite some of the older guests to go fishing too."

"I love that idea!" Jessie beamed. Then her face fell. "I probably better hold off on that until I know what's happening with Drago's income." Her eyes filled with tears and she put her head down on the desk.

"That's no problem. Something like that wouldn't need

to be ordered until about three weeks before the big day," I said. "You have plenty of time to decide and think over lots of ideas."

Jessie lifted her head; tears ran down her cheeks and dripped from her chin. "Sometimes I wonder if Drago and I should just wait. Everything seems to be going wrong."

Uh-oh, this conversation definitely was taking a turn for the worse. I couldn't blame her with Drago's situation, but I also didn't want her to back out, for more reasons than just my own paycheck. Jessie was in love with Drago, and with Gavin, they would make a beautiful family. They all needed each other, and I wanted them to have that piece of happiness to hope for in the midst of all the problems that kept multiplying around them. "I've heard that a time or two in my line of work, so you're not alone. Almost every bride has second thoughts. Money doubts we can handle, but do you still want to marry Drago?"

"Yes, of course." Jessie sniffed. "I love him. Gavin loves him. We need him."

"Well, then, I'm sure we can make this work." I patted her hand.

My heart went out to her. I'd been in plenty of tight financial corners. Getting my business off the ground was like walking a tightrope above a pool of great white sharks. There were several times that I nearly called the whole thing off, but my never-quit attitude pulled me through. I'd worked two jobs and liquidated all my savings to start my business so that I could help brides like Jessie plan their dream weddings—that special, once-in-a-lifetime day that every girl imagines.

I tucked my smile back in place and flipped through a

few pages in the binder to find Jessie's finance sheet. "I know it's hard not to worry about money, but please, don't worry." I pulled my finger slowly down the expense sheet, noting the conservative amounts we'd listed for each of the venues. Jessie hadn't wanted anything over the top, but she did want a nice wedding. There wasn't a lot of wiggle room, because we'd cut out anything extravagant at the second planning meeting. There was still something I could do, though. "I'd like to give you a fifteen percent discount."

Jessie's eyes widened, and she shook her head. "No, Adri. I couldn't let you do that. I know you're not overcharging me."

"Thank you, that means a lot to me, but I'm already writing it down and I like my wedding planners to stay neat and tidy." I noted the discount and flipped the binder around to face her. "See? There isn't any more room on the line, so it'll have to stay."

Jessie smiled, and her chin wobbled. She stood and hugged me so hard I nearly fell out of my chair. "Thank you. Really, thank you! You're the best!"

"You're welcome." My chest warmed with goodness. The light in Jessie's eyes was genuine. Maybe she wouldn't end up needing the discount in the long run, but the important thing she needed now was to know that someone was on her side. "Just keep it on the down low, okay?" I put a finger to my lips.

Jessie mimed sealing her lips, and then mouthed, "Thank you."

Chapter 23

CROCKPOT BARBEQUE PULLED PORK SANDWICHES

2 lbs Pork Roast with 1 ½ cups water. Cook on low overnight or until meat shreds easily. Then add barbeque mixture and cook on low for 4 hours.

1 chopped onion, 2 diced green peppers, ½ tsp salt, ½ tsp pepper, ¼ tsp. paprika, 1 cup ketchup, 1 Tbsp ground dry mustard, 2 Tbsp vinegar, 4 Tbsp brown sugar, ½ cup water. Heat mixture through and serve with warm Kaiser Rolls or homemade buns. Delicious paired with Janeen's Perfect Potato Salad and a fried pickle.

Courtesy of www.mashedpotatoesandcrafts.com

Lorea and I spent the rest of the afternoon packing up

my Mountaineer with everything we needed for the booth. We'd opted to rent a tent so we wouldn't have to worry about setting up our own. I'd also ordered a banner and some foam core posters to be printed up highlighting some of my wedding package options. My mom had made her own signage for Mashed Potatoes and Crafts, and the pictures she'd sent me were darling. The art festival just might turn out okay.

Luke called just before I was ready to close up my shop. "Adri, why didn't you tell me that Javier was harassing you last night?" His voice was worried, but held no hint of accusation.

"Sorry. I thought Tony would fill you in, and then I got busy today prepping for the festival tomorrow. It slipped my mind, which is actually a good thing because he kind of scared me."

"That makes me so angry that he would even talk to you," Luke said. "And Tony did tell me, about five minutes ago when he caught up to me. I've been gone all day, trying to do some exploratory work on my next case. Are you sure you're okay?"

"Yes, I've been under a lot of stress and he took me off guard."

"Did he say or do something inappropriate?" Luke asked.

"I think he was mostly looking for you and he thought I knew where you were. Maybe he wanted to scare me into telling him. Have you talked to him?"

"Three times today. He wants to try to appeal his case. I chewed him up and down for coming to my house and bothering you. He said to tell you that he's really sorry."

"Well, he's kind of a strange guy."

"Yes. I'm really sorry about everything."

"Don't worry about it. I'm trying to forget about it too."

"Was tonight the night you invited me over to your place for dinner?" he asked.

"Yes, will that still work?" I'd put dinner in the crockpot before I left. "Barbequed pulled pork and a salad sound pretty good about now."

"Man, I'm so hungry, I could eat this file folder. I had a granola bar for lunch."

That reminded me of Gavin and my daydreams, and a blue-eyed girl. I put a hand to my heart to stop it from leaping out of my chest. What was happening to me?

"Adri? You still there?"

"Oh. Yes. Sorry, I'm distracted today getting everything ready." I flipped the window sign to "Closed" and turned off a few lights.

"How do you do it all? You are pretty incredible, you know. And I can't wait to see you." I could hear admiration in Luke's voice, and something else too. A good thing—maybe love.

I probably smiled and waved at everyone on my way home, because Luke's words had left me floating on a cloud somewhere next to Cupid. My mouth watered when I walked into my kitchen, the scent of barbequed pork heavy in the air. We probably could have gone to Smokehouse BBQ, but we had originally intended to celebrate a win on Luke's part. I didn't want to bring up anything that would make him feel worse about the loss. Besides, my grandma's barbeque recipe could likely rival Clay's, especially when it was paired with the bakery kaiser rolls I'd picked up on my way home.

I had just finished setting the table when Luke knocked on my door at 5:56. He was early, and I didn't know why that made me happy, besides the fact that I was excited to see him. I opened the door, and smiled when Luke handed me a bouquet of zinnias. "For the lovely hostess. But I have to say your house smells better than these flowers."

I took the flowers and held them to my nose. "They're beautiful. I love zinnias. Did you know that?"

"Lucky guess." Luke winked.

As we walked into the kitchen, Luke moaned when he caught the full aroma of the barbeque slow-cooking to perfection.

"You really should eat more often. Three meals a day is recommended."

Luke picked up a plate from the table. "You are definitely right. What do I need to do to get some of that—" He pointed at the meat, and then to his plate. "—here?"

"If I wasn't so hungry, I'd say you needed to work on your manners, Mr. Luke."

Luke's cheeks turned pink, but he laughed and stepped aside. "Ladies first."

Soon we were sitting at the table, enjoying the mouthwatering meal. Luke told me a little bit about the case he was working on involving a successful farmer's estate, and I filled him in on the happenings with weddings and the festival tomorrow.

"Can I come over and help you set up in the morning?" Luke asked after I listed off the dozens of items my parents were bringing to add to the booth.

"No, I can't ask you to do that. You sleep in. Lorea and I can handle it, and my parents will help us finish up." I didn't say that if my mom and dad saw him there helping me, they would start planning a wedding. My mom loved Luke; she'd been rooting for him ever since I said I didn't want to date a divorce attorney. My mom liked to root for the underdog. "But you can definitely come by during the festival. That'd be fun."

"Are you sure?" Luke asked around a bite of barbequed pork.

"Yes. If it's not too busy, I might be able to sneak away for some lunch with you while someone else mans the booth."

Luke nodded. "Okay. I'll come by around noon and see if you're free."

"I'll watch for you."

"The only thing that would make this meal better is some fried pickles," Luke said after he'd dished up his second sandwich.

Knowing what he was referring to with the fried pickles, I reached out and touched his arm. "I'm really sorry about the Benavidez case."

He shook his head. "Thanks. It's only the third case I've lost since moving here."

"Oh dear. That hurts."

"Not so much as it hurts to think about that little girl. Jasmine deserves to have her father, even if he isn't perfect. I shouldn't share my opinion like this, but I think Rose is an unfit parent."

"Then why did she win?"

"I'm still not sure what happened in there. It almost smelled like blackmail to me."

"Blackmail? But who could hold anything over Javier?" My mind spun through the possibilities. Sure, Javier had a fiery temper, but from what Luke said, he was an all-around good guy and hard worker, and he appeared to keep his nose clean.

Luke put his head in his hand and slowly massaged his temples. "From what I've heard, Phil could absolutely be involved in this."

"But Rose hates him."

"What makes you say that?"

Uh-oh. Here was my moment of truth. I hadn't told Luke about my visit to Lost Trails Construction and I could probably keep it that way, but now it seemed wrong. I chewed on my bottom lip, trying to decide how to explain what I'd done. Tux wound around my legs and gave a plaintive mew, as if to tell me to keep quiet.

I patted Tux and glanced at Luke, then I rolled my shoulders back. I hadn't done anything wrong; I went to Lost Trails to talk about a possible remodel of my office space. I took in a quick breath through my nose and blurted out, "I went to Lost Trails Construction and happened to meet with Rose the other day."

Luke's eyes bulged and he leaned back. "You talked to the opposing side of my case?"

"I didn't plan on it. I didn't even know she would be there."

"Why would you do something like that?

"I told you, I didn't even know I was going to see Rose," I insisted, my voice raising a few decibels.

"Well, what were you planning to do there if you didn't want to see their head designer?" Luke snapped.

"I was just curious about how they ran the business, and–"

"Are you trying to get yourself killed?"

"What? How is talking to someone going to get me killed?"

"You're asking questions at a prime suspect's place of business. Phil Andrus is a suspect, whether the public knows it or not. From what I've heard, he's capable of many things that you and I can't even fathom." His voice was firm, but held a note of desperation.

That reminded me of what Phil had said at Trixie's wedding. *"People are capable of many things that we could never imagine."* I swallowed as I looked at the conversation with Phil from a different angle. At the time I thought he was referring to Tim, but maybe he had been referring to himself. I shuddered.

Luke was fuming. He leaned back in his chair, and I could almost hear him mentally counting to ten. "I didn't see Phil," I assured him. "I talked to Rose. I wasn't even planning on asking questions about Lily, but then the secretary took me right to Rose."

"But Phil probably knew that you were there. He's a smart guy. He'll make the connection if word gets out that you're talking to Tim, scoping out Phil's business, talking to his employees. Or did you forget Drago?"

The way he lined things up made it look like I was doing a full-blown investigation. "It's not like that. I just asked a few questions."

"Adri, why can't you stop this insane desire to be a detective?" Luke threw his hands up in the air.

"I'm not insane!" I yelled. "Tim really is innocent."

Luke shook his head. "I don't get it. Do you think it will help Lily if you end up getting hurt?"

"I'm not hurt." I held out my hands. "How is asking a few questions going to get me hurt? I'm not being stupid. I stay in touch with Tony if I have questions, and I'm not breaking any laws. If anything, I think Tony might actually admit that I've helped him a little bit with this case." I stood up and took my plate to the sink. "It's not my fault that I keep running into people that have information about Lily."

Luke knew I was referring to Gladys and how the police had taken that tidbit seriously. "That's different. Gladys came to you. But you went to Lost Trails by yourself."

"Nothing happened," I said. "Why is it such a big deal for me to ask a few questions?"

Luke clenched his fists and pressed his lips into a thin line. The tendons in his neck popped out. I took a step back, unsure if I'd ever seen him this angry before.

My voice trembled. "I think we both need some time to cool off."

"No, don't go." Luke reached for me, but I brushed off his hand. I grabbed my car keys from the side table and hurried out my front door. He didn't follow me, even though I'd left him standing in my own kitchen.

Tears stung my eyes, but I held them back until I reached my car. Everyone wanted me to keep my nose out of Lily's murder, but I couldn't. I didn't even consider myself an amateur detective, but for some reason I had collided with this investigation and uncovered information, and I couldn't ignore what was happening. Someone had killed Lily, but it wasn't Tim.

I sped away from my house, unsure of where I was headed. I took a tissue and dabbed under my eyes, blinking several times to keep new tears from falling. Luke wanted me to be safe because he cared about me, I knew that—or at least the logical side of me knew that. But I hated being bossed around or treated like I didn't know the value of life. I wished I had kept my mouth shut. Luke wasn't in the state of mind to consider what I had to say today; losing the case was a huge blow to him. I groaned. Why did I have to be so honest? If I would have just kept that visit to myself, I would probably be inside chatting with Luke, trying to help him feel better.

I traced my fingers over the curve of my lips, thinking of the way Luke had tried to kiss me before we got jumped by Mike the dog. The way Luke had looked at me so tenderly, I had felt cherished, even loved. But maybe I had read too much into things. We'd had plenty of spats since the first time I'd met him, but today felt different. There was much more at stake, and I was afraid that I'd just ruined everything.

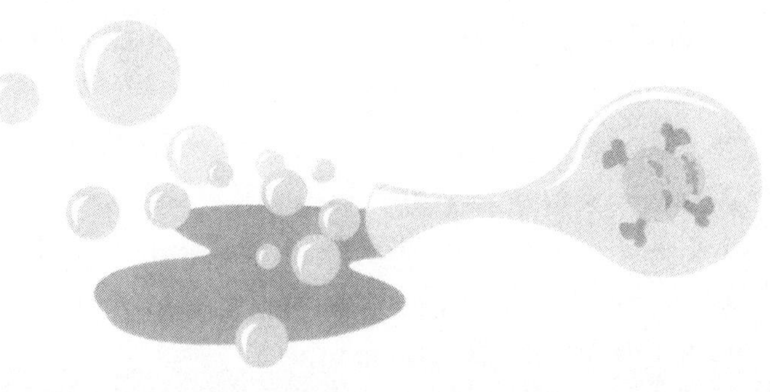

Chapter 24

LEMON LIME REFRESHER

2 lemons

2 limes

¼ cup stevia or sweetener of your choice

2 quarts ice cold water

Slice the lemons and limes in thin rounds. Add them to the pitcher of water with stevia. Stir vigorously to release lemon/lime juice. Serve with a half slice of lemon/lime to garnish.

Courtesy of www.mashedpotatoesandcrafts.com

The parks that I usually frequented were filled with lots of happy people enjoying the summer weather, so I drove over to the cemetery and put my car in park. With the air conditioner on max, I sat there feeling like a dork. I had just run out of my own house, away from Luke, when I knew that he was only being overprotective because he cared. I did know that, didn't I?

"So what are you going to do about it?" I asked myself. I closed my eyes and carefully analyzed Luke. Not just the outward part of Luke that was definitely worthy of "hottie" status, but the inward part. I knew him because he'd let me in far enough to see his vulnerable side.

After a few minutes, I felt like an even bigger dork, sitting in my car while I burned up gas to keep the air conditioner going. I pulled back onto the street and drove the few miles to my house. My stomach sank when I noticed that Luke's Harley was gone. I hated that we had ended the evening on a fight. It was supposed to be relaxing and stress free, and I'd ruined it. Well, Luke had helped ruin it too, but still.

I parked my car and trudged up the front steps. It was seven thirty, so there was still plenty of time to get some work done, even if I wanted to take a break.

I'd just hung my keys on the peg when a knock sounded on the door. I peeked out to see it was Luke. A little thrill shot through my heart at seeing him, even though part of me was still mad. "Hey, did you forget something?" I swung the door open.

He stepped in and pulled me into an embrace. "Yes, this." He covered my mouth with his, kissing me with an intensity that had sparkles of heat bursting from my fingertips. I grabbed onto his arms to steady myself. He caressed my lips and pulled me closer, shutting the door behind him.

Every question I'd had about Luke evaporated as I kissed him back. All the hurt and angry feelings drained away. Luke's arms around me tightened, and I wrapped my arms around his neck. My fingers threaded through his hair, and Luke deepened the kiss with a soft moan. The heat sparking inside me could've rivaled the sun. Kissing Luke wasn't like anything I'd experienced before. I could feel from the gentle way he held me that he cared for me.

My senses were heightened to his every movement as he pulled me closer, his mouth caressing mine. He broke contact for a second, and then kissed me once more.

"I'm sorry. I let my stress get the best of me," he murmured.

"It's okay. I know where you were coming from."

"I care about you so much, Adri."

"You too." I traced his jawline and had an irresistible desire to kiss him again. "I'm sorry that I can't keep my nose out of trouble."

"I talked to Tony. He assured me that you haven't been looking for trouble," Luke said. "Should I believe him?"

"Maybe," I ventured.

Luke chuckled. "Okay, I trust you. I know you're not trying to get into trouble. Just please, will you be even more careful, for me?"

His plea turned my insides to mush. All the fight left me. I just wanted to be with him. "But what about you, your case, and everything?" I asked. "Will you be okay?"

"See, that's what I mean?"

"What?" Had I said something wrong?

"You." Luke took my hand and caressed it. "It's so nice

to be with someone who notices me." Luke swallowed. "I feel like you really see me."

My throat was thick with emotion. I did see Luke. I'd seen him from the very beginning, even when he tried so hard to hide himself from me and the rest of the world. But the best part was that he saw me too. "I feel the same way." I took his other hand and clasped it tightly. "You took the time to really get to know me."

My brother had teased me that only a divorce attorney would be brave enough to date a wedding planner because he would know an easy out, but I knew that Luke was tentative and cautious because he took marriage seriously. For all the jokes, he wanted a good marriage. He'd had one until his wife died—something that most people in the Sun Valley area still didn't know.

"Does this mean you really are my boyfriend?" I asked, knowing he would understand the reference to the crazy bride from my shop.

Luke chuckled. He pulled me in for another kiss. My senses were jumbled, and all I could feel was the heat of his fingertips on my back, the softness of his lips against mine, the coarse curls at the nape of his neck.

Luke pulled back. "Does that answer your question?'

"Almost," I teased.

He led me to the sofa in my front room, and we sat down next to each other. "Yes, Adri, you're my girlfriend, if you'll have me. Sorry I took so long."

"I think the timing is perfect." After all we'd been through in the past year, we were finally at a place of healing, strength, and stability. My toes tingled as the future blurred across my vision. I wanted to be with Luke. I didn't want him to be just my boyfriend. I wanted more. My stomach flipped, and I shushed my inner thoughts and acted as if I hadn't just contemplated marrying Luke. I needed to lighten up the conversation. "But it seems amoral to date a divorce attorney."

"Hey, we could go into business together."

"How?" I scrunched my nose.

"You get them married and I'll help undo the mess," he said with a lilt to his voice.

I shook my head. "You attorneys give marriage a bad name."

"Well, it's your fault I'm in business at all."

I put a hand on my chest. "My fault?"

"Haven't you heard?" Luke leaned toward me. "Marriage is the leading cause of divorce."

I couldn't help it: the laugh escaped from my lips in a spurt, almost like I was blowing a raspberry. Luke laughed so hard he snorted, and then we were both laughing until tears ran down our faces.

When the giggles faded, Luke sighed and pulled me close to him. "You're all right, you know that?"

I touched my fist to his cheek. "So are you." I leaned my head on his chest and took a deep breath. "I like laughing with you a whole lot better than arguing."

"Yeah, we should probably try it more often."

I tipped my head to look up at him. "I'd like that."

"Me too." Luke dipped his head toward mine, and I didn't breathe, didn't move, because I couldn't believe that this was really happening. I'd been waiting for this moment—the one we'd just shared—wanting him to kiss me for way longer than I'd admit.

His lips brushed against mine and I kissed him back, putting my arms around his neck. He angled his body closer to mine, and I put one hand on his chest to steady myself. His lips on mine ignited the slow-burning embers into a spark of desire. He pulled away, kissed me again, and rested his forehead against mine. "You're sweeter than you look," he whispered.

I giggled. "I'm full of surprises once you get to know me."

"I'd like that." Luke embraced me and I reached my arms around his neck, breathing in the woodsy scent that had grown familiar to me. I wanted to curl up in his arms and have him hold me forever. I could never go back to being just friends with Luke Stetson. "Thanks for letting me in," he said.

"I didn't hear you drive up on the Harley."

"That's because I moved it so you would think I was gone. I was afraid you wouldn't come back if I was still here."

I put my hand on his cheek. "Thank you for not leaving."

"You're welcome, but now I think it's time for me to kidnap you for thirty minutes."

"Um?"

He tilted his head toward the window. "Remember a while back when you promised to go for a ride with me on the Harley?"

"Was that a promise?" I teased.

Luke pulled me close and brushed another kiss across my lips. "Please?"

"Okay, okay, but then I have to get back and pack up the

food and drinks for tomorrow. Everyone at the booth will need some sustenance, you know. It'll be a long day."

"So you'll come?" He looked like a kid who'd just been given a new bicycle.

I stood up and tugged on his hand. "I'm ready when you are."

Luke revved the engine of his Road Glide and I tightened my purple glitter helmet. He drove through the streets of Sun Valley and then headed up past the Sun Valley lodge toward Lost Trail Pass. I put my arms around his waist, enjoying the freedom to be close to Luke. He was my boyfriend, and he kissed like nobody's business.

I leaned my head against his back and enjoyed the view of the Sawtooth Mountains rising in the distance. Baldy, the popular ski mountain for Sun Valley resort, was lush and green this time of year, but if we didn't get rain soon, August would find the mountainsides losing their vibrant color.

The sun was dipping down closer to the horizon, but we still had plenty of sunlight left on that July night. The heat had decreased significantly, and the higher we drove up the mountains, the cooler the air became. I was just starting to feel a chill to the wind whipping across my arms when Luke turned around and began coasting back to the valley.

The ride took closer to an hour, but I didn't complain when Luke dropped me off at my house at nine o'clock.

"Come in and have some lemon-lime refresher before you go." I took his hand and we walked up to my doorstep.

"That sounds delicious," he said. "Thanks for going with me. It was a perfect night tonight."

I poured up the drink I'd put in the fridge to chill before

we left, and dropped in a few pieces of ice. "Couldn't have planned it better."

Luke downed half his glass. "This is delicious. I like the lime flavor."

"It's one of my favorite summer drinks."

He watched me sip my drink, a contented expression on his face. The sour sweetness made my tongue tingle, and I licked some of the sweet drink from my lips. He set his glass down and took mine from me, setting it carefully on the counter. "Can I see you again tomorrow after the festival?"

My stomach fluttered at the thought of spending more time with Luke. I put my arms around his neck. "You're coming for lunch and you want to see me after?" I kissed his cheek. "Yes please."

Luke touched his forehead to mine and we stared at each other for a charged moment. The electricity zinged back and forth between us. His mouth hovered next to mine, our breath mingling, before slowly caressing my lips with his. Heat surged through me, and I let him pull me closer. The distance between us that had been looming for so long fell away, and I dared to hope that something was happening to him, to us. The way my heart was thrumming couldn't be ignored.

The kitchen heated up and my air conditioning kicked on. Luke released me with a smile. "It's a good thing I got a new case, or else I might stay here and kiss you all night."

"And I have loads to do for the art festival tomorrow." I leaned forward and whispered in his ear, "I'll see you tomorrow."

With one last kiss, Luke sighed and then hurried out the front door. I locked it behind him and moved to the front room, standing with my fingers on the window ledge, peeking out between the curtains. Luke turned and waved with two fingers before climbing on his motorcycle. My cheeks lifted in a smile and I waved back, even though I knew he couldn't see me standing there in the dark.

I could still feel his kiss lingering on my lips as I heard his Harley roar out of the parking lot. My life had just switched tracks. I wasn't riding the train of doubt, insecurity, and broken dreams anymore. I couldn't wait to see Luke tomorrow and kiss him again.

Chapter 25

CROCHETED SCALLOPED HEADBAND

Materials: *Medium weight yarn in desired color, Size G/6 (4 mm) crochet hook*

Begin by Chain 57.

*Row 1: 4 dc in 3rd ch from hook, sk 2 sts, *sc in next st, sk 2 sts, 5 dc in next st, sk 2 sts * 8 times, sc in next st, sk 2 sts, 10 dc in last st.*

Note: The following row is worked on the opposite side of the foundation ch.

*Row 2: Sk 2 sts, * sc in next st, sk 2 sts, 5 dc in next st, sk 2 sts * 8 times, sc in next sc, sk 2 sts, 5 dc in next st. Sl st to top of first dc. Fasten off.*

Add Ties: *Ch 21.*

Row 1: Sl st in 2nd ch from hook and each st across (20 sl sts). Use yarn needle to attach a tie to each end of the headband and weave in ends.

Courtesy of www.mashedpotatoesandcrafts.com

PROPOSALS AND POISON

I had a little trouble sleeping the first part of the night because I kept reliving the moment when Luke walked through my door, swept me into his arms, and kissed me. When I finally did fall asleep, it was deep and dreamless and I awoke with Luke's name on my lips. A craving for him burned in my chest, and I couldn't resist sending him several good morning texts when I woke at six o'clock that Friday morning.

It took two coolers to hold all the snacks and food I'd prepared for the festival; one cooler was full of water bottles, lemon-lime refresher, and soda to keep us hydrated during the heat of the day. I wasn't looking forward to that part of the festival. Temperatures were supposed to be in the low nineties, so I had pulled my hair back into a messy bun and applied sunscreen.

The festival meadows were beautiful that early morning. The grass was still dewy and cold on my sandaled toes. I dragged one of the coolers and a large, overstuffed bag filled with tablecloths over to the booth.

"Good morning," Lorea said. "Your hair looks cute."

"Thanks. You look the part of a dress designer today." I indicated the scissors and measuring tape hanging from her neck, and the pencil tucked behind her ear, poking out of the dark strands of hair.

"I'm prepared, and even excited for today," she said.

"Me too. Surprising after how much I've been dreading it," I admitted. "Maybe it's the atmosphere."

Lorea and I paused to look around at the meadows. The backdrop of the rugged mountains covered in pine was breathtaking. There were tents and tables going up everywhere we turned. A murmur of conversations drifting along the air held a note of apprehension as people worked to get their booths set up before the first patrons arrived at ten. There were always a few early birds, or so I'd been told.

"Hopefully we can trade off, because I'd like to take a look around today," I said.

"I'm planning on it," Lorea replied. "Tony said he'd try to come by this afternoon and we could go get a funnel cake."

"Luke's going to stop by around lunchtime." I didn't try to hide the grin that perked up my cheeks when I said his name.

"Now that's a smile. What's going on with you two?"

"Last night I found out that Luke is pretty much the best kisser in the world."

Lorea squealed. "Finally! He kissed you?"

I saw a woman look up from the load of multicolored skirts she was carrying and smile. "Hush, you don't have to tell the whole world." I lowered my voice. "Luke is officially my boyfriend."

"What? Does he know that?" Lorea straightened the tablecloths and adjusted her portfolio and business cards.

"Yes, he knows, and he wants to be with me," I said. "It kind of feels like a dream. He's been so good to me lately."

Lorea gave me a knowing look. "I think he was worth waiting for. Tony, too."

We finished unloading our boxes and I made a few more trips to the car. When I returned to the booth with the last boxes, my parents were there, and my mom was in a frenzy.

"So sorry we're late!" she said. "I hope we can get it all set up in time. There was just so much to do."

"Good morning, Mom and Dad." I gave each of my parents a hug.

"How's my girl?" my dad asked. "You ready for this?"

"Yes, Lorea and I were just saying that we're kind of excited for today."

"Kind of?" my mom asked. "I couldn't sleep last night 'cause I kept double-checking if I had everything ready."

I surveyed the pile of boxes that my dad was opening. There were about ten of them, and they all looked overstuffed. "I think you remembered everything."

My dad smirked. "She brought enough stuff for the entire county."

"Oh, you." Mom nudged Dad with her elbow. "Let's hang these scarves up here. I know it's hotter than Hades this time of year, but I always do a little Christmas shopping when I come."

"Great thinking," Lorea said. "I love these little crocheted headbands. Did you make all of these?"

"Yes, finished the last batch two nights ago." Mom beamed. "Do you think they'll sell?"

"I want one, so definitely." Lorea selected a pink headband and slipped it over her hair.

"That suits you perfectly," Mom said.

All four of us worked until just before nine, hanging, arranging, and unboxing items. When the booth was ready, we stepped back and I snapped a few pictures.

"We have over four hundred items in that little tent," my dad said. "Hope some people show up."

"Dad, don't make Mom more nervous." I stepped over and gave my mom's arm a squeeze. "I can see people lining up already." I pointed across the meadow to the entrance, where a cluster of people gathered behind a roped-off section.

"Oh, do we have everything ready?" Mom asked.

"Yes." I smiled. "Do you two want to take a minute to walk around?"

Thankfully, my parents agreed so that my mom could walk off some of her nervous energy. I couldn't wait for my turn to check out the booths. I loved walking along looking at all the beautiful paintings in oil, acrylic, and watercolor that were produced by dozens of different artists. My dad was fascinated by the different styles of photographers who came to the festival, and he usually purchased a couple pieces. And of course, my mom could never get enough of all the handmade, hand-sewn items offered by so many talented Blaine County residents.

I had just ducked under the table to straighten the remaining boxes when I heard a familiar voice. "Is Adri here today?"

"Yes, she's right here," Lorea answered.

I swallowed my inner groan and raised my head above the purple tablecloth to see Gladys standing with one hand on her hip. Today she wore a blue blouse that accented her eyes, and denim capris. The look suited her, even if women half her age were wearing the same thing.

"Thank goodness you're here." Gladys leaned over the table. "I didn't know that you two were setting up a booth. What a great idea. Everyone's getting married these days. At least, it seems like all of Hank and my friends are—it's not a first marriage for any of us, mind you, but that's what happens when you get old. Nobody likes to be a widower."

She stopped for a breath, and I found my opening. "It's good to see you Gladys. Do you have your bath salts for sale today?"

She nodded and pointed to the booth straight across from ours. "I have dozens of different scents and colors in these cute little jars. You'll have to come and see. I can even mix up your favorite flavor today. I have all the ingredients and different cards that show the combinations. I thought it might be a new angle for the festivalgoers."

"That's a great idea," Lorea said, and I could tell her compliment was sincere. There was a lot more to Gladys than either of us had noticed at first. Behind the chatty gossip was a shrewd and talented businesswoman.

"Do you happen to have bergamot?" I asked.

"I sure do," Gladys replied. "I have over thirty different essential oils, and about that many perfumes."

"That sounds wonderful. I'll come by around noon."

Gladys paused and puffed up her frizzy hair. "Will you look at me? I came over here to tell you something important and nearly forgot."

"Oh, what's that?"

"I didn't want to be the bearer of bad news." Gladys huffed. "But I've been worried sick ever since I talked to that grouchy woman."

"I think you're getting ahead of yourself," I said. "What's the matter?"

"The matter is that a young lady by the name of Vickie doesn't like you in the least, and I'm worried she might try to sabotage your booth."

"Vickie with short blonde hair and a big frown who works at the animal clinic?"

"That's the one." Gladys nodded. "I was simply making small talk, telling her all about how you helped me with my weddin', and she turned sour."

I held in the cringe at getting credit for Gladys's wedding, though I guessed there were worse things. "I know Vickie doesn't like me. I've talked with her a few times. She works for Tim Esplin."

Gladys gasped. "The veterinary murderer?"

"Well, I don't think he's a murderer, but yes, he's been accused."

"Oh dear. He looks innocent, but he had the poison that killed Lily." Gladys clenched her fist. "And he had motive."

I tilted my head. "What motive?"

Gladys ducked her head and mumbled, "Hank told me to keep my mouth shut and not spread any more rumors. I'd best follow his advice." She turned to go.

"But wait." I grabbed onto Gladys before she could leave. "Why did you think I was in danger?"

Her eyes widened, and she stepped closer to me. "Some people you can just tell, and that Vickie is no good." Gladys glanced behind her and whispered, "She said that one way or another you were going to learn your lesson about snooping into other people's lives."

I shivered. I couldn't stop the cold dread winding through my body. One part of my brain reminded me that Gladys was a busybody and enjoyed stirring up a little mischief with words, but the other part of me remembered the way Vickie had looked at me and demanded that I keep away from Tim.

"I'll see you later." Gladys hurried off.

My parents returned after that and I gave Lorea a look that said to keep quiet about Gladys. It wasn't until later that I realized I didn't get a chance to ask Gladys where she had seen Vickie. The thought heightened my senses, and I suddenly felt like someone was watching me. I looked up at the throng of people walking the grassy meadows between the booths, and nearly laughed at myself. There were hundreds of people looking at me as they passed our booth.

But then I saw Phil Andrus leaning against a pickup with his poodle on a leash. He was staring right at me.

I shivered and ducked behind Lorea, pretending to straighten a few items.

"Adri, grab me some more of those card packets out of the little box," my mom said. She turned to me and whispered, "I can't believe that we've already sold seventy-five items. It isn't even lunch yet!"

I grinned. It was good to see my mom in her element. I tried to focus on the booth and working with my parents and Lorea, but talking to Gladys had brought up all of the incidents and questions I had about Lily's murder. Luke wanted me to stay far away from the investigation, and I was trying. But it seemed like everywhere I went, another murder suspect was waiting around the corner.

Chapter 26

KILLER FRY SAUCE

4 Tbsp Mayonnaise

1 Tbsp Mustard

3 Tbsp Ketchup

¼ tsp Garlic powder

¼ tsp Onion powder

½ tsp Season All or favorite BBQ Seasoning

Whip together and serve in dipping bowls. Makes about 4 servings.

Courtesy of www.mashedpotatoesandcrafts.com

My stomach grumbled while I rang up another purchase, and I glanced at my watch. It was already twelve thirty. Luke would probably arrive soon, and there were six people inside our booth at the moment. During the next five minutes, I hurried to help a young woman fill out an information card to get a bid for her upcoming wedding, while answering questions from Lorea about ordering in some kind of silk that another woman requested, and I even sold two more card sets.

I looked up and saw Luke walking toward me with a smile on his face. Swiping my brow, I straightened and moved past a customer to greet him.

"Hey, beautiful." He said, grabbing my hand and pulling me close. "Are you surviving?"

"Barely. I'm starving, and it's been so busy."

"What about all those snacks you packed?"

"Maybe if it dies down a little, we'll have a chance to eat some of them." I turned back toward the booth. "I'm going to lunch with Luke; call me if things get too crazy."

My parents called out a quick greeting to Luke, but there were three more customers lining up, so there wasn't time for chitchat. Luke laced his fingers through mine, and we ambled down the aisle of booths. The sun glared down on me now that I was out from under the shade of our tent.

"Hang on, it's way too hot out here. I need a drink." I stopped and guzzled a water bottle I'd nabbed before leaving.

"It looks like a success out here, but how are things in your booth going?" Luke asked.

"Way busier than I would have predicted, but that's a good thing."

"What are you in the mood for?"

I wanted to say "lots more kissing," but I knew he was talking about food and I was really hungry. "I could go for a cheeseburger and onion rings right about now."

We walked past the live band playing a bluegrass type of music. We paused for a moment to appreciate the banjo and fiddle players accompanied by a guy with what looked like a ten-gallon hat pounding on the piano. The music was loud enough that we could hear it all the way across the meadow.

"I want to try one of those triple-decker burgers." He pointed out a food wagon that had a line of about fifteen people in front of it. "I noticed it on the way in. It might be a few minutes' wait, but do you want to try one?"

My stomach was gnawing itself from the inside out, and my mouth watered as the aroma of the juicy burgers filled my nose. "I hope the wait isn't long, because that smells fantastic."

Luke squeezed my hand and we moved into line. We talked while we waited, and thankfully, ten minutes later, we sat down in the shade behind a booth to eat our lunch.

"So, I saw Phil Andrus today. Someone told me that Rose was thinking of suing him for misappropriation of funds. Have you heard anything about that?"

"No. I'm not sure that's right. The only way she could sue him was if she was part owner." Luke wiped his hands on a napkin. "I guess she could be."

"Hmm, maybe." I took another bite of the hamburger, with cheese dripping off the sides. "This is so good."

Luke swirled a piece of onion ring in the fry sauce. "I agree. This fry sauce is out of this world."

"It reminds me of my mom's recipe." I dipped my onion ring in the creamy fry sauce and took a bite, savoring the tang and spice mixed together.

"There's a recipe for fry sauce?"

"There's a recipe for everything." I took another bite of onion ring and closed my eyes.

"So what time do you think you'll be done tonight?" Luke asked. "Can we still get together?"

I smiled. "Do you want to go out for ice cream with my parents? My dad is treating all of us. He said after melting all day in the sun and being suffocated by crafts and wedding junk, he deserves it."

Luke laughed. "Your dad sounds like my type of guy."

"Yeah, my mom and dad both want a chance to get to know you." Luke had met my parents and talked with them over a year ago, but it was under different circumstances. It'd be nice for him to have a conversation with them outside of the hospital where I was getting stitched up. I pushed that memory out of my mind and focused on the present.

"Do you want to text me when you're about ready and I can meet you wherever?"

"Sure. I think it'll be about seven. We'll clean up some things, but most of the display will stay overnight."

"I probably better let you get back to work," Luke said.

I glanced down at my empty wrappers. I'd devoured my hamburger, but I was still thirsty. "I want to refill my pink lemonade. How about you?"

"Sure, that'd be good. I'll take care of all the trash while you do that." Luke stood and began gathering up the wrappers and napkins.

I had to wait in line for a couple minutes to refill my drink, but a sip of the ice-cold sugary lemonade tasted great in the heat. The grass was uneven in some places, so I walked carefully with the two drinks, trying not to let them slosh over the sides.

I was about fifteen feet from Luke when I saw a familiar bleached blonde heading straight for him. I gritted my teeth as Zara sidled up next to Luke, grabbing onto his arm and batting her lashes. I wasn't jealous. The way Luke jumped back was kind of funny, but it was also evidence that he didn't want anything to do with Zara. I didn't understand who she thought she was, or why she was intent on Luke when she was supposed to be engaged. As I got closer, I noticed the ring was off her finger again.

"You want to play hard to get, huh?" she cooed. "I like to play games."

"I have a girlfriend. And I'm also a lawyer, so it's not a big deal for me to file a court order against you." Luke's tone invited no argument. "You'll stay away from me and Adri from now on. Is that clear?"

"Gosh, you're no fun." Zara pouted. She turned, and when she saw me, her eyes narrowed and she stomped off.

Luke wiped his hand across his brow as I gave him his drink. "That woman is insane."

"I'm sorry. Maybe we *should* file a complaint. There's something wrong with her," I said.

"Don't worry. If I see her again, I'll definitely follow through on my threat." Luke took a sip of his drink, wiped his hands on a napkin, and stared at something in the distance.

"What is it?" I moved to look in the same direction.

"I don't know. I thought I saw Javier a minute ago," Luke said. "Just hoping that Rose is nowhere in the vicinity."

"I bet you'll be glad when Rose leaves town."

Luke swiveled his gaze to me. "What do you mean? She can't leave town. That was part of the custody arrangement."

I swallowed, knowing I was treading on dangerous ground, but I'd already confessed to talking to Rose. "When I saw her, she said she was quitting her job and leaving town. So you're saying she has to stay here?"

"Well, not exactly. But she can't move more than one hundred and fifty miles away, or custody will immediately revert to Javier. I can't imagine that she'd try to move somewhere else, but maybe if it was within range."

"Hmm." I thought about what surrounded the Sun Valley area. Some people would joke that only deserts surrounded the valley, and in one direction they would be right, but there weren't any major cities close by.

"What are you thinking about?" Luke asked.

"I'm just wondering why there are so many conflicting stories going around. Rose says she's moving. You say she's not. Someone else says she's going to sue Phil. Could Javier be causing trouble to try to force her to leave?"

Luke shrugged. "I don't think he'd stoop that low, but there are a ton of rumors circulating. Probably best not to pay attention to most of them."

I took his hand and we walked back toward our booth. We'd already been gone for forty-five minutes, and although I would've liked to stay with Luke all day and analyze the mysteries in our town, I needed to get back to work so Lorea could have a break. "Thanks for coming by. Lunch was delicious."

"I don't know if I'd put it up there with your cooking, but I'm glad I could share it with you," Luke said.

"Thanks." I leaned forward and gave him a quick peck on the lips.

He grabbed hold of me and kissed me again. "See you tonight," he whispered.

I waved and walked quickly back to my booth, resisting the urge to skip.

My parents took a lunch break, followed by Lorea, so the next time I had a free second to check my watch, it was already four o'clock. When Lorea returned, we both spent a few minutes restocking and arranging the display.

"I thought today was supposed to be a slow day," Lorea said. "It's going to be nuts tomorrow."

"I know. I've already gone through half of my stack of information cards," I said. "And a lot of these gals are really nice. If I book even half of the weddings, I'm going to have to hire another assistant because you're going to be up to your eyeballs in pins and needles."

Lorea smiled, and nudged my mom. "Maybe Laurel will have to come up and help me, because I have six new wedding gown requests.

My mouth dropped open. "You're kidding. What kind of deadline?"

"The farthest one is eight months away, but I might have a buyer for the dress I've been working on." Lorea rolled up her measuring tape and tapped the table. "It's really happening."

"I'm so happy for both of you girls," my mom said. "What an accomplishment, to be able to start your own business and be successful at it."

"Spoken from the source," my dad said. "Look at you, Laurel. You've been whining for the last week over if anybody would want to buy your stuff, and it looks like a third of it is gone already."

"Thanks, honey." Mom kissed Dad on the cheek and gave him a hug. "You're a sport to come with me. Even if you only hope I make money so you can spend it on that cowboy hat I saw you checking out."

My dad smiled. He wasn't wearing his usual straw cowboy hat in the booth because of close quarters, but it was pretty much a part of him—that, and the shiny, gem-studded belt buckles he liked to wear.

Someone cleared her throat. "Excuse me, are you Adri?"

I turned toward the young woman who had spoken. "Yes, that's me. How can I help you?"

Her pink lips turned up in a smile. "Well, I'm hoping to have a reason to talk to you."

I glanced at her left hand. No diamond sat on her finger, but she must be in a serious relationship. "A wedding might be in your future?" I asked.

She blushed, and lowered her voice. "I think so. I wanted to talk to you because I'm sure you're getting booked up. I don't want a year-long engagement."

I immediately liked her open and honest face. She was beautiful. Her chestnut-brown hair was braided and fell halfway down her back, and when she smiled her dark eyes sparkled. She looked a bit young, maybe only early twenties, but her flawless skin probably hid her true age. "Let me have you fill out an information card. I brought them with me today and I'll follow up with everyone in the next week to see if we're a match or not."

"My name's Maggie Williams." She extended her hand, and I shook it.

"It's nice to meet you, Maggie. This is my assistant, Lorea Zubiondo, and my parents, Carl and Laurel Pyper."

"Hello," my parents said in unison.

"Adri is the best wedding planner in the state," my mom said.

"Mom, don't get her hopes up," I said.

"Oh, I know," Maggie said. "I've seen her work, and I love it." She picked up a pen and a card and put a star at the top. "If there's any way to fit me into your schedule, I hope you will."

"When do you think the big day will be?" I asked.

"I'm not sure, but maybe November or December. And depending on a few things, Jackson and I would like to do a destination wedding. I'd like to talk to you about some of your packages."

I tried to keep my face from showing any emotion. A destination wedding was a huge undertaking and difficult to do with a full client list. "That might work. I look forward to talking with you more."

After Maggie filled out her card and left, I circled the star she'd made. There was something sincere and sweet about her, and I hoped we'd be able to work together.

"She's a keeper," my mom said. "Hope the boy she's dating puts a ring on her finger soon."

I smiled and filed the card with the others in my bag. I let my mind wander for a moment to some of the destination wedding locations I'd researched. Tahiti would be fabulous in December. Costa Rica might also be a great choice. If she didn't want to leave the States, a visit across the country to the southern coast could provide a warm and tranquil setting.

I was envisioning sunny beaches in December when I looked up. There stood Vickie, about fifteen yards from my booth.

Chapter 27

HOMEMADE LAUNDRY DETERGENT

Makes 300-500 Loads

1 (4lb 12 oz) box Borax

1 (3lb 7 Oz) box Super Washing Soda

1 (3lb) container OXY clean (you can adjust this amount to your preference. I use a little less.)

2 bars soap grated–one Fels Naptha, one other favorite soap

1 (2lb) boxes Baking Soda

1 bottle Downy Unstopable Scent Booster

Dump all the boxes into a large bucket to mix together. Mix outside to avoid inhaling soap powder.

Use a fine cheese grater to grate your soap. Use a large wooden spoon to stir all of the ingredients together, making sure that your soap flakes are blended well.

2 Tbsp each load for Super Capacity top-load washer

1 Tbsp each load for Super Capacity front-load high efficiency washer

Video Tutorial available at www.mashedpotatoesandcrafts.com

I blinked and squinted to be certain it was her. I wasn't sure if it was coincidental or not, but Vickie stood in front of Gladys's booth. Gladys was talking nonstop as usual, and Vickie stood still and straight. How much of what Gladys gleaned from other people was inadvertent because she got them talking, and how much was skilled extraction via gossip?

I continued to stare until my eyes watered, but Vickie didn't do anything. It didn't even look like she was speaking to Gladys. Maybe Gladys had read more into Vickie's curt and abrupt manner. From this distance she looked harmless, but I would keep my distance just in case.

Another customer came to our tent, and I helped her purchase a lovely centerpiece patterned after the one my mom had made for Natalie and Brock's wedding last year. A chunk of wood with greenery attached to it surrounded a handmade candle. The candle had different layers of colors, and the woman was excited about how it would look on her mantel.

My mom tucked a card in with the purchase. She'd printed up five hundred business cards with our website and details of her services. We made sure that everyone who stopped by received a card. I wondered if we'd run out before the festival ended on Sunday.

"You have quite an assortment at this booth," the woman said. "Very talented."

I turned to my mother, who had overheard and was

beaming. "Yes, my mom is the heart and brains behind this business." I motioned to the Mashed Potatoes and Crafts logo behind us.

"I'm going to find my friend and make sure she stops by," the woman said.

"Thank you." I smiled at her as she turned to go

"Only one more hour to go," my dad announced.

"Wow, the day has gone by fast." I surveyed our work space and the pile of wrappers, bags, tags, and other garbage under one of the tables. "I'm going to throw this trash away."

The large bins were situated behind Gladys's booth, so I waved at her on my way to dispose of the bags. In response, she called, "Adri, come over here and look what I have for you."

I stopped, holding the trash bag at my side. "What is it?"

"I mixed your bath salts with bergamot and a hint of lavender. See?" She pointed at a blue glass bottle that contained the mixture of salts. My name was printed neatly on the label.

"That looks lovely," I said. "I can't wait to try them out."

"All I need to do is give it one more good stir and check the consistency, and it'll be ready."

"Okay. Let me throw this trash away, and I'll be back in a few minutes." I left before she could continue talking my ear off. The trash bins were nearly overflowing, so I walked to the next set and dumped my bags in.

I heard someone shout right after the lid of the garbage slammed shut. When I walked around the corner of Gladys's tent, there was a commotion. I edged past someone and saw Gladys clutching at her throat and coughing, or choking, or what looked like a painful combination of both. Someone else was near her, asking if she was okay.

Pushing back my shock, I approached to see if I could help, but before I could even pat her on the back, she collapsed. Someone screamed as I knelt beside Gladys. She wasn't moving anymore, and I couldn't tell if she was breathing.

"Gladys!" I yelled and shook her arm, but she didn't move. I looked up. "Someone call for help!"

"They have already, but let me take a look at her." The artist from the next booth over felt for a pulse, and leaned closer to her. "She's still alive, so maybe not a heart attack."

"She was choking or coughing, and then just collapsed."

A couple minutes later, the paramedics arrived and immediately began mouth to mouth. Horrified, I stepped back. I hadn't even realized that she wasn't breathing. I heard one of them say something about her airway and possible blockage.

One of the paramedics was a woman, and she turned to me. "Did you notice if she was eating anything?"

"No, she said she was mixing up some bath salts for me."

The table Gladys had been standing behind when I'd last seen her was filled with her bath salts. In the center stood my bottle. The lid was off and a wooden spoon poked out, with bits of salt spilled around the table. I gasped and covered my mouth. The paramedic gave me an odd look before returning her attention to the other male paramedic, who was performing mouth to mouth.

I took another step back, and then another, until I bumped into the frame of our booth.

"Oh, Adri, there you are?" Lorea grabbed my arm. "Did you see what happened to Gladys?"

"Call Tony," I said. "Tell him we need to inspect Gladys's bath salts. I think someone may have been trying to poison me."

"I'm not sure what's in this that could have caused a problem," Tony said. "But I got word that Gladys had some sort of reaction to something and went into anaphylactic shock."

"So she ate something that she was allergic to?" I asked.

"Well, that's what it looks like."

"Or maybe, that's what it's supposed to look like. What kinds of poison mimic a severe allergic reaction?"

Tony bagged another sample. "A lot of them. But tell me again why you think someone was trying to poison you?"

By now the festival hours were officially closed for the day, but there were still plenty of people moving about, cleaning up booths and prepping for tomorrow. The police had cordoned off the area around Gladys's booth and the two booths next to her while they investigated. Hamilton had peppered me with questions when he first arrived, and now it was Tony's turn.

"Gladys told me that Vickie had said something mildly threatening about me—you know, relating to my visit to Tim."

Tony nodded. "When was that?"

"That's the thing. I don't know. Gladys was all flustered about it this morning, so maybe it happened yesterday? She doesn't seem like the type to want to wait on a piece of gossip.

She searched me out first thing today so she could tell me all about it." I chewed on my bottom lip as I surveyed the remains of Gladys's booth. "I didn't take her seriously."

"So what changed your mind?"

"I talked to Gladys just before she had her reaction. She was mixing up my bath salts. Maybe ten minutes before that, I saw Vickie standing in front of her booth. She wasn't talking or buying anything when I saw her—just standing there, watching. I thought it was strange at the time, considering Gladys had said how ornery Vickie was."

"Did Vickie handle any of the bath salts?" Tony asked.

"I wasn't close enough to see. And it was only for a minute; then I got sidetracked with another customer. Sorry, I know that isn't much to go on."

Hamilton walked up next to Tony. "I haven't been able to locate the woman Adri's talking about. Tim Esplin said the clinic's closed today. An officer went by her house, and Vickie isn't home."

Tony glanced at me, and then back at Hamilton. "Have we figured out if Gladys is allergic to anything?"

Hamilton shook his head. "Her husband didn't know of anything."

"Let's get these samples sent off to the lab." Tony handed off a few of the bags to Hamilton. "Adri, don't go off snooping, okay?"

"Okay, but I wasn't snooping. Give me some credit," I protested. "And you'd better not tell Luke that I was involved in this, because I wasn't. I didn't even order the bath salts. Gladys was mixing them up when I got here."

"That's true. Any other orders?" Tony gave me a mock salute.

I rolled my eyes. "You're still invited for ice cream later if you think you can make it. Wes and Jenna are coming into town tonight with their kids."

"Depends on what happens with Gladys's condition, but probably not," Tony said. He frowned and lifted the sample bags in his hands. "It'll take a while to get this entered in, and then I'll have more paperwork to fill out, but tell Wes I'll try to catch up with him tomorrow if I don't make it tonight."

"Sounds good." I ducked under the police tape and headed back to the booth, where my parents and Lorea were packing up some of the items. We finished up, and my dad pulled the flaps of the tent down and tied it securely.

"Everything should be safe until tomorrow morning," Mom said. "The police will be here all night, I'm sure."

"Yes, poor Gladys," Lorea said.

"All kinds of crazy things are happening in this town," my dad mused. "We heard about the murder of that young lady. Lorea told us she was your neighbor."

"And your client," Mom added. "Why didn't you tell us?"

"I didn't want you to worry. I hoped they would have figured things out by now, but nothing is happening."

"Odd that they arrested her fiancé and then let him out on bail," Dad said.

"Yes, it was terrible. I feel so bad for him."

"Well, let's get this load of stuff down to the car," Mom said. "Wes texted me a half hour ago to say they were ten minutes away. Those kids will be going through the roof waiting on their ice cream."

"I'll be coming right after you," I said. "Let me help you

with your stuff, Lorea." I picked up a box and followed Lorea to her car.

After we loaded it up, Lorea looked as if she wanted to say something, but then she swallowed and opened her car door.

"Wait, what's the matter?" I asked.

Lorea pursed her lips and swallowed again.

"Are you upset about something with the festival?" I asked.

"No, no, it's not that at all," she replied. "This was definitely a smart move for our business."

"Well, what is it, then?" I prodded.

"I think I discovered something important, but I wasn't supposed to figure it out."

"Okay, that's cryptic and unhelpful. Do you want to play a game of *Clue* later on?"

She swatted at me. "I'm trying to keep my promise to Tony not to get you any more involved than you already are."

"That's not fair," I said. "I didn't have anything to do with Gladys. I think it might have been an accident . . . hopefully."

"See?" Lorea wagged her finger at me. "You're already coming up with ideas, and I bet you have a plan to go ask more questions."

I shook my head, even though I did want to talk to Hank and see if he could provide a clue to what might have happened. "What is this about?"

Lorea took my non-answer as some kind of proof, because she ignored my question and pulled out her cell and pushed a button.

"Who are you calling?"

"Tony," she said. "I'm pretty sure that Phil and Vickie are related."

I sucked in a breath as every cop drama I'd ever watched came to mind. Two criminal masterminds with a joint cause of gaining Lily's life insurance money? "But wait, how are they related?"

"They're first cousins."

"But how did you find that out? And why would it be a secret?"

Lorea ended the call, obviously unable to reach Tony at the moment. She tapped out a text and slid the phone into her back pocket. "I bumped into Javier Benavidez today when I was looking at some jewelry."

I frowned. "I bet that was pleasant."

"Actually, he was really friendly. He had a necklace for his daughter, and started talking about how he was going to make a bracelet to go with it using stones he got from Phil's friend Vickie."

My eyebrows shot up into my hairline. "Phil's *friend?*"

"Yeah, I didn't pay much attention until later with Gladys. Then I heard Tony talking to Hamilton. He said they needed to find Vickie Larson."

"And?" I was trying to follow Lorea's train of thought, but I was getting derailed.

"Phil's mother was a Larson. I remembered reading about Lily's step-grandmother in her obituary. She was related to tons of people in the valley, and her sister Meredith Larson is still living."

"And who is she?"

"I had to do a little checking, but Meredith is Vickie's mother." Lorea looked triumphant after her revelation.

But I still wasn't following it. "I don't see why that's important."

"The important part is that Phil claimed not to know Vickie when Tony questioned him tonight," Lorea said.

"Wait, Tony questioned Phil tonight?"

"Yes, he was in the vicinity when Gladys had her attack. I heard him ask Phil if he'd seen Vickie near the table, and Phil said he didn't know who she was."

"That's really strange, but I'm not sure that it proves anything."

"Besides my theory that Tim and Phil were working together?" Lorea asked. "And maybe it means Vickie was involved too. She had access to the euthanizing agent, right?"

"I already covered that angle. Tony said she has an alibi corroborated by several people. She was getting her hair done."

"I still think she was involved somehow," Lorea said.

It was a lot of information to digest, and my stomach was grumbling with hunger again. "I'm not sure, but you're right. I'll stay out of things and let Tony handle it."

Lorea's shoulders slumped. "You still don't think I'm on to anything?"

I chuckled. "Hey, I'm supposed to be the detective. Sounds like you've been working this case overtime to come up with that many connections."

"Well, maybe something will help Tony so he can get off work early one night this week."

"Hopefully. Are you still coming for ice cream?"

"Let me call Tony again, but yeah, I'll probably be there."

"I'd better run. My family's waiting."

Lorea waved goodbye and pulled out of the parking lot. I hurried to stash the rest of my bags in the Mountaineer. I guzzled another water bottle on my way out of the resort. It was nearly seven o'clock by the time I left the festival meadows and headed down to Frozen Tundra Treats. Part of me wanted to go home and put on my pajamas, but my brother was already waiting with his little family.

I called Luke on the way, and he said he'd be there. "I might be a few minutes late, though," he said. "Do you want to order me a hot-fudge-and-caramel sundae?"

"Sure, that's a good idea. See you there."

After I hung up, I wondered if he was nervous at all to meet the entire family and hang out tonight. He seemed okay, though, and that made me happy.

My family filled half of the little diner, and we made a lot of noise greeting each other and reporting about the happenings of the Ketchum Arts Festival.

"Hey, sis, did you have to go and get involved in another crime? I was looking forward to seeing Tony tonight." Wes gave me a hug.

"It wasn't my fault. And hello to you too."

"Where's Lorea?" he asked.

"I thought she'd be here by now, but she did say something about checking at the station to see if Tony could come."

We got in line, and I received big hugs from my niece, Bryn, and my nephew, Ethan. "I'm glad you could make it, Jenna." I hugged my sister-in-law. "The kids look like they're happy to be here. Did they sleep on the way?"

"They did for part of the way, so with a late nap and sugar, I'm sure they'll be up late."

"Maybe they'll surprise us and crash early. If not, we'll have to keep them busy."

"I've been using this treat as a bribe all day." Jenna smiled ruefully. "Sort of sad to see my tactics come to an end."

We squeezed a few of the red and white tables together, and the waitress filled them with several kinds of ice cream, brownie sundaes, and milkshakes. My blackberry malt with pecans was a little piece of heaven, and the sugar would probably keep me from passing out too early tonight. We all laughed when Bryn balanced a giant scoop of ice cream on her spoon and licked it.

Luke arrived just as I was taking the third bite of my milkshake. I swallowed fast and had a brain freeze, but I managed to stand up so that I could introduce him to the rest of my family.

"Thanks for coming," I said. "I saved you a seat."

He put his arm around me and smiled. "I wouldn't miss it."

"Luke, this is my brother, Wesley, and his wife, Jenna." I raised my voice a bit. "And their darling kiddos, Bryn and Ethan."

Bryn waved an ice-cream-covered spoon at Luke. "Hello," she said.

"Hi there, cutie," Luke replied. Bryn gave him a big smile and returned her attention to her ice cream.

Wes stood and shook hands with Luke. "It's great to meet you. I've heard a lot about you." He winked in my direction, and I blushed like a schoolgirl. How did my brother still do that to me?

"All good things," Jenna assured him. "It's great that you could come tonight. Adri said you've been so busy at work this summer."

"Yeah, we hardly saw each other during June. But I'm hoping to have a reprieve soon."

Luke sat down, and we continued to eat and chat over ice cream. The conversation flowed comfortably, and Luke talked about his work, his Harley, and several other things with Wes and my dad. When he finished his ice cream, he leaned back and put his arm around me. I loved how that simple movement said that I was his. I leaned in closer to him, enjoying the feeling that he was mine.

Everything felt right, like the pieces of my puzzle were finally coming together. Luke was my missing piece. I watched him, how easily he conversed with my parents and Wes and Jenna. His laugh was quick and bright. Ethan kept smiling at him every time Luke waggled his fingers in the direction of the ice-cream-covered baby.

Luke turned and held me tighter. He bent his head toward mine. "How am I doing?"

"Perfect," I said.

"Just like you."

A little thrill went through me as I gazed at Luke. Then my phone rang, breaking the magic of the moment. Tony's number came up on my screen, and I groaned. "I hope I don't have to fill out any more statements today." I flashed the phone at Luke, and he nodded.

"Hey, Tony," I said.

"Adri, did Lorea make it over there to have ice cream with you guys?"

"No. I thought she was coming to pick you up?"

"Dang, I must have missed her. I'll try calling her cell again. She wasn't picking up, so I thought maybe it was too loud in the diner for her to hear and I'd try someone else."

"She was kind of iffy on coming, so maybe she went home to bed. I know that's kind of where I want to be right now," I said.

Tony chuckled. "Don't we all. Well, if you see her before I do, tell her to give me a ring."

"Will do." I hung up the phone. "Tony was just looking for Lorea," I explained.

Luke nodded, and then he leaned back and patted his stomach. "That hit the spot. So what's the plan for tomorrow?"

"We'll be at the festival all day, and then we want to go to dinner. Are you game?"

"Sure. Do you want me to come up and help with anything?"

"No, not unless you're really bored," I said. "I think we'll be able to keep up, unless you want to meet for lunch again."

"Well, I did have my eye on a couple of those Mexican food booths. I could be persuaded to try one out if you'll let me treat you to lunch."

"I think that's a great plan. Same time as today?"

"Sure," Luke said.

"Oh, Bryn, look at your shirt," Jenna said as she lifted Bryn from her chair. Bryn's light-pink shirt was smeared with chocolate sauce and ice cream. Jenna grabbed a handful of napkins and began wiping it off. "I'll probably have to toss this one."

"Not if Adri still has some of her homemade laundry

detergent," Mom said. "That stuff works wonders. We'll rinse it out and start a load when we get home."

"Okay, that'd be great, because his clothes are pretty much drenched with ice cream." Jenna pointed at Ethan.

"Yeah, that won't be a problem," I said. "I have a big glass jar of the soap sitting on my dryer. You're welcome to wash whatever you need."

"Thanks, Adri." Jenna scooped up her kids and handed Ethan to Wes.

As my family scattered out to their separate vehicles, Luke walked me to my car. "You're going to have quite the houseful."

"Yeah, I'll be sleeping on the couch so my parents don't have to," I said. "It's a good thing I have a spare room and an air mattress."

"Let me know if you're too crowded. I have plenty of room," he said.

"Careful, I might take you up on that."

"Well, as long as it's not you I think it'd be totally fine."

"Hey!"

Luke leaned closer and nuzzled my neck. "You know what I mean."

Heat flared up in my chest; I did know exactly what Luke meant. He kissed me tenderly and then helped me into my car. I watched him walk across the parking lot and straddle his Harley. I wouldn't admit how much I wanted to climb on with him and go for a ride—I just couldn't get enough of Luke.

My phone buzzed, and I swiped the screen. There was a text from Tony.

Lorea texted me that she was too tired. I'll see you guys tomorrow.

I closed that text and saw that I had a missed text from earlier. It was from Lorea.

Just in case, I had an idea. Tony can't get mad if I ask the questions.

I stared at the screen, trying to get my overworked brain to catch up to the meaning. When I figured out what Lorea was hinting at, I clenched my fist. "No, Lorea. Please say you didn't do something stupid."

Chapter 28

MOM'S HOMEMADE BREAD

5 cups hot water

2/3 cup honey

2/3 cup oil

2 Tbsp Yeast

2 Tbsp Dough Enhancer (optional)

1 Tbsp Salt

About 10 Cups Whole Wheat Flour

Mix the water, honey, oil, and yeast together. Make sure the water isn't too hot for the yeast. Let sit for about ten minutes. Next add in dough enhancer, four cups flour, and salt. Mix for two minutes. Gradually add in the remaining flour, one cup at a time until dough pulls away from sides of the mixing bowl. Knead for ten minutes. Turn out onto lightly floured surface and separate into loaves. Shape loaves and put in greased baking pans. Allow to rise until nearly doubled in size.

Bake at 350 degrees. Makes 4 loaves. Courtesy of www.mashedpotatoesandcrafts.com

My insides were tied up in knots with the feeling that something was wrong. I called Lorea's cell three times, disconnecting just as it went to voice mail.

Then I told myself not to panic. I sent Lorea a text asking where she was, but she didn't answer that, either. I waited a moment, tried calling, and left her a brief message asking her to call me back. Then I texted her. Three more times.

By then several minutes had passed, and anxiety had a stranglehold on me. Where was Lorea?

I almost called Tony before I remembered the find-a-friend app Lorea had made me download on my phone before I went to Kauai. She was able to track me on the island and google some of the places that I saw. I wondered if it was still active on her phone.

I scrolled through my apps, and a few seconds later a green circle popped up, showing Lorea's location. She was on her way up the canyon, it looked like. Then I noticed the circle wasn't moving. I gasped when I recognized the area above the Sun Valley resort where Phil Andrus lived.

Pressing hard on the gas pedal, I sped through town toward Phil Andrus's house. Probably half the town had driven by the mansion at one time or another, hoping to get a peek, but from what I'd heard it was located down a private drive that was usually closed. If Lorea was there, did she call and get an appointment to talk to Phil?

I thought about the connection that Lorea had told me about earlier between Vickie and Phil. If the police couldn't find Vickie and she really was related to Phil, could he be helping to hide her from the police? That sounded far-fetched, but it was the only thing I had to go on.

Once I reached the general area, it took me ten more minutes to find the right lane up to the private drive of the Andrus residence. The light was fading fast, but thankfully there was still enough that I could see I was headed in the right direction as the big house loomed before me.

When I pulled into the driveway, my breath lodged in my throat. Lorea's yellow Volkswagon bug was parked to the side of the imposing three-story mansion. Lorea hadn't answered any of my calls or texts, which sometimes happened, but given her location, I expected the worst. I opened my car door and stepped onto the asphalt.

My phone was in my pocket, and I wondered if I should call the police. I hesitated, trying to decide if I had overreacted again. Knowing that Tony would be angry if I even breathed in unsafe territory, I pulled my phone out of my pocket. Phil had probably seen me arrive—I'd noted the camera installed on the light pole as I came up the driveway.

I began typing in Tony's number as I walked up the elaborate tiled pathway and was almost to the front door when I heard someone screaming. The blood pumped hard in my ears, and every sound intensified. I tried the front door, but it was locked. I turned and ran down the steps, around the side of the house, looking for another entrance. There! I spotted a door next to the steps that led up to the huge balcony overlooking the backyard.

I still gripped my phone with only part of Tony's number entered on the screen. I made an impulsive decision and dialed 911 instead. As soon as dispatch picked up, I identified myself and hurriedly gave my location. "Please send the police. Tell them Lorea Zubiondo may be hurt and it involves the Lily Rowan murder case."

"Are you hurt?"

"No, but I'm going in the house."

"Miss, please don't enter the premises if you think there is danger."

"My friend is in there. I have to help her."

The operator was asking more questions, but I hung up and silenced my phone. I stepped quietly, my movements mimicking Tux when he was on the hunt for June bugs every night. The handle turned easily, and the door swung open without a sound. I stepped into a dim hallway in the basement of the massive home. I lifted my head, listening for any sounds, remembering the scream. How many minutes had passed? One, maybe two? My fingers tingled with anticipation, and I shook them out as I rounded the corner and looked up an imposing set of stairs.

The stairwell was dark and enclosed. It must have been a service entrance. I thought I heard voices filtering down the stairway, so I began climbing, only putting weight on the balls of my feet. One of the stairs creaked. I froze, holding my breath, instantly transported back in time to when Wes and I would sneak around the house after our bedtime. Wes knew all the creaks on the steps and how to avoid them. I remembered one of his tricks was never to put weight on the middle part of the stair; he walked near the wall or on the edges of the steps. I licked my lips and continued climbing the stairs like my brother had taught me.

Near the top of the stairs, light illuminated a hallway on the next level. I stopped at the top of the stairs, taking shallow breaths and straining my ears for any sound. To my left, I heard someone speaking, but it was too far away for me to make out any words. Blood pounded in my ears, muffling the sounds even more. My right foot was on the threshold of the stairs when I heard a grunt, followed by a thump. I closed my eyes, afraid that the thump was the sound of a body falling. The thought of Lorea kept me moving.

I peeked around the corner and took a few more steps into the hallway. I rounded a corner to my right, and the light reflected off a pair of gleaming amber eyes. I swallowed the scream that filled my chest. A mountain lion was poised to pounce on a jackrabbit hopping over a log. What looked like real sagebrush and Indian paintbrush was planted in the rocks and sand of the cat's hunting ground.

My heart was triple-timing the beats, ready to burst from the adrenaline coursing through my system. I heard a man shout, and there was another loud thump. I shrank back against the wall, wondering what was happening and why Lorea had come here alone.

It was at that moment I realized I didn't have a weapon. Luke would never let me hear the end of this. I looked back at the wildlife display; there were a few logs under the jackrabbit, one that was about twice the width of my forearm. I bent and tugged at the piece of wood. At first it didn't budge, but then I lifted it straight up, and with a clink of metal it came loose. There were two metal rods sticking out of the piece of wood where it connected to the display. The wood was only moderately heavy as I hefted the weight in my hands. If I needed to use it, I figured I could wield the makeshift weapon, but I still hoped that this was all a misunderstanding.

That thought vaporized when I saw the pair of feet sticking out of the doorway of the next room. The dark leather shoes belonged to a man, maybe Phil. Where was Lorea?

It was some kind of office—the light spilled over a massive desk and into the hallway. I peered around the corner and saw Lorea on one side of the desk, facing a woman with dark hair on the other side.

"You shouldn't have come here. What did you think you could do, *señorita?*" The woman's tone was icy.

"I came to warn Phil about Vickie," Lorea answered, and her voice trembled. "I didn't know it was you. The police don't suspect you. Just let me go, and I won't tell anyone."

I took another step forward and recognized the profile of Rose Benavidez. The gears in my mind click-clacked to a stop, then began spinning in every direction as the bits and pieces of the mystery came together. Rose had killed her own sister.

"It's a little late for that," Rose spat. She took a step toward Lorea, who was tied to a straight-backed chair. How in the world had Lorea walked into this mess? Rose didn't have a gun, or any weapon that I could see.

"So, Tim? It wasn't his fault—he didn't kill Lily?" Lorea was trying to keep Rose talking, but the fear in her voice was almost tangible, hanging onto the end of each of her words.

"No, but none of that matters now." Rose lifted her hand, and I caught sight of the weapon. Her hand covered most of the syringe, but the needle glinted under the light as she put pressure on the plunger. A drop of liquid clung tight to the end of the needle.

Phil groaned, and as if in slow motion, I watched Rose turn in my direction. I leapt into action before her eyes could meet mine. With a scream, I lifted the log and swung it with my entire body toward her. Rose yelped and jumped back, but there was too much force behind my swing. The log hit Rose's body with a sickening crack; she screamed, red blooming from the front of her light-blue blouse. I looked down at the weapon in my hand, and my stomach rolled over at the metal spike now covered in Rose's blood. In my haste, I'd forgotten about the metal rods embedded in the wood.

Rose covered her shoulder with her hand and lurched forward. She only made it a few steps before she cried out and slumped to the floor.

The knuckles of my right hand were white from gripping the wood, but speckles of blood dotted my fingers. I looked from Rose to Lorea, and back to Rose again.

"Adri!" Lorea squirmed against the ropes. "Help me get loose!"

I knelt by her chair and began untying the knots. My hands shook, and I struggled to get the rope loose. "How did she tie you up with Phil here?"

"The gun. She made Phil tie me up." Lorea swallowed. "It must be on the desk somewhere."

My heart collided with my chest as I leapt to my feet to search for a gun. "Keep an eye on her," I said, motioning to Rose as I searched the desk. The soft gleam of a dark gray handgun caught the low lights of the office. The weapon was sitting next to a pile of books. Something about it looked different; the barrel was slightly longer than other handguns I'd seen. "Why did she have a gun if she was planning to use poison?"

"I don't know, maybe she thought she'd need it to keep Phil from fighting back. Don't touch it," Lorea said.

I glanced at Rose lying on the floor. She wasn't unconscious, and I couldn't risk her getting to the gun. I grabbed a file tray and used one of the books to slide the gun onto the tray. Stepping carefully around the desk, I set the tray with the gun on a shelf above Lorea's head.

"Can you untie me yet?" Lorea whimpered.

"Hopefully." My hands shook as I again knelt beside the chair and fumbled with the ropes.

"How did you know?"

One side of my mouth turned up, and I shook my head. "I finally figured out the clue."

"You did? But how did you find me?" Lorea's voice sounded like she was on the edge of a panic attack.

"That little friend location app you downloaded on my phone," I answered. "You better never play hooky from work, 'cause I'll know if you aren't at home in bed."

Lorea's eyes widened. Then she laughed. Her face was pale, and my hands felt clammy. Some part of my brain registered that we were both probably suffering from shock.

I tugged at the rope but still couldn't get Lorea's hands free. Shakily, I stood and looked for something that might help me cut the ropes. My eyes darted from the blood pooling on the floor by Rose, to Phil lying quiet halfway in and out of the room. There was an angry red-and-purple goose egg on the side of his head. My foot bumped the blood-spattered log, and the room seemed to tilt. I sucked in a breath, commanding myself to stay with it.

"Adri, are you okay? Rose is moving," Lorea whispered.

I held on to the back of the chair and focused on Rose. "Don't move, or this time I'll go for your head," I growled.

Rose didn't look up, but she lay still.

It felt like much longer, but only a couple minutes later the police burst into the house. I grinned when I saw Tony in the throng of officers, figuring that when he heard Lorea's name on the police scanner, he'd led the pack. I saw him take in the area. There were paramedics and officers surrounding both Phil and Rose, so he made a beeline for Lorea. He sliced the ropes with a knife from his utility belt and snatched her up into his arms.

"What happened? Are you hurt?" His voice was tinged with hysteria.

"I'm okay. Adri got here just in time." Lorea bit her lip, and the tears she'd been holding in flooded out. She buried her head in Tony's uniform.

He looked over her head to me. "Are you hurt?"

"No, but I feel kind of lightheaded." I turned to look behind me, and collapsed into the sofa along the wall of the office. I watched two paramedics working on Rose. They helped her from the room and onto a stretcher. Two cops followed, handcuffing her right hand to the stretcher's metal bar.

"Miss? Miss! Take steady breaths." One of the paramedics was at my side, checking me over for injuries. One part of my brain registered what was happening, but everything seemed to float around me, the voices muffled.

A light shined in my eyes, and I jerked back. "Sorry about that," the paramedic said. "You're experiencing shock. Can you put your head between your legs and take a few deep breaths?"

"Yes. I'm sorry I hit her so hard," I mumbled.

I saw the paramedic motion to Tony out of the corner of eye as I hung my head over my knees. "She said something about hitting someone," the paramedic said.

Tony helped Lorea sit on the sofa next to me, and then he crouched down beside me. "Can you tell me what happened, Adri?"

I lifted my head a couple inches. "I snuck in the basement and came upstairs. I heard a thud and found Phil in the doorway of the office." I paused to take a deep breath. "Then I heard Rose threatening Lorea. She had a syringe. She was going to kill her. I didn't know what else to do."

"It's okay," Tony soothed. "Where's that syringe?" He raised his voice toward another officer. I lifted my head enough to see the officer delicately handling the syringe with gloves. Tony nodded and turned his attention back to me. "You did the right thing. What did you hit her with?"

"The log from the mountain lion display. I forgot that it had metal spikes in the wood. Is she going to be okay?"

"Yes. Puncture wounds bleed a lot, so maybe it looks worse than it is," Tony replied.

"Oh, the gun is on top of that shelf. I didn't touch it." My voice sounded hollow and emotionless.

Tony jumped up and made a beeline for the shelf. The commotion sounded far away. I wondered how close I was to passing out, and sucked in a few big breaths.

"Adri, good work on not touching the gun. It's actually a tranquilizing gun."

"Did she steal it from Tim?" I asked.

"No, he wouldn't really have a need for something like that at his animal clinic," Tony said. "I wonder how she got her hands on that poison."

I blinked and turned to Tony. “She killed Lily,” I whispered.

“I know.”

“For the life insurance money?”

Lorea cut in. “No—at least, I don’t think that was the reason at first. It was because Lily found out Rose was embezzling money from Lost Trails Construction.”

“How did—”

“Rose said something about her stepdad’s money, and that he was running the business into the ground anyway,” Lorea said. “I remembered how Drago got accused, and it all made sense. Rose pretty much confessed to me before you got here.”

“Will Lorea have to testify?” I asked Tony.

“If Lily found a paper trail. I’m sure we’ll find it,” he answered. “Lorea, why in the world did you come here?”

Lorea looked down at her hands. “I wanted to warn Phil. I thought he was in danger.”

“What kind of danger? You couldn’t have guessed Rose would be here.”

“No, I thought it was Vickie.” She looked over at me and frowned. “After I talked to you, I kept thinking how strange her behavior was today, and how possessive she was of Tim. I thought maybe she and Tim were working together to get all of the life insurance money. With Phil out of the way, Tim was the next in line to receive the payout on at least one of the policies.”

“And you knew this how?” I asked.

“Terese.” Lorea’s voice was small. “I never would have come if I thought I’d be in danger. While I was talking to

Phil, we heard a door slam and Rose came storming into the office talking about Phil stealing her money."

Tony closed his eyes. "You could have been killed."

"I know, and I'm sorry. It all made sense in my head." Lorea sank back into the couch. "It was really stupid."

My head was feeling less like a throbbing watermelon, so I slowly sat up and leaned back against the sofa. "It wasn't my fault this time." I looked over at Lorea, and she pulled her bottom lip through her teeth.

"You're a bad influence, Miss Pyper," Tony said in his official cop voice. "Luring innocent civilians into your amateur detective business."

"Hey, I didn't lure anyone. She ran headlong into trouble trying to prove that Tim was guilty." I poked Lorea in the ribs.

She rolled her eyes. "I heard that."

"Heard what?" Tony looked from her to me.

"She was saying *I told you so*," Lorea said. "It was practically vibrating off her."

I laughed. "Okay, but I did tell you so."

"Yeah, next time I'll listen," she said.

Tony cleared his throat. "Um, ladies. There won't be a next time, right?"

Lorea turned to me and arched an eyebrow. I smiled and stood slowly. "I think I need some water if we're finished here."

"Yes. Finished as in final, no more investigating," Tony said.

I patted his arm. "You're a good cop. Now quit being bossy and go take care of your girlfriend."

Tony smirked. “I’m afraid that you both have a lot more explaining to do, statements to fill out—you know, all that fun stuff.”

Lorea and I both groaned.

Chapter 29

PEANUT BUTTER & CHOCOLATE GRAHAM CRACKERS (STRESS RELIEF)

Spread peanut butter on a graham cracker. Sprinkle with chocolate chips or chunks of your favorite dark chocolate. Enjoy with a glass of cold milk.

Courtesy of www.mashedpotatoesandcrafts.com

It was nearly ten thirty before we got the okay to go home. I'd had a moment to call my parents and fill them in on what was going on, and then I'd called Luke. He was on his way over now.

"How are we going to function tomorrow at the festival?" Lorea whined. She rubbed her wrists, which were red and chafed from the ropes.

"Wes and Jenna said they could take a shift in the morning for us." Even though the thought of my brother in a craft booth was pretty scary, I planned on accepting his offer. My entire body felt shaky. Someone had offered me an orange juice to sip, and that helped a little, but right now I needed sleep.

"Are you sure you don't want someone to drive you home?" Tony asked.

"That's why I came." Luke stepped into the office and knelt by the sofa. "Are you okay?"

I couldn't answer, because seeing him there undid me. All I wanted was Luke. I wanted to feel his strong arms around me, to hold me up in the chaos surrounding us. I shook my head.

"Oh, Adri, you scared me to death." Luke held out his hand and helped me up. He wrapped his arms around me, and I melted into his embrace.

"These girls are a lot of trouble," Tony said.

Lorea pouted. "Hey, I just solved your case for you."

"Yeah, and it's a good thing I love you, or else I would arrest you." He touched his fingers to his lips, then pressed them against Lorea's cheek.

She stood on her tiptoes and boldly kissed him. "I don't care if you're on duty. I love you."

Tony hugged her. "Let's get you home." He looked at Luke and me. "Text me when you get home."

I saluted him. "Yes, sir." I turned and gave Lorea a hug. "Are you going to be okay?"

"Yes. Tony said they'll have a few more questions for me tomorrow." Lorea squeezed my arm. "And for the record, I'm sorry that I didn't listen to you."

"It's okay. I understand."

"Good. I'll get there as soon as I can in the morning," she said.

"Don't worry about setup. We'll handle it. Get some rest, please."

Luke helped me into his pickup. "I'll come back with your dad and get your car after I drop you off, okay?"

I nodded.

"Are you sure you're okay?" he asked as he pulled out onto the road.

"Just a little woozy from all the adrenaline."

"I can't believe it was Rose." He shook his head. "It changes everything."

"That's right. The custody case. What will happen to Jasmine?"

"It might be sticky, because the judge ruled in Rose's favor. There will be some hang-ups depending on who she has that might want to take care of Jasmine. Javier may still have to appeal, but hopefully they'll grant him full custody now."

"That poor little girl."

Luke pulled up to my house and cut the engine. "Do you want me to come in for a minute?"

"Yes, please." I grasped his hand. He grinned and jumped out of his pickup, trotting around to open my door. "We'll have to keep it down, but hopefully the kids are asleep," I whispered.

Luke nodded, and we walked through my house quietly.

My parents both came in from the kitchen and scooped me into a bear hug as soon as they heard the door click shut. "Adri, are you okay?" Mom's voice was muffled against my shoulder.

"Yes, everything's okay."

"You ever thought about moving back home to Rupert? 'Cause it's a lot safer there," Dad said.

I smiled. "I'm glad you guys are here. Is everyone else asleep?"

"Yes, the kids were restless, so Wes and Jenna had to lie down with them. But honey, we've been worried sick," Mom said. "Are you hungry?"

"No. I'm thirsty, though."

"Let me get you some ice water." Mom hurried into the kitchen, flicking on the light.

Luke approached me, and his eyes widened. "Did you get hurt?" He motioned to my chest.

I looked down, and jumped at the sight of blood spattered across the front of my green shirt. Why hadn't Tony mentioned it? The red speckles were small and infrequent, so maybe he thought it would freak me out even more. Lorea must have noticed too. "Wait, is it on my skin?" I rubbed my hand along my neck and shivered.

"No, just those few small spots on your shirt. What happened?" Luke asked.

I looked from my parents to Luke. "Let me go change, and then I'll tell you the whole story."

"Okay. Do you want me to make you a cup of tea or something?" Mom grabbed my tea kettle before I could answer.

"Actually, that would be nice. There's a honey chamomile in the cupboard above the sink."

I heard Luke speaking softly while my mom filled the tea kettle as I hurried down the hall into my bedroom. I tossed my shirt in the trash. It was ruined. Even if the blood came out, I didn't want to remember that squelching sound when the metal spike impaled Rose's shoulder. I shuddered and tried to think of something else as I pulled one of my running shirts over my head, smoothing down the silky hot-pink fabric.

Tux bumped up against my ankles and I scooped him into my arms, his purrs reverberating against my chest. For some reason, he made me think of Tim and that visit to his office only a couple weeks earlier. I had believed in his innocence, and I had been right. I only hoped that his practice wouldn't suffer because of the investigation, his arrest, and everything related to Lily's death.

When I returned to the kitchen, Luke was sitting in a chair at the kitchen table, spreading peanut butter on a graham cracker while talking to my dad. "What's that?" I asked.

"Stress relief, if you have some chocolate chips," he answered with a smile.

I grabbed the bag out of my pantry and dropped it on the table. "I could definitely use some stress relief."

"Me too," my mom said.

Luke finished spreading a thick layer of peanut butter on the cracker and then dotted it with chocolate chips. He slid it onto a plate and pushed it toward me. "I like to have mine with milk."

I moved to get up, but my mom beat me to it. She grabbed the carton from the fridge and four glasses. My dad poured the milk while Luke finished smothering the next graham cracker. The kitchen felt cozy as I sat next to him, his presence filling the room with a security that I craved, especially after the evening's scary end to the murder investigation.

I bit into the treat, and the crunch of the cracker mixed with the creamy peanut butter and chocolate was delicious. "Wow, you need to patent this. It's better than I thought."

Luke swigged some milk as the teapot began to whistle.

"I'll get that." Mom jumped up again and bustled around by the sink.

I finished off my cracker while the tea steeped, and brushed a few stray crumbs onto my plate. "Mmm, this tastes so good for some reason."

"Adrenaline letdown. Everything sweet tastes good," Luke said.

"Are you going to tell us what happened?" my dad asked between bites of graham cracker. "Or do we have to wait until morning?"

"Nope. It's quite the story." I told them about Lorea's cryptic clues and hunches, and how I figured out something different than she had. Luke and my parents listened, and then I sipped the soothing chamomile tea as we talked about the craziness that was Rose Benavidez.

"I probably better let you get home," I said to Luke after we had all discussed theories of Rose's motive for murder–killing her sister to hide embezzling didn't seem like enough, unless the sum she'd stolen was even larger than the life insurance.

"I'm going with him to pick up your car," Dad asked. "Do you have your keys?"

"On the table by the door, but you can wait until tomorrow if you want."

"No, it won't take long. I'll go now," Dad said.

Luke nodded. "Good idea. We don't want it stuck there when the police seal everything off." He stood and I did too, because I really wanted another hug, and maybe a kiss. He took my hand as he walked toward my front door.

"Thanks for being here," I said.

"I want to be here. Please, don't ever hesitate to call me." He squeezed my hand and ran his fingers up my arm. "I would have felt so bad to find out all of this tomorrow. I'm glad I could help."

My parents were still in the kitchen, so I leaned toward him and kissed his cheek. "Thank you," I murmured.

He turned his head and kissed me on the mouth, then once on each side of my lips. "I'm glad you're safe. I'll see you tomorrow."

I touched his cheek, resting my eyes on his for a moment. "Good night."

After he and my dad left, I found my mom in the kitchen scrubbing my stove. "Mom, it's midnight. Stop cleaning my kitchen."

She turned and waved her rag at me. "I can't sleep. Not after seeing you kiss Luke. Now tell me all about him."

I smiled, not even caring that they knew I was head over heels in love with Luke Stetson.

Chapter 30

CLEVER WAYS TO ANNOUNCE AN ENGAGEMENT

Take a fun photo of the couple kissing in the background with a tag clipped to a tree, "She said Yes!" Use Scrabble pieces to spell out FOREVER replacing the 'O' with your engagement ring. Create an announcement card with each of your fingerprints in the shape of a heart and the word ENGAGED along with your engagement date.

Courtesy of www.mashedpotatoesandcrafts.com

It took superhuman effort, but with my family's help we survived the Ketchum Art Festival's Saturday crowd. We received word that Gladys was recovering, after the surprising revelation that she was allergic to one of the perfumes she had used to mix up bath salts. I was relieved to find out it had nothing to do with me or Vickie. She'd never used the scent before, and what I had witnessed was an extreme allergic reaction. I made a note to visit Gladys soon and purchase some bath salts to make up for her loss at the festival.

Luke came for lunch and helped get rid of our empty boxes and trash. He stayed for a little over an hour, and then left to go into his office for a couple hours to catch up on a few things.

Tony stopped by when we were packing things up for the night. He was off duty, but he had a couple questions to ask Lorea and me.

After he questioned us, I had one of my own for him. "I thought you said Rose had an alibi for the whole day on the day of Lily's murder." I put my hand on my hip.

Tony lifted his chin. "She did, but that's because she had a temp worker take her place at the design event in Boise. She was instructed to introduce herself to everyone as Rose Benavidez, and since the event was out of town, no one was the wiser."

"Wow, so this really was premeditated," I said.

"Yes," Tony said. "And I'm glad Rose went ahead and confessed."

"It's official, then?"

"Yep," Lorea chimed in. "So I don't have to testify."

"That is a very good thing," I said, nodding sagely.

"She took more than half a million dollars from Phil over the past five years, and somehow Lily found out," Tony said. "We're studying all of the files that were on Lily's computer even though Rose thought she'd cleaned it up. We found a hidden file with the evidence of how Rose had embezzled right under her stepdad's nose."

"Tim did say Lily was incredibly smart with numbers," I said. "I'm glad that he can have some closure."

"Are we still on for tonight?" Tony asked, bringing my attention back to the grassy field where we stood.

"Yes, we're meeting at seven on the dot for dinner," I said. "And there won't be any distractions tonight." We were all gathering for dinner before Wes and Jenna left home. Tony had already double-checked with me twice; he must have been anxious to catch up with Wes and celebrate the successful resolution of his investigation.

When we closed the flaps of the tent that evening, my mom was bursting with excitement over how many items she'd sold with still one day left of the festival. "I think we should do this again next year," she said.

"Minus the murder investigation," my dad said, pointing at Lorea and me.

"Hey, I'm not taking any responsibility for this one." I put my arm around Lorea. "It's so nice of you to take the heat."

She chuckled. "That'll be the last mystery I try to solve."

"It's still a pretty good twist that Rose was involved in all the rumors we heard about," I said.

Tony nodded. "I couldn't believe it when we confirmed that Rose's name was listed as the second beneficiary on Lily's life insurance policy. Tim's name was only under condition of marriage. He won't get any of the life insurance money, after all."

"So that syringe was meant for Phil?" I asked. "Rose

didn't have enough money from embezzling, so she was going to kill him too?"

Lorea nodded. "I think Phil figured it out, because one minute he was sitting there listening to Rose talk and the next minute he went after her. She slammed his head into the desk. Maybe she thought she killed him." Lorea paused and shuddered.

"And that way she could use the euthanizing agent on you," I said, completing her thought. "Hey, how did she get access to the poison?"

Tony lifted his eyebrows up and down. "That's another mystery that we just solved today, but I can only share what'll be released to the press."

I groaned. "It wasn't Rose?"

"Wait, it was Vickie, wasn't it?" Lorea jumped up and down. "I knew it! I knew it was a partnership of some kind."

I watched the exchange with a half-smile. "Vickie was working with Rose?"

Tony nodded. "She claims she didn't know what Rose was going to do with the poison, but I have a source who says Vickie was madly in love with Dr. Esplin and hated Lily for stealing him from her."

"So she helped Rose kill Lily to get to Tim?" I shook my head. "Then why would she frame him?"

"How's that saying go?" Tony asked. "Nothing burns as hot as a woman scorned?"

Lorea and I both laughed. "Something like that." Lorea patted his cheek.

"Whatever. Anyway, if she couldn't have him, then no one could," Tony said. "It's sick. I'm not sure of Vickie's mental state, but she'll do time for this."

"That's an accomplice to murder, isn't it?" Lorea asked.

Tony nodded. "Rose rolled over on Vickie, and we arrested her outside of town in a cabin this morning."

"Wow," I said. "That is nuts. But if she took the euthanizing agent, then why did you think it was Tim?"

"Vickie was pretty smart. She took the first dose from a bottle in their locked supply so Tim would be accountable. Vickie's alibi was solid, although she's always been a suspect. We discovered that for some time now she's been gathering the empty bottles and extracting the bit of poison left inside after Tim euthanized animals."

"From the trash?" Lorea made a face. "Don't they have to dispose of those kinds of things in a certain way?"

Tony nodded. "Yes, and Vickie was in charge of disposal." He shook his head. "Tim explained it to us. He said that after a dose is administered, there is still liquid in the bottle that runs down the sides and settles in the bottom. Vickie collected that so Rose could inject Lily with more poison and have enough left over for a second dose."

"That's why they left the empty bottle at the murder scene, so you'd find Vickie's alibi and look elsewhere," I said. "And the whole time she was smuggling out the poison, bit by bit."

"At least there's no question that it was premeditated," Lorea said.

"Yes, and even though Tim's clinic will be under investigation by the Board of Veterinary Medicine, I think he'll be okay," Tony said.

"So Tim knows everything?" I asked.

Tony nodded. "Yes, we've kept him informed of everything that we've discovered. It won't bring Lily back, but at least they aren't running the streets."

"I wonder if his animal clinic will make it."

"I'll be surprised if he sticks around. He was talking about going back to Florida with his family."

I scuffed my toe along the grass. "What a tragedy. Everything in his life was about to start."

Lorea and Tony fell silent as we mused over the events. We stood in the meadow, staring up at Baldy. The rugged mountain looked over the valley, and for some reason it made me think of Lily. Rose wouldn't ever be able to fully pay for her crime because she couldn't bring Lily back, but we could do our best to honor the beautiful person that Lily was. I sniffed, feeling grief roll over me again. Lorea gave me a hug, and we both felt an unspoken peacefulness. I felt certain that Lily was grateful for our meager attempts to solve her murder. And Tim could at least walk away from all the false allegations, though I still felt acute sorrow for him and all he'd been through.

It made me think of Luke. Before his wife died, his life was about to start too. Luke would understand how Tim felt, the horrible loss he would continue to face. Hopefully, in time, Tim would be able to move on, to find someone new, and start over.

My heart flipped when I thought of seeing Luke in a few minutes for dinner. I felt like life was just beginning for both of us.

"How are you holding up?" Luke asked as we slid into our seats at the restaurant.

"I think I need a vacation."

"Do you have any more destination weddings planned?" He winked.

"It doesn't count as a vacation if I'm working, silly," I retorted.

"That's true. Hmm, maybe we'd better plan one." He squeezed my hand and I held on tight, happiness bubbling up at the way Luke had said "we."

Everyone talked nonstop and ate while analyzing the crazy motives of Rose and Vickie. I'd just taken the last bite of my pasta when Tony cleared his throat and stood up. "Hey, I know we've all been discussing this case a lot tonight, but I have one more bit of information I can share."

Immediately the room was silent, every person focused on Tony's words. He coughed and wiped his hands on his pants, then looked down at Lorea.

"Hey, Lorea," Tony said, and his voice was strangely soft. "I have a question I've been wanting to ask you for a while. I kept putting it off 'cause I thought I knew how you felt about certain things, but now I'm hoping I was wrong."

Tony knelt down, and it was the first time the giant police officer appeared shorter than the spunky, barely-over-five-foot Lorea. I gasped and looked at Lorea's face to see if she was panicking. She wasn't. Her dark eyes were bright with happiness, and it was as if the rest of us weren't even in the room.

"Lorea Zubiondo, I love you and I want you to be my wife." Tony lifted his hand up, and I recognized the ring box from Walter's shop. "Will you marry me?"

Lorea's mouth hung open when she saw the ring. Then the corners of her mouth turned up into a huge grin. "Yes. Yes!" She threw her arms around Tony's neck, and he stood, twirling her around in a circle.

Everyone cheered when he set her down and slipped the ring on her finger. When he tipped her back over his arm and kissed her, she kissed him back, and the cheering grew louder.

She pulled back and held her ring up, taking a closer look. "Thank you!" She jumped up and down and then kissed Tony again.

"I can't believe he did that," Luke murmured. "I thought he was going to wait until next week."

"What?" I turned to Luke. "You knew about this?"

Luke smiled. "Client-attorney privilege."

I swatted him. "He's not your client."

"Well, he's definitely happier than most of my clients."

I turned back to Tony and Lorea. "C'mon, let's go tell them congratulations." We stepped around the table, and I gave Lorea a hug. "I'm so happy for you!"

"Me too," she said. "He totally surprised me. I mean, we've kind of been talking about things, but I had no idea he already picked out a ring."

Tony pulled Lorea close to his side. "I couldn't wait another day."

"An open-and-shut case, huh?" I smacked Tony on the arm. "You little liar."

Tony took the ring box out of his pocket and opened and closed it with a snap. "I didn't lie."

We all laughed.

I hugged Lorea again. "I can't believe you're engaged! I'm thrilled for you two."

"I bet you are," Lorea said with a smile. "You finally converted me, and I'm going to be eating crow for a long time to come."

I shook my head. "I would never. Besides, I saw this coming."

"You did not," Lorea insisted.

"I did. I even caught Tony coming out of Walter's store."

"What? And you didn't tell me?"

"I didn't want to get arrested for interfering with a police investigation," I said, mimicking Tony's authoritative tone.

Lorea turned to Tony. "You threatened to arrest my best friend?"

Tony pulled out a pair of handcuffs. "All in the line of duty."

Lorea laughed and kissed Tony again. "It's a good thing I love you."

I glanced back at Luke to see if he would pull an "Ew, yuck" face, but he was all smiles. He winked in my direction, and I felt my middle warm as if he'd just lit a match with that look.

"Stick around, everyone," Tony said. "We have lots to celebrate tonight. I ordered an orange chiffon cake for Lorea. Hey, Adri, do you want to tell them to bring it out?"

"Sure."

I moved toward the door, but Luke grabbed my hand. "Can I come along and help?"

I paused and studied him. His smile was genuine, and his hand was warm in mine. "Sure."

We walked out of the room, and I flagged down a waitress who said she'd bring the cake right out. Luke tugged on my hand when I turned to go back in the large room where we'd gathered to eat. He pulled me over to a little alcove by a picture window that overlooked Sun Valley.

"Step outside with me for one minute," he murmured. "I need to tell you something."

"Okay." I followed him out to the parking lot, my stomach buzzing with anticipation of what he wanted to tell me.

"I just wanted to say that I'm sorry again for getting after you about looking into this case. I should've listened to you when you said Tim was innocent."

"Don't worry about it." I waved my hand. "Everything's good now."

"Almost," Luke said. He put his hands around my waist and pulled me closer. "I'm feeling inspired after witnessing that proposal. I was thinking that maybe it was time for me to make a proposal to you."

"What?" My ears must have been playing tricks on me. Luke's eyes were intent, but he couldn't possibly be thinking of proposing to me.

I started to step back, but Luke pulled me forward again. "I'm glad you're my girlfriend and I'm not going to be afraid to say it anymore. I love you, Adri."

His eyes were that intoxicating deep shade of blue that always made me think of a summer thunderstorm. I leaned in close and whispered, "I love you too, Mr. Luke."

He smiled and kissed me in the parking lot as the July heat emanated from the blacktop. And I kissed him back, because that's what you do when you're really in love.

Book Club Discussion Questions

1. Were you aware that the vet's euthanizing agent can also kill humans?
2. How did you feel about Tony and Lorea dating?
3. What were you hoping to see with Luke and Adri's relationship?
4. This book is set in Sun Valley, Idaho, just like the first book in the series. Discuss how the setting is similar or different from where you live.
5. Who did you suspect as the murderer, and why?
6. Adri and her mom were at work creating crafts and delicious eats in this book. What were some of your favorites?
7. The Ketchum Arts Festival is an actual annual event with a wonderful selection of items. The event is free and includes live music, great food, and more. It includes a free kids' booth with fun activities and something for everyone. Learn more at this website: www.ketchumartsfestival.com. What is one of your favorite events in your local community?
8. Have you ever been to a wedding that offered something unique or had a creative theme?

Learn more about Adri and her crafts at www.mashedpotatoesandcrafts.com.

Acknowledgments

I'd like to thank you for picking up my book. I'm grateful to each of my readers who spread the word about my books and offer me encouragement. Writing is a difficult and often solitary job, but connecting with readers like you makes it worthwhile!

A huge thank you to my family. My husband, Steve, is rock solid and I'm so grateful for his belief in me and my abilities. Thank you to each of my five children for understanding how hard Mom has to work to "make" books. I'm grateful to my parents, Tim and Andrea, for their unwavering support and for letting me come visit for write-ins at their house! I'm grateful for the sacrifices my family makes to help me achieve my dreams.

Thank you again to my amazing beta readers and critique group. This book wouldn't have developed without the help of Patrick and Necia Jolley, Cami Checketts, Mindy Holt, and my speed-reading dad, Tim Jolley.

Kristie Maynard is a wonderful friend and genius crafter who has helped me since the beginning with MashedPotatoesandcrafts.com. Thank you Kristie!

Every book requires research and first-hand knowledge of specific situations. My thanks to my good friend,

Dominique Etcheverry, and her family for help with Basque phrases and information. Thank you to Matt Schramm who helped with details about Croatia, the language and dialect. Veterinarian Jeff Heins, DMV, provided crucial information on euthanizing procedures and answered questions about the murder plot. Thank you to Corporal Leonard for answering questions about police procedure, and the Blaine County Sherriff's office for help and a tour of the courtrooms.

I appreciate the expertise of many talented individuals in this book's production. Kimberly Anderson illustrated the perfect cover for *Proposals and Poison* and Kelli Ann Morgan designed the cover layout. Jenna Roundy is a superb editor and thank you to Heather Justesen for a beautiful typesetting job.

I am thankful for the gift of life and the blessings that my Heavenly Father gives me daily. I'm grateful for talents that require hard work and determination to develop, and for the opportunity I have to practice something that enriches my life each day.

Sneak Peek of Silver Cascade Secrets

Enjoy this sneak peek of Rachelle's novella, Silver Cascade Secrets, available now in ebook.

"SILVER CASCADE SECRETS by Rachelle J. Christensen is an exciting romantic suspense novella. I loved the park setting and the creepiness factor. Jillian meets Travis during one of her master landscaping projects at the park where his brother-in-law was killed and they both try to find answers about the murder. Great writing, a sweet romance, and an intriguing mystery all rolled into a single story."

Heather B. Moore
USA Today Bestselling Author of *Finding Sheba*

Chapter 1

"Again!" a little girl squealed as she brushed leaves off her pants.

I smiled and continued digging in the flower bed,

planting tulip bulbs. Silver maple trees lined the sidewalks of Silver Cascade Park, where I worked five days a week as caretaker. My nails were bad because I didn't like gloves, and I had perpetual dirt stains on my knees, but it was my dream job.

I watched the girl sail into the pile of leaves and seconds later run to a man screaming, "Again! Again!"

As I wondered if they were father and daughter, a woman approached and hugged the girl. The man put his arm around her in a side hug, and they talked for a few minutes before the woman left with the little girl.

Hmm, didn't seem like a divorced couple, but then my people-watching skills had proven that there was always more than meets the eye. The man sauntered down the sidewalk. I thought I heard him humming something. Carpenter jeans with a good fit were a weakness of mine, and his retreating form was straining my eyes, so I put some muscle back into the flower bed and grabbed another handful of tulip bulbs.

A few minutes later, a light wind picked up several leaves and sent them skittering across the sidewalk. The points of the maple leaves made a distinct sound, signaling that autumn had taken root in Boise, Idaho. I watched the leaves swirl and ignored thoughts of raking and leaf blowing.

I saw some out of the corner of my eye and noticed that the man had come back and was on his hands and knees, searching through the grass. His carpenter jeans had a dark wash, which complimented his olive-toned skin. He appeared to be in his late twenties, maybe a few years older than my twenty-five years. I approached him, kicking a few leaves up as I walked.

"Not to ask the obvious, but did you lose something?"

He looked up. "Yeah, my keys."

"I'm Jillian Warren, Silver Cascade Park caretaker and finder of many sets of lost keys. Would you like some help?"

He stood and brushed his hands on his pants then held out his hand. "Travis Banner. I'd love some help, because it helps to have keys if you want to drive home."

With a laugh, I shook his hand then knelt in the grass and began combing through the leaves. I stole a few glances in his direction. With dark hair and stubble along his jawline, he reminded me of Hook on my favorite TV show, *Once Upon a Time*, minus the sexy accent. "I saw you playing with that little girl. Is she your daughter?"

"My niece. I'm not married, but I like playing favorite uncle."

"It looked like you were definitely in the running."

Hook, or Travis, looked even better with that info, and I had to remind myself I was searching for keys, not a date.

"Four-year-olds are pretty easy to please." He nodded toward the flower bed I'd been digging in. "So do you like your job? The park is beautiful, by the way."

"Thanks. I do enjoy working here. I graduated in landscape architecture, and this seemed like a great stepping stone into the field. My grandma was a bit underwhelmed— not many bragging rights— but I really do like it more than I thought I would." I ducked my head, embarrassed at all the information I'd just given a stranger. Well, I knew his name, so he wasn't a complete stranger.

Travis met my gaze, picking up on my admission. "It's okay to love your job, even if it's different from what everyone else expects. I'm a diesel-engine mechanic. My white-collar dad definitely didn't approve of me donning the blue collar, but I love what I do and hope to have my own shop one day."

My hands stilled in the leaves, and I looked at Travis. He had dark-brown eyes unlike Hook, so surely he couldn't be an evil villain. "It's so nice to talk to someone who understands."

He paused, brushing a hand across the stubble on his chin. "I was thinking the same thing."

My heart felt jittery, and a rush of heat came to my cheeks. "Um, don't laugh, but I'm going to use my favorite trick to try to find your keys."

He raised his eyebrows. "I can't make any promises. I might laugh."

I shrugged. "Fair enough." Glancing behind me, I saw the remains of the leaf pile Travis had been tossing his niece into. The leaves crunched under my feet as I walked to the pile; I kicked some of the leaves then backed up a few paces. Travis was hot, so it was worth embarrassing myself to find his keys. I lay flat on my belly and squinted at the millions of blades of grass and crumbled leaves scattered in the distance. A few strands had come loose from the knot of hair I'd fixed earlier, so I tucked them behind my ear. I heard Travis chuckle but ignored him and continued using the Warren Secret Spy Method, angling my head so my view skimmed along the ground.

Leaves crunched beside me, and I looked over to see Travis mimicking my pose. He winked at me. "I know this trick. My brother and I used to do it to find stray marbles in the gravel."

"Most kids know it, but most adults have forgotten."

"Or maybe they have more pride than we do."

I giggled and rolled over in the leaves, moving to a different vantage point. The sun chose that moment to break through the mass of cumulus clouds scattered across the sky. The leaves turned from red to golden, and I caught a glint of metal about ten feet in front of me.

"Aha!" I shouted and jumped up, keeping my eyes trained on the sparkle I'd seen. When I picked them up, the keys jingled together. "Found 'em." I dangled the keys triumphantly as Travis approached.

"Thanks, Jillian." Travis held out his palm, and I dropped the keys into it. "You're amazing." His tone was light, but I chose to find a deeper meaning in his words.

"Glad to be of service."

"I really appreciate you helping me out." Travis pocketed his keys. "There's this great café a couple of blocks down. They serve the best Mexican hot chocolate. Could I treat you to some?"

"I love The Sugar Cube. Let me just finish up with these bulbs."

"Ah, so you know the place. Let me help. I owe you big time." Travis followed me to the flower bed and plopped a tulip bulb into one of the holes I'd dug.

"Thanks." I examined his work with a nod. "I'm impressed you knew which way to plant the bulb. My brother doesn't know anything about flowers."

"I may be a bachelor, but my mother had a prized flower garden, and she taught me a few things." Travis pointed at my fingernails. "Her hands always looked like that in the fall—mine, too. She's been gone for almost ten years, but for a while, I had my own bulb garden in her honor."

I had started to curl my fingers inward at his attention, but the affection in his voice made me proud to show my work-worn hands. I patted the earth down around the new plantings. "Really? What was her favorite flower?"

"Daffodils. She must have had a dozen varieties. I always liked these little miniature ones she used to plant around the tulips." He got a faraway look in his eyes as he grabbed a handful of bulbs. "How about you?"

"Hyacinths. I'll be planting a pink variety tomorrow that I think smells a little like heaven."

As he reached for the last tulip bulb, his hand brushed mine. He liked the dirt under my fingernails. I almost laughed at the thought. Too many dates with business men, lawyers, and would-be doctors had me feeling ashamed of my chipped nails. Travis was different. We'd just had a conversation about varieties of flower bulbs. He was handsome and looking better by the minute.

We stood and brushed the dirt from our clothes. "Thanks for the help. I usually don't work this late, but I got a little carried away with this flowerbed."

"I'm sure it'll be beautiful. I'm glad you were still here." His smile widened. "I have to say, I'm kind of glad I lost my keys."

The blush tinting my cheeks had me feeling like a school girl, so I hurriedly gathered my tools and tossed them in the back of the Gator— my golf cart on steroids. I loved driving it around the park.

"Can I give you a ride to The Sugar Cube?" he asked.

I looked at my dirt-smudged jeans and wrinkled my nose at the dark smear of mud on my t-shirt. "I'm kind of a mess."

"I think you look cute." He motioned to his right knee. "And look; I have a matching stain."

My resistance melted when he proudly showed off his grass stain. "Okay, let's go." I stowed my tools and followed Travis to his car.

Chapter 2

The sunset tinged the sky with purple as we drove to the city center. Travis opened my door and led me inside the cozy café. We grabbed a booth in the back corner where it was quiet and the lights were dim. A few minutes later, we were warming our hands on mugs of hot cocoa topped with whipped cream. The jitters in my stomach were pleasant, but I wasn't ready to give in to them yet. This was a thank you, not a date— it had been too long since I'd had a good date.

"Have you lived in Boise long?" Travis asked.

"I'm pretty much a full-blooded Idahoan. How about you?"

"I've spent some time in Montana, but I'm back to my roots. It's nice to be close to family, especially since, well, Heidi is growing up fast."

I could tell he meant to say something else, and judging by the shadow that crossed his face, it was something painful. My curiosity reared its persistent head, but I sipped my cocoa and steered the conversation elsewhere.

"Guess how many bulbs I'll be planting in the park this fall."

Travis looked up and pretended to calculate. "Three-hundred."

I laughed. "I wish."

"More than that?" he asked, his eyes bright with interest.

"Only about five times more."

Travis whistled. "That'll mean a beautiful park come springtime, but that's a ton of work."

"I don't mind. We've never had this many to plant before, but someone donated money for a special memorial garden. I'm thrilled with the plans I've drawn up. It really is going to be beautiful."

"That's nice." Travis sat up straight and clenched his fingers into a fist.

"What's wrong?" I blurted before remembering that I barely knew him.

He swallowed, and when he looked at me, I could see a sparkle of moisture in his eyes. "I wasn't going to say anything, because it kind of kills light conversation, but I know about that memorial garden. The reason I moved back here has to do with my sister and my niece. It's a part of my reality that I can't get away from no matter how hard I try."

Again, I swallowed back my questions. "I'm sorry. We can talk about something else." I was ruining things by dominating the conversation with talk of bulbs and gardens. Did I really think this gorgeous guy would be interested in my fall planting plans?

"No, it's okay. That memorial garden is for Craig Simmons."

"Did you know him?" Something pinged in my brain at the name. The guy had been some kind of business consultant, and his firm had made the donation for the garden. I couldn't remember all of the details, but judging by the look on Travis's face, he was going to tell me.

"He was my brother-in-law. He was murdered six months ago."

I gasped. "That's terrible. I'm so sorry. I didn't mean to dredge up sad memories."

"Not at all. It's kind of a neat coincidence to meet the person in charge of Craig's memorial. His firm, True Assets, wanted to do something for the family. Kami suggested the park, because Heidi loved to go there with her dad."

I thought of the sloping ground covered with gravel on the north edge of the park, which had been cleared of crabgrass, dandelions, and June grass. It had been a sore spot in my park for the past two years, and I was happy to make something beautiful out of the offensive weeds.

"I'm sorry for your loss." I licked my lips before continuing. "I'll work extra hard on that garden."

"I'm sure you will. More than one person in this town has bragged about their beautiful park, and that's thanks to your care of it."

"Thank you." The boost to my ego was almost enough to drown out my curiosity. Almost. "Did they catch the person who killed Craig?"

Travis shook his head. "And they don't have any leads." He pushed his mug forward and rested his forearms on the table. "Before Craig died, he told Kami that she'd always be taken care of. The last time she saw him, he said that when the time was right, she'd understand everything. He died that afternoon. Kami said it was like he knew that he was facing death, but there was nothing he could do about it."

"That's terrible. I remember hearing about the murder.

I'm so sorry."

Travis swallowed. "I feel bad for Heidi. That's why I bring her to the park a couple of times a week."

"She's lucky to have such a wonderful uncle."

"Thanks. I wish I could help her more." He turned his mug slowly in his hands and took another sip. "Kami thinks Craig knew his killer— and that it wasn't random."

"Have the police included her in their investigation— you know, to see if he left a clue she'd recognize?"

He tightened his fingers around his mug, the tension of the conversation flowing out of his fingertips. "As much as they can," Travis answered. "It's been tough on her. She said that every time she searched through his stuff, it felt like he'd died all over again."

My heart hurt for the young mother I'd seen in the park with Travis. His sister had looked so innocent holding her daughter's hand. I'd had no idea of the weight she carried in my simple observance. "That's awful. Is she doing any better now that you're here?"

He nodded. "She seems to be coping. She says it's helpful to see Heidi smiling more."

"I hope the police can solve the case, so you all can have closure."

He pressed his lips together then exhaled slowly. "We may have to find closure another way. I wish the police had more evidence to go on."

"How frustrating." I wanted to ask more questions, but I could see that the conversation was taking a toll on him. I sipped my cocoa and waited for him to take the lead.

He stared off into space for a moment, and I took the

opportunity to study the flecks of gold in his brown eyes. His hair looked light brown from the front, but it darkened as it approached his collar. It was a bit on the shaggy side and I surprised myself with the sudden impulse to run my fingers through the thick strands. He looked up and gave his head a gentle shake. "See? I told you it was a conversation killer."

"Not at all. I'm glad you shared it with me. It'll put more meaning into my work."

"So what do you do for fun?" he asked.

I jumped at the chance to lighten the mood. "Anything outdoors. Hiking, mountain biking, a little white-water rafting."

He smiled and nodded. "Sounds like my kind of fun."

My stomach flipped. "What's your favorite?"

"Hard to choose, but my bike hasn't seen any action since I moved back. Would you like to go for a ride with me?"

I nodded. "Sure. There's a path that runs along the river. It's beautiful this time of year." I tried to tone down the grin spreading across my face, because Travis had just asked me on a date to go mountain biking *and* he liked the dirt under my fingernails.

"When do you get off tomorrow?" he asked.

"I was hoping to get an early start so I could finish up by three."

"Oh, do you already have other plans?" The disappointment on his face made my cocoa taste even sweeter.

"Just some errands. Nothing that can't be rearranged." I watched a smile return to his face. "But I'll need time to change. I could meet you at the park at four." It was mid-September, but already the nights were chilly. Afternoon was the perfect time to enjoy the outdoors. Biking was much more fun when I wasn't freezing.

"Sounds great. I'm only working a half day tomorrow, because I've pulled too much overtime lately." He stifled a yawn. "This cocoa is making me sleepy."

"Me, too." I glanced at my watch and was surprised to see that an hour had already passed. It was almost eight o'clock. "Thanks for the treat."

"Thank you," Travis replied. "I'll give you a ride to the park."

On the way back we shared mountain-biking stories. He told me about being chased by a "bear" that ended up being a large and friendly dog. I laughed until my sides hurt and found myself wishing the park was farther away so that I could enjoy his company longer.

Travis offered me his arm as he walked me to where I'd left the Gator. I could feel his bicep underneath my fingertips, and for a minute I forgot where we were headed.

"You're so easy to talk to, Jillian. I'm looking forward to seeing you tomorrow." He covered my hand with his and gave it a gentle squeeze.

"Me, too." I liked the feel of his hand on mine. He released my fingers and took a few steps back as he fished his keys out of his pocket.

"I'll hold on to these." He jangled the keys and chuckled.

I pulled my keys out and held them up before sliding into my seat. Travis waved goodbye as I started the engine and turned the lights on his retreating form. Those carpenter jeans looked even better in the headlights.

Thrills for the Heart

FOR A LIMITED TIME

Sign up for Rachelle's
VIP Mailing List
to get your *FREE* book.

Get started here:
www.rachellechristensen.com

Enjoy this sneak peek of Rachelle's new romance, the Kindle Scout winning novel,

Chapter 1 – The Music Box

March 1943 — Evelyn

Evelyn stood in the one-bedroom apartment looking at a music box on the kitchen table. Slightly larger than a shoebox, constructed of pressed paperboard, and covered

with ivory parchment, a narrow line of embossed gold decorated its outer edge. It wasn't extravagant or expensive, but Evelyn held it close—it was her most precious gift in the world.

"Oh, Jim, it's beautiful! Is this to celebrate—"

"Our five month anniversary." Jim finished her sentence.

"You remembered." Evelyn touched his cheek.

"Always." He kissed her, and then bent over the jewelry box. "Look at these compartments." He lifted the lids of the two side compartments, each lined in cheap red-velvet paper.

"I like the color," she said. She brushed aside the foreboding gloom that haunted her as she counted down the time they had together. Five days left.

"I hoped you would. Push this lever over." Jim pointed to the center of the jewelry box and let his fingers glide over her hand.

When Evelyn pushed the metal button on the raised middle compartment, the center of the jewelry box clicked open to reveal a narrow chamber with padded ridges to hold rings and other precious treasures—things that nineteen-year-old Evelyn did not own. A tiny ballerina on a dais near the back popped up and began dancing an elegant pirouette in front of a mirror attached to the inside of the lid.

"Oh, it plays music. Jim, where did you find this?" Evelyn located the brass windup key at the side of the box as it busily churned out a melody she'd never heard before. The music climbed tentatively up the scale and then scattered down with a resonance as deep as Jim's voice. The wind seemed to listen, too. It took the tune and carried it on a lilting breeze out the window above the kitchen sink.

"Now, that's my secret," he replied.

"You and your secrets." She put her arms around her husband and kissed him, then pulled back to look into his clear blue eyes, seeing the love he felt for her. "I love it. Thank you." They swayed to the music and listened, and she wished that time could stop in that moment.

"Now you'll have a place to keep that locket and know my heart is with you." Jim held her close and hummed along with the tune. He'd given her the heart-shaped locket with his tiny portrait inside on their wedding day. They'd started their life together in the shabby apartment in Colorado Springs with hopes of a bright future, but the war had changed their plans.

Evelyn swallowed her tears as she felt the rumbling of his bass voice against her cheek. She leaned back to look at him. "You keep your heart right in your chest beating strong and come home to me."

Jim chuckled. "But don't you know? I gave my heart to you for safekeeping the day we met."

She laughed, determined to hold on to the echoes of their happiness blending with the melody. She thought of her good husband, the man who made her a cup of peppermint tea every evening, kissed her first thing in the morning, and sang with her in the church choir. Jim wanted to be a father, and he would be a great one, but he was leaving, and Evelyn felt like they were running out of time even though their life together had just begun.

Maybe the war would end soon. She rested her head on his chest. Her hair fell in soft auburn waves over his hands. "My mama told me not to believe everything you read in romance novels 'cause there ain't a man off the paper that comes close.' But she didn't count on a flesh and blood, real-life hero like you, Jim Patterson."

Her words blended with the music drifting on the sweet sounds of spring. The words were what Evelyn's romance novels called true love, like two pieces of a puzzle coming together to form a perfect picture. Evelyn loved how Jim could nearly finish her thoughts and almost read her mind by the expression on her face. She knew he loved her—mind, body, soul—the same way she loved him.

Nearly two months later, Evelyn woke up with her stomach full of the turbulence Jim had often described from his flight training. She counted back the days on the calendar and trembled with the news she would write to Jim—that he would be a father. Good news she would send that there would now be two people in the Patterson household loving and praying for him while he was away. Her heart rose into her throat.

She was alone and scared of the future, but she wouldn't write those words. She'd always pictured a complete family when she'd thought about her future as a wife and mother. Evelyn put a hand to her stomach and squeezed her eyes shut. She would bring this baby into the world by herself, but one day they *would* be a complete family.

Evelyn opened her eyes and pushed herself to do something absolutely normal, like scrubbing the kitchen sink. Trying to get used to Jim's absence was like wearing shoes a size too small. It pinched at the edges of her life and made everything feel tight and cramped. Staying busy didn't help—walking in too-tight shoes only caused blisters.

She had a cool cloth on her face when she heard a knock at the door. Rising on shaky legs, she breathed in and the edges of her mouth turned up in a hopeful smile. Maybe it was Lucy from the post office. She was always the first to hear the news. Evelyn put a hand to her stomach thinking of her own developing news. She opened the door. The world tilted when she saw the messenger—not Lucy—holding a yellow card. A telegram. Not bright yellow like welcome-home ribbons. Dark yellow. Like death.

The laces of those too-tight shoes wound, wound, wound around her body. They hardened the hollow spaces of her heart into one deep cavern. They pulled her nightmares of losing Jim into focus. They choked the breath caught in her throat. The melody of her life went silent, and Evelyn's world went dark.

December 1943

Evelyn sat on the loveseat in the fading light of her parent's front room. She'd moved from her apartment near Peterson Air Force Base in Colorado Springs to live with her mom and dad in the secluded town of Aspen Falls, Colorado. The reports said Jim's body hadn't been recovered, but nearly everyone in his company had been killed. Evelyn shuddered, remembering details she wanted to forget. Her fist tightened around the slip of paper that held her happiness hostage.

Jim's captain had sent a letter written in her husband's familiar script. It said, "I love you, Evelyn. If I don't come back, look in the music box. I left you one of my secrets."

She had looked inside and listened to the tune several times since reading Jim's letter, each time watching the graceful ballerina with its tiny bit of tulle swirling. She hadn't found anything—maybe he wanted her to remember he had given her his heart for safekeeping, and she still held it in the locket she wore.

She did remember it—all of it—and when his voice began to fade from her mind, she wound up the music box and listened. The memory came back with the tune they'd danced to, and she could almost hear his hum, feel it vibrating in his chest against her cheek. But she still hadn't discovered the secret.

Thirty-nine weeks after Jim left full of life and courage on his way to fight the Germans, Evelyn gave birth to their son. She cried when she held him and recognized Jim's strong chin and confident brow—or maybe she just wanted to see those things—features that would keep Jim alive in their new son. She named him Daniel, but everyone called him Danny.

Her arms were no longer empty, and Danny began filling up the cracked spaces in her broken heart. She held on and listened to the memory of Jim coming from the music box. When the melody swelled higher and the petite ballerina danced, Evelyn let her heart believe that Jim would come back to her—maybe that was his secret. She nursed the hope of her lost love and cuddled her baby boy in the hollow space in her neck. Danny rested there as she hummed the tune, and her teardrops fell on the dark crown of his head.

Living with her parents in the same house she grew up in provided some distraction from her heartache. Endless days of nursing and rocking her infant replaced the time she had spent staring at the dust particles in the air, thinking of all she had lost when Jim died.

During one of Danny's naps, Evelyn took a cloth and dusted all of the compartments of the music box. Every time she heard the melody, it took her back to that day when Jim held her in his strong arms. She slid her finger over the fuzzy lining. She felt a connection to Jim whenever she opened the padded chambers. The box held keepsakes—a lock of Danny's baby hair, the tarnished key that went with her first roller skates, the bottle caps from her first date with Jim. In the bottom drawer, she kept the few letters Jim had written. She rubbed the cloth along the inside of the right compartment and it caught on a piece of the red velvet paper, pulling it back.

Her hand shook and she dropped the dust cloth. Silently berating herself for her carelessness, she pressed the corner back down, hoping it would stay in place. It curled up stubbornly, and she noticed something beneath the lining. A piece of her favorite stationery—light blue with tiny silver birds embossed on the edges. Curious, she peeled back the corner to reveal her name printed in bold caps—Jim's handwriting. She pulled it free and sank to the floor.

Evelyn,

I wanted to come back to you. I hope you know if you're reading this that I'm so angry at myself for failing you by not coming home. Believe me, I did everything I could to make it back to you. Still, life has a purpose and people live or die for a reason. I don't know those reasons. I only know that I love you. I hope you never have to read this, but if you do, please, will you do something for me?

Be happy. Give my things away or sell them. Even the music box. There's a secret to this music box, but you'll only find it by passing it on. Give your heart a second chance. You'll always remember me, but you don't need anything but your own heart to do it by.

I'm sorry we never had much money or time, but I hope you'll have more of both those things in the future. I'm so sorry, Evelyn. Please don't let me be the reason people don't see your beautiful smile or hear your sweet laughter. Please don't die with me.

Forever loving you,
Jim

Evelyn pondered Jim's words for several weeks. The silver birds were all but worn down from reading his letter over and over. She didn't want to give the music box away. She couldn't do it, and the tears came in torrents when she listened to the music play. She didn't understand why Jim would ask her to give away the last gift he'd given her.

In February when Danny was three months old, Evelyn took him to the new memorial Aspen Falls had dedicated to fallen soldiers. The chilly air carried the scent of winter on its back. Wrapped tightly in layers of clothing and blankets, her son whimpered when Evelyn bent closer to the stone representing Jim's empty grave in Colorado Springs. She pressed her cheek to the shock of dark hair covering Danny's warm head.

"Daddy's not coming home." She cried and rocked her baby while humming the tune that reminded her of his father. An icy blast lifted Danny's blanket. Evelyn heard something and stopped rocking.

"Hello?" Evelyn listened for an answer. The wind sang through the trees, and although she knew no one would believe it if she told, it whispered something to her. *Don't die with me.* And she heard the tune, Jim's music—his voice—a song on the wind.

Evelyn clutched Danny and hurried back to their home. She climbed the steps to the front door and walked inside. She stood with her crying infant in the entryway. Her feet throbbed, but not from the cold. The winter in her heart refused to let the blood pump to her extremities. It stopped her frozen soul from feeling. It halted her steps across the thin ice leading up to each new day. If her heart wasn't so heavy, she could take a step forward, cross the ice, and find safety. She closed her eyes and felt a warm breath of air brush the tendrils of hair from her face, repeating those words—Jim's haunting words. A tingling in her feet drew her attention. Evelyn looked down at the puddle of water dripping from her boots, steam rising from the melted ice. It was time. Time to live—really live—for Jim and for Danny.

Chapter 2 — Trading Sorrows

April 1944 — Evelyn

"Mother, I put Danny down for his nap, and I'm heading over to the church swap meet." Evelyn paused at the front door.

Marie looked up from her sewing. "It's time then?"

"Yes, it's what Jim wanted."

Marie nodded, and Evelyn let herself out and walked two blocks to the whitewashed building in silence. A gentle spring breeze caressed the back of her neck and reminded her of the day she and Jim stood in the kitchen one year ago. So much had changed since then. Her hair stayed tight in the clip and refused to play with the wind.

The town of Aspen Falls was much as it had been for the past twenty years–moving at its own pace. If one knew what to look for, change would be evident, but a passerby wouldn't recognize the handful of new shops and the remodeled park the town boasted in its claim to progressive growth.

Evelyn carried the music box under her arm. Her heart seemed to beat with the rhythm of the music held inside.

Maybe it would always keep time to Jim's melody. She had copied his message and pasted it inside the box under the red velvet paper to remind her of what she'd heard in the cemetery. Jim had hinted at a secret, and if it wasn't for that, Evelyn would never have ventured out with the music box.

Tugging at the heavy door, she cradled the music box and stepped inside the church. Her eyes adjusted to the dim lighting of the entryway. She crossed the hall and entered the Sunday school room. With some hesitation, she eyed the gleaming wooden benches surrounding tables overflowing with donations.

Evelyn meandered through the church, looking at the tables filled with trinkets and treasures from the community and the larger neighboring town of Callaway Grove. She rubbed the ivory paper on the box in a circular motion, and her voice resonated with a hum—something she did almost without realizing.

The double doors at the back of the church swung open. A gust of wind pushed through and collided with Evelyn. She stood there staring as a woman struggled to carry a large cradle inside. As the wind died down, the current of air tickled her ears with the sounds of the earth coming alive, and Evelyn walked toward the woman.

The cradle was marvelous—solid maple with little birds carved in the sides—and polished to a pale sheen. The woman closed the doors, and the last bits of wind pushed the cradle until it rocked gently. Evelyn smiled at the woman.

Her cheeks were flushed from the exertion of carrying the load inside. A tangled mess of dark curls fell halfway down her back. She glanced at the cradle, then at Evelyn. "Do you like it?"

Evelyn saw something familiar in the woman's eyes. "I, uh, I do, but it's so beautiful–I don't know if I have enough."

"My name is Rhonda Halverson." She motioned to Evelyn. "What did you bring to trade?"

"I'm Evelyn Patterson." Her throat tightened and she held out the box with trembling hands. "This is a music box." She set it on the table and popped open the compartment. The miniature ballerina stood up gracefully and pirouetted to the music.

The two women stood still and listened. Rhonda bent down and peered at the reflection of the ballerina in the mirror. "Beautiful. I've never seen one like this before. Where did you get it?"

Evelyn hesitated. "It was a gift. I'm not sure where it came from."

Rhonda's fingers grazed the tulle skirt of the ballerina. "My daughter would've loved this. That was her cradle, or bed as she called it. It's big enough that she slept in it until she was nearly eighteen months old."

Evelyn swallowed. "Your daughter?"

"Yes, she passed on two years ago. She was three." Rhonda squared her shoulders and gazed at Evelyn.

"I'm so sorry." Evelyn shook her head and murmured, "My late husband gave me this music box and asked me to give it away to help me move on with my life if he died." She touched the velvet padding and looked at Rhonda, understanding what she had recognized in her eyes. "He died in the war before I could get a letter out that I was expecting."

"Seems like we have a connection then," Rhonda said. "I'd like to trade you my cradle if you feel up to it."

Evelyn knelt down beside the cradle and traced the lines carved into the wood. "I think my baby will fit better in here than in the music box." She laughed and the tinkling sound echoed through the hall.

"And I think I'm ready to pour my sorrows into something smaller." Rhonda cleared her throat. The music stopped playing, and the ballerina stood still in a half turn away from the mirror, her face painted in an everlasting smile that looked up at the two women who knew about heartache.

A few hours later in the quiet of her room, Evelyn battled second thoughts. She closed her eyes for a moment and hummed Jim's tune. Her heart beat in time with a loss she thought might never leave. She knew Jim wanted her to trade the music box so her heart would not be haunted by the song of his love, but it didn't matter what material possessions she gave away, it wouldn't rid her heart of the pain of Jim's loss. She didn't want to—wasn't ready—to give up a love that had barely begun.

She rocked her baby in the cradle until she felt a draft coming from the window. Stepping close to the sun-streaked pane, she saw it was open a half inch. Evelyn closed it tight, and the wind tapped against the glass once and then twice before turning back to blow in another direction. The wind seemed to know something that she didn't. If only it could whisper what the next step was for her and Danny. Evelyn hummed and Danny smiled in his sleep, unaware of the past and with no concern for the future.

The wind blew down the street to a two-bedroom house with a picket fence and a rusty tricycle in the yard. Leland Halverson nursed a bottle of beer in the back bedroom and looked at the empty spot on the wood floor where the cradle had been. He groaned, remembering those happy times when he could breathe without hurting. Leland had built the cradle for their baby girl, Jessie.

He felt the current of air enter before he heard Rhonda's light step in the kitchen.

"Leland, I'm home. I traded the cradle for something special."

He winced, took a long pull from his beer, and tossed it in the corner. The glass shattered, and the amber liquid trickled over the pile of bottles he had consumed. No matter how much he drank, he'd still hear Jessie's scream. He'd hear the haunting cry of his baby girl and remember that horrible day.

He heard Rhonda move around the kitchen and then a clicking noise, like a windup toy. A melody—ethereal yet alluring—traveled toward him and filled the room. Rhonda must have left the door ajar, for Leland could still feel a light breeze moving down the hall. And for just a moment he thought he heard something besides music.

The cool air sent a shiver through him. He cursed and slumped against the bedroom wall. The music continued to play and he rubbed his hand along the coarse stubble framing his jaw. He couldn't remember the last time Rhonda had made him shower and shave. The whiskers on his cheek were matted. It must have been over a week.

"Would you like to come in the kitchen?" Her voice was

almost a whisper, but he still flinched. Rhonda stood in the doorway and Leland took a shallow breath.

"Why?" He glanced at her and then back at the floor. He waited for his wife to answer that he stunk of liquor and needed something running through his veins besides alcohol, but she only sighed. Then he heard the wind blow the screen door shut and the music stopped playing.

"I picked up something today I think Jessie would've liked."

Leland cringed and covered his eyes with his hand. Rhonda crouched beside him and touched his arm. "It will only take a minute. Come on." She tugged on his sleeve.

He curled his toes snug in his woolen socks and bit his bottom lip. Slender fingers grasped his hand and pulled. He looked up into the clear blue of Rhonda's eyes and tried not to see Jessie there. She paused and he knew she was doing the same thing—trying not to see Jessie in the dimple under his left eye or the red highlights in his hair. She pulled again, and he allowed himself to rise with the momentum and follow her out of the bedroom.

"I'm tired," he complained as he shuffled down the hall.

Rhonda turned around and looked at him. "Me, too." She gave his hand a gentle squeeze and nudged him into the kitchen. "Here it is."

She pointed at the music box open on the table with a ballerina frozen mid-twirl. Leland swallowed, but his throat didn't seem to be working right, his saliva caught and he choked. His chest burned, his eyes blurred, and still he was choking.

"I need a beer." He gasped for breath and moved toward the icebox.

"Wait." Rhonda put a hand on his arm and pushed him into a chair situated directly in front of the music box. She leaned over the ballerina and turned the brass key until the melody began again and the ballerina finished her pirouette and started another.

He watched her spinning to the tune emanating from the music box and shook his head. "Why?"

"Because it's time for us to heal." Rhonda sank into the chair next to him. "I traded the cradle to a woman who lost her husband in the war. She has a baby boy who'll never know his father. She smiled at me anyway, Leland, and said she needed to give this music box away so she could keep on living." Rhonda motioned to the music box. "We still have a chance to live. I don't want to give up on that."

The table in front of him was polished with a satin finish, and the grain of the wood was hardly noticeable, lost in the deep mahogany. Leland rubbed his finger along the edge of wood he had sanded and shaped so carefully, the same way he'd shaped Jessie's cradle. The music played on, and the melody climbed higher to sweeter notes that reminded him of Rhonda's lullabies. He sucked in a breath, fighting the tightness in his chest. The chair scraped along the floor as he pushed it from the table and stumbled toward the icebox.

"It was an accident. Drinking won't change that. Jessie's gone."

His hands closed around the beer bottle squeezing nearly hard enough to break the bottle and crush the shards of glass into his hands—the same hands that would never hold his little girl again. He choked, this time on a great ball of tears rising up his throat. Woolen socks made it easy to shuffle down the hall, and he leaned against the door frame for a moment, his chest heaving with sobs.

After prying the top from his beer, he drank and swallowed his tears then sank into a heap on the floor. Grimy fingers rubbed the jagged edge of the bottle cap and flipped it into the air. It bounced along the hardwood floor—ping, ping, ping—in perfect time with the music box as the notes reached for the sweet strains of a lullaby again. Leland held his breath, listening to the tinny music, and stared at the mound of brown glass in the corner. The bottles rested against each other like a graveyard of lost hopes and dreams.

The screen door slammed and a whoosh of air rushed down the hallway. It lifted dark strands from Leland's head like little fingers once did when his baby girl rode on his shoulders through the woods. Closing his eyes, he leaned his head against the wall and listened to the music dance with the wind. The smell of lavender overtook the scent of liquor, and the sound of small feet pattered against the floor.

Thrills for the Heart

FOR A LIMITED TIME

Sign up for Rachelle's
VIP Mailing List
to get your *FREE* book.

Get started here:
www.rachellechristensen.com

About the Author

Photo by Erin Summerill

Rachelle is a mother of five who writes mystery/suspense, nonfiction, and women's fiction. She solves the case of the missing shoe on a daily basis. She enjoys raising chickens and laughing with her husband. She graduated cum laude from Utah State University with a degree in psychology and a minor in music.

Rachelle is the award-winning author of ten books, including *The Soldier's Bride (a Kindle Scout Selection)*, *Wrong Number*, *Diamond Rings Are Deadly Things*, *What Every 6th Grader Needs to Know*, and *Christmas Kisses: An Echo Ridge Anthology*. Her novella, "Silver Cascade Secrets," was included in the Rone Award–winning *Timeless Romance Anthology, Fall Collection.*

Join Rachelle's VIP mailing list to learn more about upcoming books & get your free book at www.rachellechristensen.com

CPSIA information can be obtained
at www.ICGtesting.com
Printed in the USA
LVOW07s1821061217
558856LV00005B/973/P